THE SAGE'S TOWER

M.A. ROTHMAN

PRIMORDIAL
PRESS

ALSO BY M.A. ROTHMAN

Technothrillers: (Thrillers with science / Hard-Science Fiction)

• Primordial Threat

• Freedom's Last Gasp

• Darwin's Cipher

Levi Yoder Thrillers:

• Perimeter

• The Inside Man

• Never Again

Connor Sloane Thrillers:

• The Patriot

• The Death Speech

Epic Fantasy / Dystopian:

• The Plainswalker

• The Sage's Tower

• Agent of Prophecy

• Heirs of Prophecy

• Tools of Prophecy

• Lords of Prophecy

- Running From Destiny

- The Code Breaker

- Dispocalypse

CONTENTS

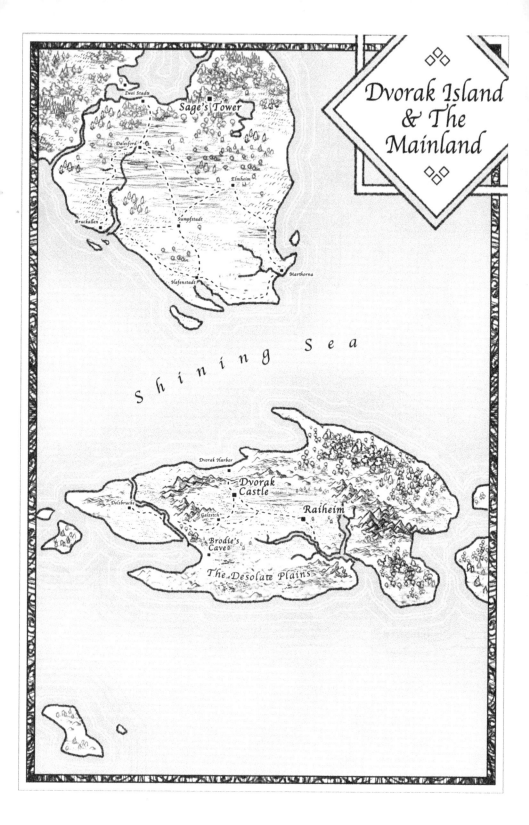

Dvorak Island
& The
Mainland

Zwei Stadt
Sage's Tower
Dalesford
Elmheim
Bruckallen
Sumpfstadt
Hafenstadt
Marthorna

S h i n i n g   S e a

Dvorak Harbor
Dvorak
Castle
Delsbrucke
Galzstch
Raiheim
Brodie's
Cave
The Desolate Plains

CHAPTER ONE

Standing in a giant cavern deep in Myrkheim, Peabo watched three platoons' worth of soldiers organize themselves in a manner that was very familiar. With his Special Forces background, he was used to working in small groups, but this brought him back to his infantry days, when the entire company would get rousted to go on maneuvers. But there were two key differences between now and then: the majority of these soldiers were less than four feet tall, and there wasn't a firearm in sight.

Nicole, a tall blonde blood maiden who could literally kick his ass from one end of this cavern to the next if she chose, came over and draped her arm over his shoulder. "Are you doing okay?" Both the tone of her voice and her furrowed brow clearly expressed her worry.

"I'm fine," he lied. "The headache isn't that bad right now."

"Liar." She never minced words. "You bled all over the pillows last night. You're nothing resembling fine."

That was true, and Peabo didn't argue the point. Instead he nodded at the soldiers and changed the subject. "I don't understand why the prelate needs such a big escort," he said. "Do we really need this many people to get to the mainland?"

Nicole gave him the look she reserved for when he'd said something particularly stupid, but she spoke with an uncharacteristically warm tone. "You've never made this trip, so you'll just have to trust me when I say that yes, it's necessary. With a group of this size, even the stupidest creepy-crawly will stay out of our way."

Brodie, the high priest of the Nameless One and their mutual friend, joined them. "You look like week-old garbage," he said, looking Peabo up and down.

"Gee, thanks." Peabo shook his head. Brodie was always griping. In fact if he ever stopped, Peabo would be worried about the old man. "Perhaps you can explain why we aren't just taking a boat to the mainland. We wouldn't need this many people for a boat ride."

The dwarf snorted. "First of all," he said, poking Peabo's chest with a thick finger, "we Myrkheimers aren't fans of being up in the aboveworld more than we need to be. Second"—he poked Peabo again—"there's not a boat made that'll survive an attack by a kraken. Third"—another poke—"I'm not risking my hide on the skills of some sea captain I don't know. Fourth—"

"Okay, stop poking me! I get the picture." Peabo rubbed at the sore spot on his chest. "What's a kraken? I've memorized the monster manual from front to back, and there's no mention of it."

Brodie waved dismissively. "There's a second edition, but don't you worry about that yet. You're not ready for that."

Peabo was still a newbie in this world, and he often wished Brodie would just tell him everything he knew so he'd have a clue about what was going on.

The sound of crunching gravel echoed throughout the cavern, and Peabo turned to see a large wagon rolling into view at the entrance. It was pulled by three red-eyed behemoths that looked like a cross between an ox and a Clydesdale, if an ox and a Clydesdale were about eight feet tall at the shoulder.

"Ah, there it is," said Brodie.

"What's the huge wagon for?" Peabo asked.

"It's for you," Brodie and Nicole said at the same time.

"Me? I don't need a ride. I'll march with everyone else."

Nicole did what she always did when trying to calm him: she began rubbing his shoulders. "Peabo, I know you think you're fine, but you're not. It's a long journey across the island, under the ocean, and to the mainland. You're getting worse—I've seen it—and believe me when I say you won't survive this march if you don't ride in that wagon."

The wagon continued through the cavern, soldiers stepping aside to create a path that led directly to Peabo. It was clear that everyone had known the plan except for him.

He took a deep breath, let it out slowly, and tried to remain adult about this. Nicole was right. Even standing upright made him feel lightheaded, and the nausea that came with his damned headache was constant now. He was in crap condition.

If he marched alongside the others, he'd only slow everyone down.

The soldier at the head of the wagon, cracking a whip and flicking his reins, maneuvered the vehicle around so that its back faced Peabo. Two soldiers unlocked the back gate, and it yawned open on a set of well-oiled hinges.

"Plainswalker," one of the soldiers said, offering his hand. "Let me help you get on."

Peabo ignored the hand and climbed onto the wagon by himself. He was sick, but he could still step onto a wagon. Nicole hopped up beside him, and the soldiers closed the gate behind them.

Brodie cupped his hands to his mouth and announced to the assembled group, "In the Nameless One's service, let's get moving!" He then began rattling off orders like a competent captain might do in the army. He assigned one platoon to take point, another to cover the rear, and the rest of the soldiers to serve as a protective barrier surrounding the wagon. They certainly weren't taking any chances.

With a cloth in her hand, Nicole dabbed at Peabo's upper lip.

"Damn it," Peabo groaned. He was bleeding again.

"It's okay." Nicole cupped his face with two glowing hands, and he felt something high up in his nose get hot as she tried healing him… again.

The wagon began to move, and Peabo sighed. This was going to be a long trip.

Waking from a fitful sleep, but keeping his eyes closed, Peabo sensed the rocking of the wagon traveling along the underground path through the underground caverns of Myrkheim. He tried to find sleep once more, but couldn't; the voices of everyone around him were so damned loud. It was like a hammer pounding incessantly on his temples.

"I think there's another four hours before our next rest break."

"He doesn't look like a plainswalker. Where are his markings that I read about in seminary?"

"I wonder if the high priest realizes he's got a failed blood maiden sitting next to the plainswalker. The woman can't be trusted."

That was when Peabo realized he wasn't hearing conversations, he was hearing people's *thoughts*. Nobody would have said anything like that about Nicole out loud—at least not within earshot of her. Not if they valued their lives.

But—wait, that couldn't be right. He shouldn't be able to hear their thoughts. He could peek into low-level minds, but these were seasoned soldiers, certainly past level four, the point at which the mind closes itself off from being spied on.

He started to sit up, only to realize he couldn't. He couldn't move at all, not even to open his eyes. And yet... he could see everything around him. He could see Nicole beside him, sitting cross-legged, staring down at the ring in her hand, but he wasn't seeing her from his place within the wagon—he was seeing her from above. He was somehow hovering over the moving vehicle, looking down, watching everything from that vantage point. He could even see his own body, still asleep.

He'd heard of out-of-body experiences back on Earth, and had never put any stock in it. But evidently it wasn't all nonsense, for he was quite clearly having such an experience right now.

Brodie was sitting across from Nicole, and they were having a silent conversation with their paired communication rings, tapping the equivalent of Morse code to each other. Though their messages were silent, he could hear their thoughts.

"I hope they've got an answer at the tower," thought Nicole, tapping the message to Brodie.

"You seem to lack confidence in the women of the tower, despite the prelate's recommendation that we take him there," thought Brodie as he replied.

"Brodie, I lived there for a decade, and I know what goes on behind those walls. I wouldn't subject anyone I cared for to such a thing, ever."

The dwarf gave her a quizzical look. *"You care for him? I didn't think such a thing was allowed."*

"Shut up, Brodie. I'm still my own person, regardless of my vows. Do you think it's coincidental that all of this started right after the castle incident?"

"I think not. The essence he gained from Lord Dvorak must have been immense, and he leveled immediately. I'd wager that something up in his head was unlocked at level five, and he's missing some key training that we know nothing about."

"I'm worried for him."

"You should be. Is the sedative you gave him strong enough to last the trip?"

6

"Yes. I hated doing it, but he's stubborn, and he'll hurt himself without even realizing he's doing it."

A sedative, Peabo thought. So that was why he couldn't wake up.

Testing his abilities, Peabo immediately found that he could shift his point of view and his position by just willing it. He glided forward, like a ghost flying across the train of soldiers, and as he neared the point of their procession, he discovered that there was some kind of assault taking place, though it seemed he had only caught the tail end of it. He watched as a dwarf soldier felled some sort of humanoid creature with a pig-like snout, nearly cleaving the creature's head off its shoulders in the process. There were already a half dozen other corpses on the ground.

Orcs.

Peabo recognized them immediately from his studying of the monster manual. They were nothing like the orcs in the Lord of the Rings movies, though—these were pathetic, scrawny things. Clearly they hadn't given the dwarven escort much reason to pause.

As the orcs were dragged to one side of the cavern and the procession continued, two of the soldiers stood over the corpses and muttered some prayers of dedication. Peabo listened in on their thoughts, and then on the thoughts of the other soldiers. These weren't just work-for-hire guild members; they were the prelate's men, the equivalent of some kind of papal guard—an elite unit, and proud of their service.

Suddenly Peabo snapped back into his body. He still couldn't move or open his eyes, but he felt Nicole dabbing at his nose and heard her crying. He sensed her fear. She was terrified he was going to die.

Brodie whispered beside him, "He's fighting the sedative. That's likely what's causing him to bleed. Scoot over—I'm going to put him into a deeper sleep."

Peabo felt Brodie's hand touch his forehead. A warmth enveloped him, and the world went dark.

When Peabo woke again, it took a few minutes for his eyes to adjust to the brightness. The wagon must have climbed up from the underground realm of Myrkheim and into the daylight. When he breathed in deeply and detected the scent of the ocean, he knew they must now have arrived on the mainland.

Nicole smiled at him from the other side of the wagon, then scooted over to hand him a waterskin and some dried meat jerky. "You've been asleep for over a day. You need some energy."

Peabo bit off a chunk of the jerky. It tasted like chicken, but flavored with a combination of unknown spices that left his lips tingling and his tongue feeling numb.

"Where are we?" he asked when he finished chewing.

Brodie's voice sounded from the front of the wagon. "We're passing through Elmheim," he said. "Just relax. We'll be at the tower soon enough."

Peabo pushed himself to a sitting position and saw that the wagon was now winding its way through a city that made the Castle Dvorak area look like a humble village. Despite the medieval technology of this world, the buildings stretched up into the sky, their architecture all spires, pillars, and ornate masonry. It reminded him of the old buildings in Vatican City. In fact, it was strange how similar the construction was to Roman, baroque, and even Gothic styles, yet this world's architecture had its own unique flair, giving the city a familiar and alien quality at the same time.

"What's got your interest?" Nicole asked.

"I'm just amazed at the buildings. They're all so much bigger than the ones back in Dvorak."

"Bigger than the buildings where you're from?"

Peabo shook his head. "In our biggest cities, like New York, the buildings are taller. But they're less... I'm not sure how to say it. I guess these buildings are more intricate. More unique. Most of the buildings where I'm from are very similar to each other. How old is this place?"

Nicole shrugged. "Very old." She turned toward the front of the wagon. "Brodie, do you know how old these buildings are?"

The dwarf, who was sitting next to the driver, pointed at a building that reminded Peabo of the Parthenon. It had pillars and a triangular roof profile. "That's one of the oldest buildings here. There was a land quake almost five hundred generations ago that leveled much of this province. Not much remains from before then. But that building was constructed during the rebuild."

"Roughly how many years is a generation?" Peabo asked.

Brodie shrugged. "Twenty or so."

Peabo did the math. Five hundred generations was almost

ten thousand years. There certainly weren't any buildings back home, or structures of any kind, that were still standing after that many years. If he remembered his history lessons correctly, even Stonehenge and the pyramids were at best half that age.

Nicole took his hand and held it between hers. She was becoming very touchy-feely, which was unlike her.

"Are you okay?" he thought at her.

She gave him a lopsided grin and projected her thoughts into his head. *"Just worried about you."*

"I'm fine." And it was true. Other than a dull ache at the base of his neck and feeling sore from having slept on the wagon, he felt fine.

"There she be," Brodie announced as the wagon crested a rise and a series of towers loomed large ahead of them. "The Sage's Tower. You wanted to see old buildings, Peabo? The tower complex is among the few buildings in the province to have survived the land quake."

"How old does that make it?" Peabo asked.

"I can't say precisely. I know it's a construction from the First Age though, so at least one hundred thousand turns of the season."

One hundred thousand years? "How is that even possible?" Peabo asked.

Nicole looked surprised by the question. "The stones are resistant to wear, if that's what you're asking. You seem shocked by this."

"I am," Peabo admitted.

The towers rose higher as they approached. Together they

resembled a castle, but without outer walls. There were five towers in all, with four of them set on the corners of a large square, and the fifth, the tallest, set directly in the center.

As the wagon rolled to a stop within the complex, a group of a dozen women exited the center tower, led by a tall blonde who radiated a white glow.

Nicole whispered in a shaky voice, "That's Ariandelle, the headmistress."

As the women approached the wagon, Peabo felt his nose begin to bleed. Nicole quickly brushed at Peabo's face with a glowing hand.

Rather than walking up to Brodie, Ariandelle came forward and stopped directly in front of Nicole. "Nicole," she said with a smile. "It is a surprise to see you. Weren't you paired with...?"

A red-faced woman next to her whispered in the headmistress's ear, and Ariandelle looked sad for a moment before turning to face Peabo.

"Plainswalker. Yes, I can see who you really are." She shook her head. "It's a good thing you've arrived. I see that the bleeding has already started, and I can sense the pain within you. Despite all that you've been through to get here, I'm afraid your journey has only begun."

The woman's voice had an airy, almost ethereal quality to it, much like the unnatural glow of her skin. Peabo felt the urge to reach out and poke her to verify that she was flesh and bone and not some kind of weird spirit.

She pulled out a metal card, about the size of a credit card, and held it out to him. "Please, read this aloud."

Peabo recognized the card immediately—he'd seen a copy of it earlier, back in Dvorak. But as he took it from Ariandelle's hand, he discovered this one was heavier, and warm to the touch. And more importantly, something about it felt… wrong.

It had words written on one side, in a CAPTCHA format, the same style of obfuscated writing used in his world to prove that the reader was a person and not some kind of computer. He already knew what it said, having seen these words before, yet as he looked at them again, he felt his anger rise just as it had before.

He pulled in a deep breath and tried to let go of his emotions as he exhaled.

"Reporting in for duty," he read. "I'm from STAG."

The card exploded into fine dust, and the world went dark.

A cacophony of voices erupted all around him. He felt himself being moved. Nicole cried out. But the headmistress's voice cut through the din.

"No. You may not accompany him into the tower. You are forbidden access to the plainswalker."

Peabo could see nothing, feel nothing. His body floated in a sea of darkness. But as he was taken away, he sensed Nicole's voice in his head.

"Don't admit to being paired with me," she thought at him. *"It'll keep you safer in there."*

CHAPTER TWO

A loud crack like a thunderclap exploded in Peabo's head, and he lurched against his restraints. He was still in darkness, but he heard whispers nearby, along with a faint humming noise.

"He's built like an ogre," said a woman.

"Plainswalkers are supposed to be large," said another.

"Leena, how in the world would you know? Nobody's seen one since the First Age."

"Because unlike you, I actually studied what's in the archives."

"Girls, that's enough," said a third voice, this one familiar. *"Do it again,"* she said.

The humming sound grew louder, reminding Peabo of a straining electric transformer. And then suddenly he felt like he *was* that transformer. His body was hit by a powerful *zap,* and another deafening crack of thunder erupted in his head.

His eyes flew open.

He was seated in a straight-backed chair, strapped down tightly. Three women were arrayed in front of him, their expressions ranging from concern, to curiosity, to amusement. One of the women wiped a wet towel roughly across his face. It came back streaked with blood.

The other two women studied his face from various angles for a full ten seconds. Then one of them said, "He seems to have stopped bleeding."

Peabo didn't know if that was true, but he did know something had changed. The ever-worsening headache that he'd been experiencing for weeks seemed to have vanished entirely. At least for the moment.

The woman who'd wiped his face tossed the soiled towel into an overflowing basket, then grabbed a clean one from a pile on a workbench. When she rubbed it across his face, Peabo objected.

"Easy there!" he said. "I'm quite capable of wiping my own face." Although this was obviously untrue, given his arms were bound. He opened and closed his fists, trying to improve the blood flow to his tingling fingertips.

The women ignored his outburst. All three studied the towel, which showed no fresh red blood, just hints of brown. His face was probably covered in old dried blood and who knew what else. No doubt he looked like a complete nightmare.

The women looked down at him like he was a zoo animal. Then the tallest of the three—Ariandelle, that was what Nicole had called her—nodded with approval.

"I will inform the prelate that his plainswalker is on the road to recovery," she said. "Then I'll dig through the archives and see what else a plainswalker needs. Leena, you will get him checked out by the physician. Let's put him in with the primary education classes." She glanced over at Peabo once more. "And make sure he understands the rules and limits the collar imposes on him."

The two other women nodded, and Ariandelle turned and left the room.

While one woman tidied up the towels, the one named Leena studied Peabo with her head tilted at an angle. Her eyes shone with an icy shade of blue, the same shade as Nicole's. Peabo wondered if that was a common characteristic of the women in the Tower.

Leena cupped his chin in her hand and rubbed her thumb across his cheek. "You're a bloody mess." She gave something on his neck a flick and it rang with a metallic sound. "While you're here, this collar will help us keep track of you, just in case you have an episode and pass out, or can't be found. It will also act as a means by which some doors will be unlocked for you."

She leaned forward and studied his face, almost like a scientist with a lab rat, and she shook her head. "Are the headaches gone?"

It was the first time any of them had spoken to Peabo, or even acted as if he were capable of speech.

Peabo tried nodding, but his head was trapped in a web of leather straps. "Yes, thank you," he said. "I'm sorry, but can you unbuckle me from this thing?"

Leena smiled. "There's no need to be sorry." She began undoing his straps. "Welcome to the Sage's Tower."

An elderly doctor placed a wooden tube against Peabo's chest and listened on the other end. "Plainswalker, please breathe in deeply and then slowly let out the breath."

Peabo did as he was told. Apparently this device was some kind of primitive stethoscope—which Peabo found surprising. He'd come to believe this world didn't even have doctors, at least in the sense that he knew them, much less stethoscopes. After all, in this world, there were people—people like Nicole —who possessed magical healing skills. In such a world, who needs doctors?

But this man's office looked much like the doctor's offices Peabo had grown up with, complete with drawings of the human anatomy on the walls. The main difference was, these drawings looked to be hand-drawn, and they were covered with handwritten notes that reminded him of images he'd once seen at the office of a traditional Chinese acupuncturist.

The doctor sat back and patted Peabo on the knee. "Plainswalker, you are in remarkably good health considering you were on death's door just a day ago."

"My name is Peabo, if you don't mind."

"My apologies. I wasn't given your name, and it wasn't my place to ask. Peabo, then. Do you have any questions for me before I call in one of the executors?"

"Yes," Peabo put his finger between his neck and the metal collar that had been placed on him. "How do I take this off?"

The man looked a bit startled at the question and shook his

head. "I don't believe it's meant to be taken off while you're here."

Peabo frowned. The idea of wearing something that reminded him of a dog collar really bothered him, but as he ran his fingers across the contiguous smooth metal it bothered him even more that there was no obvious way to remove it. "What exactly does it do?"

"I'm sorry, but that's not something I'm really well-versed with. You'll need to talk to the executors about that."

"Executor?" Peabo didn't like the sound of that title. "I'm sorry, but I'm new to the goings-on of the tower. What does an executor do?"

The doctor gave him a weak smile. "I'm sorry to have to repeat myself, but it is not for me to talk of the hierarchy of the tower, but I suppose it does no harm to explain who you will be meeting with. Executors are senior maidens who have come back to the tower to assist in the raising of new recruits. You have nothing to fear from them."

As he spoke, the doctor pressed a button on the wall, and a moment later the door opened and a woman walked in. Like the others, she had blue eyes, but her blonde hair was giving way to gray.

The physician looked up at her and bowed his head. "Executor Eileen, the plainswalker is in good health."

The woman looked at Peabo with an expression that would sour milk fresh from the cow. "Plainswalker, are you ready for integration?

Peabo stood. The woman was tall, but he was a good six inches taller, and at least twice her weight. Still, he had the distinct feeling that this woman was capable of knocking him on his butt in the blink of an eye.

"I don't know what 'integration' means," he said, "but sure. I suppose I'm ready."

Without a word of explanation, she led him out of the doctor's office, down a few passages, and then through a door that led outside. As he stepped outside, he felt a tingling sensation coming from the metal collar around his neck. It wasn't uncomfortable, but it reminded him that he had more questions.

"What's this collar for?" he asked. "The doctor wouldn't speak about it; he said it wasn't for him to explain."

"And he was right." Eileen shot him a glare. Or maybe that was her version of a smile. "Without it, you wouldn't be able to enter or exit any of the towers."

Peabo narrowed his gaze and felt a bubbling sense of annoyance rising within him. "I notice you're not wearing a collar. Isn't there a way for me to take this thing off and carry it around or get a key if the doors are locked?"

The woman snorted and shook her head. "There are rules you will abide by while here. And wearing the collar is one of them. The executors within the tower have other means of entering rooms that are locked."

Peabo frowned, but remained silent. For the moment, it didn't seem like he had much choice in the matter anyway.

She paused and gestured one by one to the towers that loomed over them. "The northeast tower, the one we just left, is used primarily to treat ailments that do not respond to divine intervention. The southeast tower contains the armory, and is where melee lessons are conducted. In the southwest tower we keep all things arcane, including books, enhanced armor, and weapons. Advanced classes are held there. And in the northwest tower is where the physical sciences from the First Age are housed. This is more of a museum, as such things are impractical in today's day and age."

Peabo looked around at the towers. He was particularly interested in that last one—the museum. "Now that I'm healed," he said, "is it okay if I explore—"

"You are *not* healed, plainswalker. The treatment you received is a First Age treatment, and one that you will need again—unless you learn more about who and what you are."

Eileen stepped closer to him, closer than two strangers would normally be, and closer than Peabo was comfortable with. But she spoke with an unexpectedly soft voice. "I can sense your frustration. We all mean to see you healed and able to fulfill whatever destiny you have. But this process will require your patience. I hope you understand."

Whatever frustration Peabo had felt building, it suddenly melted away. He still didn't understand much of anything, but he nodded.

"What is the next step in this process?" he asked.

"That is still to be determined. The headmistress herself is doing research on your case. But in the meantime, you'll join classes like any other recruit."

Peabo grinned. "Recruit? You mean I'll be training to be a blood maiden?"

Eileen barked out a laugh, and for a split second, she lost her sour expression. "If it pleases you to think of that way," she said. "Now follow me. I can't have you arriving late to your first class."

Peabo felt more than a little odd sitting in a class with a bunch of girls who all looked to be about ten years old. He definitely stuck out like a sore thumb, and he couldn't help but notice the girls' curious glances—or their thoughts.

"It's the plainswalker! I can't believe it."

"He has such a kind face for someone who looks like a brute."

"He doesn't have any of the markings I read about."

"He's gigantic... even bigger than Pop-Pop."

Hearing other people's thoughts was, as Peabo had learned, a feature of being a plainswalker. That was, until someone matured to level four, where they could shield their thoughts. But these girls were young, and lacked that ability—for now.

They lacked something else, too: the ubiquitous blue eyes and blonde hair of the blood maidens. The students in this class had a myriad of hair and eye colors, just like the people he'd met out in the real world.

"Peabo, what can you tell me about the First Age?"

The blood maiden at the head of the class was staring directly at him. He felt everyone's eyes suddenly turn to him, and he had a flashback to grade school.

It wasn't a good memory.

"It was... a long time ago?" Peabo said with a grimace, knowing how weak an answer that was.

"That is true." The teacher smiled warmly and shifted her gaze to another student. "Carolyn, please tell me what you know about the First Age."

The dark-haired girl stood. "The First Age started at the very beginning of time. This was before us, when the gods walked on the land we live on. We don't know much about the early and middle times, but in the late part of the First Age there were strange and dangerous powers, and the gods warred with each other. Eventually there was a war that ended the other wars, and it forced the gods to leave the lands for other planes. It was a very dangerous time for our ancestors, and it led to the dark times and chaos. But it also led to the coming of the king, and he brought peace out of the chaos and destruction."

Peabo realized with bemusement that this little girl had just taught him more about this world's history than he'd learned in all his time living in this strange land. Gods walking the world? Strange powers? He wondered what was considered "strange" to a people who didn't bat an eye at magical healing or turning a person into an undead creature.

"Very good, Carolyn," said the teacher. "Today, we're going to focus on the true beginning, when there was nothing on this world but three immortal spirits: darkness, chaos, and order. Can anyone tell me what happened to chaos?"

A half dozen arms shot up into the air. The teacher pointed at one of the girls, and she jumped up from her desk to speak. "Chaos split into the dark and light versions of itself. The twin gods."

The teacher nodded. "That is correct."

Another girl raised her hand and spoke when called upon. "How do we know about any of this? It was so long ago."

The teacher smiled. "We have records of the twin gods' escapades from the latter First Age tablets that survived the great war. And we know of darkness because it was mentioned in the First Age chronicles of the first plainswalker—the founder of these sacred towers."

The girls all snuck glances at Peabo, probably wondering the same thing he was: *What does it even mean to be a plainswalker?* The truth was, he had no idea what made him different from anyone else—other than some superficial skin markings, and even these were currently masked by a potion he'd taken before arriving at the tower.

He realized he'd zoned out for a bit, and the teacher was still talking as she walked among the students' desks. Even though she looked to be in her later years, she moved gracefully and soundlessly, with no hints of age. "… and so the darkness was imprisoned on a distant plane, one that could no longer influence our world. As for the twin gods, they died in the war that ended the First Age."

Peabo raised his hand. "You said the gods were immortal. So how could the twin gods die?"

The teacher smiled. "Excellent question, and I should be more careful with my words. We actually don't know for certain that the twin gods perished. But we do know that ever since the end of the First Age, nobody has been able to commune with either of them. Their fate, strictly speaking, is unknown."

Peabo lapsed back into silence. He didn't believe in gods.

He'd never been particularly religious in his other life, and he wasn't about to start now. But there was one thing he'd learned about this world: don't take anything for granted. There may not be "gods" in this world, but he had no doubt these legends referred to something very real. Something possibly beyond comprehension, and likely dangerous.

"That leaves us with the Nameless One," said the teacher, and Peabo's eyes widened. Peabo had definitely heard of this guy, named or not.

"The Nameless One is the deity that stands for order and equality in all things. In the Great War, he was the one that stood aside as his brethren were cast from this world. And even though in the end he too was banished to an alternate plane, it's the Nameless One who continues to hold sway over the people even to this day."

Peabo raised his hand.

"Yes, plainswalker?"

"I've seen someone communicate with the Nameless One —by writing messages in sand. How is that possible?"

"Excellent question." The teacher panned her gaze across the classroom. "Does anyone know the answer to the plainswalker's question?"

Her question was met with blank stares.

The teacher turned back to Peabo. "I'm going to assume this was a priest you saw communing with the Nameless One?"

"That's right."

"The *how* is difficult to explain... or even to understand. But I can tell you that such a thing is possible only with great skills and extensive training."

"Has anyone tried to do the same thing to communicate with the other gods?" Peabo asked.

"Oh, they have definitely tried. And always failed. As I said, chaos and darkness are either dead—or whatever fate befalls an immortal—or they have been banished to alternate planes of existence that are unreachable by any of us. At least, so it is said, according to the ancient records."

As the teacher instructed the students to open their history books, Peabo thought about what he'd just learned. The truth was, it wasn't much. He'd come grudgingly to this place because the women of the tower were said to be the only ones who knew how to save his life. And yet, in many ways, they knew not much more than he did.

And that wasn't the only thing bothering him. Nicole's warning echoed in his head: *"Don't admit to being paired with me. It'll keep you safer in there."*

What, precisely, do I need to stay "safe" from? Peabo wondered. So far, this place and the people in it seemed nice enough, but he had the creeping feeling that there was a dark underside to it all.

As Leena waited patiently, the headmistress sat at her desk, shuffling through a stack of papers, without giving the other woman a moment's glance. To Leena, Ariandelle was an enigma. Nobody knew her background, or even how old she was. But what they did know was that, at level twenty, she was one of the most powerful people walking the lands, if not the most powerful, outside of maybe the king himself.

Leena was quite powerful herself. Whereas most maidens graduated from the tower at level seven, and rarely progressed much further—they were usually paired with a figure of some prominence whose most dangerous habits involved paper cuts and overeating—Leena had taken a different path. She'd spent most of her life as one of the king's assassins, where countless victims had fallen to her deft hand. The ocean of blood she spilled allowed her to earn her levels, such that now, at age forty, she was level thirteen, making her the highest-ranked executor in the tower complex.

And still seven full levels lower than that of the head-mistress. To reach level twenty was unfathomable. How long it must have taken to achieve such a thing was beyond what Leena could guess. Each level was harder to achieve than the one before, and it had taken Leena five years to move from level twelve to thirteen. She honestly did not anticipate ever reaching level fourteen, and could not imagine the powers it must entail. The headmistress constantly buzzed with latent energy.

At last Ariandelle looked up from her work and acknowl-edged her visitor. When the woman smiled, her ageless face showed not even a hint of a wrinkle.

"Is she ready for what I'm going to task her with?" the headmistress said.

Leena wasn't sure if the headmistress intended to say that aloud. But she nodded all the same.

Ariandelle closed her eyes. "When the prelate of the Nameless One reached out to me saying that a plainswalker was walking this world and was deathly ill, I admit I thought he'd gone insane. Nobody has encountered a plainswalker in the flesh since the First Age. But here he is. And he is, indeed, ill."

On that they all agreed. The plainswalker's sickness appeared to be a stronger form of something all the blood maidens had experienced. When first coming into her skills, a young maiden would start to have dreams about using these new skills—dreams that would become an obsession, a nagging hunger to employ these skills. It was unpleasant but manageable—an irritant that drove a maiden to reach her potential.

But for the plainswalker, the negative consequences of the drive appeared to be much stronger, strong enough to cause disabling headaches... and maybe, in time, even death.

"The device you had us treat him with..." Leena said. "Has it cured him?" She knew the headmistress had discovered the secrets of the ancient device in the oldest of the archives, but not what those secrets were.

"I am afraid not. It uses magic from the First Age, applying a thing called magnetic resonance to alleviate the pressure inside the plainswalker's head. But that relief is only temporary."

"So he will start bleeding again?"

"Eventually, yes. First the headaches, then the bleeding, and then unconsciousness followed by death. The device only buys him some time—time in which we must implement a more permanent solution. We need to encourage the plain- swalker to use his skill, whatever that might be."

"Do we even know what that skill is?" Leena asked.

Ariandelle's expression turned sour. "No. Almost all the records regarding the plainswalkers were destroyed during the War of the Gods. We know almost nothing about what that creature is capable of." The headmistress leaned forward and fixed Leena with a stern gaze. "But you, Leena, will find out. It is your task to discover what latent powers he has... and encourage him to use them. Use whatever means is necessary. If he's damaged in the process, we have healers for that. We need to understand the nature of this plainswalker. He is central to learning what truly happened at the end of the First Age."

Leena smiled. "Yes, headmistress. I understand." After a pause she added, "Do you think he's a danger to us?"

Ariandelle shook her head. "He's but a child in his training, barely level five. Whatever it is that he's capable of, the training collar will keep that under control."

CHAPTER THREE

Peabo yelled as a zap of electricity surged from the doorknob and into him. He shot an accusatory look at Eileen.

The woman looked indifferent to his pain. "Now you have learned what happens when you attempt to open a door your collar isn't keyed for." She pointed to the next door down the hall. "*That* door is the one that actually leads to your room."

Peabo glared daggers at her as he opened and closed his tingling fist. That shock was no joke—no way was it a proper way to teach a lesson. If someone had tried to pull that kind of crap on him when he was back in the army, he'd have kicked the joker's ass into the next county.

When he walked to the next door, he hesitated before reaching out to touch the doorknob.

"You have nothing to fear," said Eileen. "You've already learned your lesson."

But Peabo wasn't about to so easily trust her again. He

flicked the doorknob with his finger, ever so slightly. Only when he felt nothing did he venture to grasp it firmly and turn, opening the door to reveal a small bedroom.

He spoke over his shoulder to Eileen. "How long will I need to stay here?"

"I cannot say. It depends on what the headmistress uncovers. But I do know that the illness that brought you here will bring you back, again and again, unless it is cured. Rest assured, we will make your time here fruitful. We offer all the education and training resources that are part of our mission. But for now, I recommend you rest."

As Eileen departed, Peabo examined the quarters that had been assigned to him. It was nothing fancy. Two single beds, cots really, one of which had neatly folded blankets on it. A chest at the foot of the bed contained several pairs of clothing, all in his size. And beneath the clothes lay his sheathed sword. Not that it would do him much good against these women. They could surely kick his ass before he ever drew his blade.

As he grabbed the sword's familiar handle, a voice growled in his head.

"Where've you been, pea brain? Sitting in a chest waiting for you is getting as old as that recycled hash you used to eat at the chow hall."

Peabo ignored the sword's insults. It felt odd to admit it, but he had missed that rough voice. This sword, which he'd acquired a few months back, was very rare. It had been imbued with intelligence, and that intelligence had somehow dug into Peabo's mind and taken on the personality of Max Decker, his drill sergeant from boot camp many years ago. The man had been a total ass, and yet hearing the voice in his head was comforting in its familiarity.

"Sorry, buddy. I've been laid up for a while. I'm only now on the mend." He swished the blade through the air and had a sudden yearning to spar.

The sword felt the same way. *"Let's go bite something and draw blood. I'm feeling frisky."*

Peabo grinned. "I'll see what I can do."

He belted the sword to his waist and stepped out into the hall. Retracing his steps, he found the door to exit the tower and had already grabbed the metal ring to open it before remembering the risk of getting zapped. Luckily, he felt no such shock this time, and he walked out into the main courtyard.

The shadows were growing longer as the sun drifted lower on the horizon. He walked toward the southwest tower, where Eileen had said melee lessons were held. He tested the handle with a flick, then grabbed it firmly. There was no shock, but he did feel a tingle in his collar. Eileen had said that his collar was keyed for some doors but not others. To Peabo, it felt like this world had come up with some magic version of RFID security chips and embedded it into his collar.

He opened the door and stepped inside the tower. To his surprise, the first floor was completely empty. Just a fifty-foot-wide circle with a spiral staircase on the far side. Lanterns hung from metal brackets evenly spaced on the walls.

"Hello?" he shouted.

A couple seconds later a man's voice yelled back from

above. *"If you want to talk, come up here. I'm not going to yell across three floors."*

Peabo climbed the stairs to the second story, which contained an impressive variety of armor and weapons. They gleamed with reflected light from the lanterns, and a few of them had the same sort of internal glow that his sword had—indicating that they were likely magically enhanced in some way.

"If you want any of my time, you better move it. I'm about to pack up and leave for the night."

Peabo continued up the stairs to the next level, which was also filled with armor and weapons. Except whereas the second floor was all gleaming orderliness, this floor was a chaotic mess. Nearly every inch of open space was piled high with teetering stacks of items in various states of disrepair. There was enough here to equip a small army of medieval soldiers.

The voice called from somewhere on the other side of the piles. *"Just follow the path. And if you know what's good for you, don't touch anything."*

Peabo moved carefully as he weaved his way through the unstable-looking piles. The path soon opened out into a cleared space on the far side of the floor, where he finally found the owner of the voice. A wizened old man with the bushiest white eyebrows Peabo had ever seen sat at a sturdy workbench with a variety of unfamiliar tools scattered on its surface. The man was examining a dagger, and next to his elbow was a bottle of something that glowed like a thousand captured lightning bugs.

"You must be the plainswalker," said the old man, looking up.

"How'd you know?"

The man rolled his eyes. "That's a stupid question if I ever heard one. You got into the tower, so that must be a student's collar you're wearing, and you're plainly not a woman. And it's no secret that a so-called plainswalker has arrived at the Sage's Tower." He frowned, taking Peabo in. "You don't look like what the stories describe. But then again the stories are all probably lies from the First Age."

"How did the stories describe me?" Peabo asked.

"You're supposed to have lightning etched all over your skin. I don't see no lightning on you, my boy." The man pointed at a chair on the opposite end of his workbench. "Have a seat. It hurts my neck looking up at you."

Peabo found himself immediately comfortable with this old-timer who seemed to speak his mind. The man's eyes sparkled with intelligence, and judging by this workshop, he clearly knew a thing or two about weapons and armor. Taking a chance, he unhooked Max from his belt and lay the sword on the table.

"I'm guessing you know quite a bit about enchanted items. What can you tell me about my sword?"

Without even glancing at the weapon, the old man replied, "What makes you think it's enchanted?"

"Well..." Peabo hesitated. It felt weird to say the truth out loud. "It talks to me. In my head. I'd say that's a pretty good sign that it's not an ordinary sword."

The old man looked up from his work, his bushy eyebrows shooting up into his disheveled mop of hair. He ran his gaze along the length of the sword, and when he reached for the pommel, a bluish-white haze appeared between his hand and the sword.

"Yes, indeed." The man nodded in approval. "It is most definitely enchanted. And keyed to a single person."

"What does that mean?"

"What does it mean? It means as long as the sword's owner is alive, it will be antagonistic to anyone else who tries to touch it."

"Antagonistic? You mean it'll... what? Shock them?"

The man shook his head as he pulled out a spool of copper wire and snipped off a length. "How is it you came by such a thing and know nothing about its nature?"

Peabo opened his mouth to respond, but then decided to fudge the truth. After Nicole's warning, he wasn't sure how much was safe to reveal about his past.

"I just found it," he said.

The old man seemed to find that explanation satisfactory, as he asked nothing more. He attached one end of the copper wire to what looked like an old-fashioned two-armed scale, then put on a pair of thick gloves and touched the other end of the wire to the pommel of the sword. As the wire made contact, a humming filled the air, like the sound of a transformer.

One side of the scale immediately moved down as if a heavy object had been dropped onto it.

The old man then began adding weights to the other side. One weight after another, and yet the scale didn't move. Finally the arms of the scale began to wobble.

"What are you doing?" Peabo asked.

"What does it look like I'm doing? I'm determining the

nature of what this sword was infused with." He started adding and taking away smaller weights, and finally he got the two sides of the scale to be even once more.

He looked at Peabo with a wide smile. "To make a sword like this involves a complex process. First you need a smith to forge the sword, and if you're serious about such a thing, you won't be using no journeyman smith from some village nobody has heard of. You want a master of the craft. Then you need someone like me, a conductor who can manipulate life essences and incorporate them into the forging process. And even if both smith and conductor are skilled, there's no guarantee the enchantment will be successful. But if it is..." The little man grinned. "You end up with an object that is much more than the metal it is forged from."

He removed the wire from the pommel, and the weighted side of the scale slammed down. After looking at the weights for a moment, he fixed Peabo with his gaze.

"You're very lucky to have found such a weapon. The essence with which this sword was infused is quite powerful."

His hands still gloved, he reached for a chunk of what looked like clear quartz and pressed it against the blade. The crystal began glowing with an almost blinding white light.

"Fascinating!" the old man muttered. He looked up at Peabo again. "You said the sword communicates with you in your head. Do you mean you sense emotions from it, or is it actually speaking to you in complete sentences?"

"It's not shy about telling me what it thinks, if that's what you're asking."

The wrinkled old man removed his gloves and raked his

fingers through his scraggly white beard. "Well, I can tell you this. According to my measurements, the life essence used to enchant it belonged to a creature that was level nine."

"Creature?" Peabo said. "You mean the thing that's talking to me could have been a rat?"

"Hardly a rat," the man scoffed. "I said level *nine*. And the essence would have to come from a creature of high intelligence. That's one reason why sentient items are so rare."

Peabo had only just wrapped his head around the concept of levels for himself and other humans; he hadn't really given much thought to the levels of animals. The monster manual provided numeric toughness ratings for each creature, and it suddenly dawned on him that those probably corresponded to their level. Rats were a one, while an ogre was a four. A nine would definitely be a frightening prospect.

"Can you tell what type of creature's essence went into my sword?" Peabo asked.

The old man shrugged. "That I can't measure, I'm afraid. It could be several creatures. But I checked the disposition of the essence, and it seems to be a safe one."

"Safe? What does that mean?"

"Not much, really, since it would be rare and foolish for anyone to infuse an item with the essence of a truly unsafe creature. But if, say, a demon's essence were infused into a sword... well, the sword would almost certainly try to overwhelm the will of its possessor."

Peabo didn't like the sound of that. It sounded like something out of a nightmare.

"But although I can't be sure," the old man continued,

"there are two creatures whose essences I would deem most likely for this weapon: either a bronze dragon or a silver one. The former more likely than the latter. But either one is a very powerful creature."

Peabo lay his hand on the pommel, and before he could even ask Max a question, the sword groused, *"You can tell that tower slave that he's wrong on both counts."*

The old man peered at Peabo, his blue eyes sparkling with reflected light. "Did it just speak to you?"

"Yes. He claims you're wrong about the dragons."

"Aha!" He grinned widely. "Then it's a shedu, no doubt about it. Another rare creature, one rarely found on this plane of existence."

A shedu was another creature Peabo had seen in the monster manual. The drawing reminded him of a flying centaur.

"Does the type of creature matter in what the item can do?" he asked.

"Not necessarily, but it certainly can," said the old man. "On rare occasions, some of the dead creature's memories are preserved, and if so, the owner of such an item might find himself with some unexpected insights from that being's life. A shedu spends much of its existence flitting in and out of our plane, so if it retains some of its memories... well, that sword of yours may have some tricks up its scabbard that even it isn't aware of."

As Peabo marveled at the idea of a plane-shifting sword speaking in the voice of a boot camp sergeant, the old man stood and stretched.

"I thank you for bringing me such a fascinating item, but I'm afraid if I don't leave now, my wife will think I'm dead somewhere on the road. And if I'm late for dinner, she may very well kill me herself. I'd invite you and your sword to join me, if not for that collar of yours."

"My collar?" Peabo's hands instinctively went to the metal on his neck.

"Well of course. You can't leave the tower complex with that thing on. At least, not while keeping your head on your shoulders. Didn't they tell you that?"

As the old man ushered Peabo down the stairs and out of the tower, Peabo couldn't help but wonder:

Am I a patient? Or a prisoner?

CHAPTER FOUR

As Peabo re-entered the main tower, he followed his nose toward the scent of spices and charred meat. It didn't take him long to find his way to a room filled with enough picnic-style tables and benches for a hundred people. But for the moment, all the tables were empty. This must not be the usual time to eat.

He walked past the tables to a cafeteria-style serving area, where a rosy-cheeked woman looked up from the vegetables she was dicing and gave him a gap-toothed smile. "Oy, you must be the plainswalker I be hearing about all up and around the town. Is it you?"

Peabo returned the smile. "Yes. My name is Peabo. I guess I'm a bit early for supper?"

"Aye, that you are. Another few minutes before we'll be serving. But you look like a hungry, strapping man, so I can fix you up. What would you like?"

Peabo shrugged. "I don't even know what you have. What do you recommend?"

A woman who was stirring a giant cauldron yelled over the sound of the woman chopping vegetables. "I'll take care of you, darling." She opened an oven to reveal a row of what looked like Cornish hens on a rotating spit.

The woman who'd first greeted him smiled. "Aye, that's a good choice, plainswalker. And I'll make sure you have some roasted vegetables too."

Within two minutes Peabo was seated at one of the tables with a full plate of game hen, some kind of mashed potatoes and gravy, and stewed mushrooms. As he dug in, he heard a bell clang in the distance, and not long after, students began streaming into the cafeteria—all girls between the ages of roughly eight and eighteen. Peabo watched them with amusement. He was in a different world, yet these students were lining up for a meal just like he had when he was their age. Some things were the same no matter what world you were in.

He turned his attention back to his food—which was delicious. The skin from the bird crackled as he cut through it, the meat was dark, and it tasted more like beef than chicken. The "mashed potatoes" was probably some kind of bland root vegetable, but it was infused with a ton of cream and butter. And the mushrooms had a texture that reminded him of portobello mushrooms, but juicier, with a distinct butterscotch flavor.

He was so focused on his food that it took him a moment to realize what had happened. The students had all taken their seats, packing every table in the cafeteria—except his. He continued to eat alone.

Were they that afraid of him? Or was there some social thing that he was somehow oblivious to?

As he looked around, a blonde-haired girl came racing into the cafeteria. She looked disheveled and had a bruised and puffy cheek. Maybe she'd just come from combat training. She was obviously late for meal time. After she got her food, she scanned the room, looking for an empty seat. Several times her gaze skipped past Peabo as if his table wasn't even there. Only when she was convinced there were no other seats available did she come join him—and even then, she sat as far away from him as she could, still not making eye contact.

Now that she was closer, Peabo saw that the bruise on her cheek wasn't the only one. Her arms were also covered with bruises… and her eyes were shining with unshed tears.

This girl had been beaten.

Peabo tried to reach into her thoughts, but sensed nothing. She was apparently well into her training, and probably a higher level than he was.

He opted for casual conversation.

"I really liked today's dinner," he said. "Is the food always this good?"

The girl almost choked on her food as she glanced at him, looked away, and then wiped a few tears away. "I'm not supposed to talk to you." She said it with a hushed tone and focused on her plate as she continued eating.

Her face had turned red, and he didn't need to read her mind to know she was praying he didn't talk to her again.

So that was why everyone was avoiding him. They'd been told to not talk to him. But why?

Peabo focused on the younger girls in the room. Their minds were still open enough for him to hear their thoughts. Most were focused on their meal, or classes. Others were thinking about home. Many were a bit scared about some kind of upcoming exams, which was understandable. He didn't pick up any thoughts about himself.

But he did notice something weird. Whereas all of the older girls had blonde hair, blue eyes, and pale skin—just like Nicole, and all the adult women he'd seen here—the younger girls had a variety of colorings. Brown hair, black hair, red hair. Skin tones that ranged from pink to charcoal.

Peabo suddenly recalled something Nicole had said to him long ago.

"As a part of my training, my body was infused with certain... treatments. These treatments make blood maidens immune to the effects of most spells and poison. They're also why we cannot have children."

Apparently these treatments also changed one's appearance.

How was that possible? Was it safe? Did these poor girls all sign up for this voluntarily? Peabo couldn't help but wonder.

"Plainswalker, are you done with your meal?"

Peabo looked up to discover that Leena, the executor he'd met earlier, had come up to stand behind him.

"Yes. I'm done. It was delicious."

"Good. We're going to the training floor. I've got a special exercise I want you to try."

Peabo started to pick up his plate as he stood, but Leena waved for him to put it back down. "Scarlett will take care of that." She pointed at the bruised girl, who nodded obediently. Then she walked off at a brisk pace, leaving Peabo no choice but to follow quickly.

The woman was clearly used to giving orders.

Peabo was rocked backward as Leena struck him across the face. The woman's open-handed slap had come so quickly, so unexpectedly, it was as if her hand had just magically appeared against his cheek.

She was *that* fast.

He'd encountered impossible speed from Nicole, but even she couldn't compare to Leena. This woman had to be a higher level than anyone he'd ever met.

They were in an empty room on the second floor of the main tower—a room apparently meant for sparring. Peabo was not looking forward to the exercise. He had the greater strength, but he knew that strength could easily be offset by a difference in speed. And given Leena's speed, any match between them would be like an adult sparring with a toddler.

"What skills do you have, plainswalker?" Leena asked.

Peabo hesitated. "I—I don't know what you mean."

"You've read the histories. The people of the First Age were afraid of the power of the plainswalker. What is this power that was so feared?"

The truth was, Peabo knew very little about the history of

this world, and the only time he'd ever experienced any kind of "power" was just after he'd killed the vampire named Lord Dvorak. He'd leveled up as a result, and the experience was etched in his memory. He'd manipulated light in some way, dividing it into its constituent wavelengths, weaving those wavelengths together, making them dance.

And he had no idea how he'd done it. He'd tried doing it again—countless times—but without a hint of success.

But he wasn't about to tell Leena any of this. His instincts told him not to trust her. Not to trust anyone in this place.

"I don't have any power that I'm aware of."

Leena's gaze narrowed, and she stepped closer. "That's a lie." She spoke with a menacing tone that raised the hairs on the back of Peabo's neck. "You do have power—some skill unique to who and what you are. And we believe this power is key to your recovery. It's my job to help you learn what it is— so you can be cured."

Before Peabo could respond, Leena's fist caught him with an uppercut that snapped his head back.

He tasted blood.

Leena began walking in a circle around him, speaking in a calm, professorial tone—as if she hadn't just punched him in the face.

"We have certain techniques we use when a student has difficulty expressing her innate skills. These techniques are quite effective in initiating a fight-or-flight reaction." She gave Peabo a hard shove that nearly knocked him off his feet. "And flight won't be an option, that much I can promise you."

Peabo spit a glob of blood to the floor, rolled his shoulders and took a ready stance. If this woman wanted a fight, she was going to get one.

Leena looked him up and down and nodded. "Attack me, plainswalker. You know you want to. I'll give you one free hit."

Peabo stepped in range, tingling from the dump of adrenaline in his bloodstream. Back in the real world, he was a third-degree black belt, having practiced karate for almost twenty years. If he only had one free hit, he needed to make it count.

In a sudden movement, he launched a vicious spinning back kick. But when he landed on his feet, he hadn't hit a thing. Leena had stepped out of range faster than should have been possible.

"Is that the best you can do?" she teased. She stuck her chin out and tapped it with a finger. "Come on, big boy. Hit me."

Peabo took a deep breath and let it out. She was baiting him. There was no doubt about it.

He exploded with a straight punch to her center mass.

She didn't even bother to block it or dodge it.

She just hit him first.

Before his punch could connect, she launched her own closed-fist punch to the side of his jaw. It smashed into him with such intensity that he felt something crack. He didn't even know how he found himself lying on his back, coughing up blood, but the sadistic woman was hovering over him with a look of disdain.

"That's enough for now," she said. "We'll continue tomorrow."

Then she smashed her fist once more into his jaw, and everything went dark.

CHAPTER FIVE

Peabo woke to the sound of someone knocking on his bedroom door. He sat up in bed, wincing at the expectation of pain, and was genuinely surprised that he felt okay. There was some tenderness in his jaw, and he was a bit shaky, but he wasn't seriously injured by the pummeling he'd taken the day before. Someone must have brought him back to his room, cleaned him up, and healed him.

Knock, knock, knock.

"One second," Peabo yelled through the door.

He grabbed fresh clothes from the chest at the foot of his bed and quickly got dressed and opened the door.

He found Eileen waiting outside, looking just as sour and annoyed as she had the first time he met her. For some reason the sight put a smile on his face, and he couldn't resist giving the woman a quick hug, which earned him a raised eyebrow.

"It's good to see you, Eileen."

She took a step back and handed him a slip of paper. "Your class schedule."

He scanned the list. The first class of the day was going to be a science class. That should be interesting. The science of this world was… different. But the last item on today's agenda made him groan.

Session with Executor Leena. Main tower. Second Floor. Exercise room C.

"Your first class begins in thirty minutes, and breakfast service ends in fifteen," said Eileen. "So I suggest you get moving."

She turned to go, but Peabo stopped her with a hand on her shoulder. She glared at the hand, and he immediately let go.

"Sorry, I just… I have a quick question about this collar." He touched the metal band around his neck. "You said it acted like a key for some doors in the complex, but someone else suggested that it also prevents me from leaving the tower complex. And that… well, that it might kill me if I tried. Is that true?"

The woman laughed, then immediately resumed her dour expression. "It won't kill you. But yes, you will be prevented from leaving."

"So… what would happen? Let's say I'm sleepwalking and I accidentally cross some line out there…"

"You will find yourself unable to go further," Eileen said. "The girls who study here make a commitment to see their training through to the end. There is no leaving until then. Your situation is obviously different. You're staying here for your own safety, as your condition will kill you if not properly treated. But as you're a guest of the tower, according to protocol you must be treated like any other student."

She turned to go again, so Peabo asked his next question quickly. "Why are the other students not allowed to talk to me when I'm in the cafeteria?"

"Not allowed?" Eileen looked genuinely surprised. "I'd imagine the girls would love to talk to someone from the outside, seeing as most of them haven't been outside these towers in years." She gave him what she probably thought was a sympathetic smile. "Perhaps you should talk to the headmistress. Ariandelle is the one who sets policy within the tower complex. Right now, you are going to be late. If you have more questions for me, my office is on the third floor of this tower."

With that, she turned and walked down the hall, and Peabo, taking the hint, rushed off to the cafeteria—and a full day of classes.

Peabo found himself in a class filled with young girls— probably no older than twelve. Thankfully someone had put a single adult-sized desk and chair at the front of the room. Otherwise there would have been no seat he could have squeezed into.

The girls didn't speak to him, but as they waited for class to begin, he heard their thoughts as clearly as if they were speaking aloud.

"Why can't we talk with him? He doesn't seem dangerous."

"I wonder if he's been paired with anyone yet. He's huge,

but has a kind face."

"I wonder if he's still sick."

The teacher snapped her fingers to begin the lesson. "Today we'll be continuing our discussion about the things we cannot see with our eyes. Who here can tell me the two types of weaving arts?"

Peabo actually knew the answer to this one. *Weaving* was the term people here used in place of what he thought of as magic. He raised his hand, as did several of the girls.

The teacher smiled and pointed at him. "Peabo, I'd love to hear your answer."

"The two—" he began, but the teacher cut him off.

"Anyone who is giving an answer in this class must stand and speak clearly so others can hear."

Peabo levered himself to his feet. "The two types of weaving are healing and conducting. Healing takes energy from within the healer and concentrates it elsewhere. Conducting takes force from outside the conductor's body before manipulating it."

The teacher nodded with approval. "Very good. You may sit."

As soon as Peabo sat, he raised his hand again.

"Yes, Peabo?"

"May I ask a question related to what I just said?"

"Please."

"I've never used either of these skills myself, but I've seen it done. Even though conductors use energy from outside of themselves, don't they need to use some of their own energy as well in order to manipulate the external energy?"

The teacher nodded. "Excellent question. And you're absolutely correct. The use of any of the weaving arts requires an effort on the part of the weaver. That becomes obvious when a conductor is using a lot of force against an enemy. Even though all of the force he's using is coming from outside the conductor's body, in the end, the conductor will be left exhausted. And that's a perfect segue into the topic I wanted to cover with you all today. Can anyone tell me what the energy *looks like* that's being used by someone using the weaving arts?"

She called on a girl whose hand shot up, and the girl stood. The girl had raven-black hair, but with blonde roots. Peabo wondered if she'd just undergone the "treatments" that Nicole had mentioned.

"The energy is invisible," the girl said.

"And why is that, Kailey?"

The girl looked down at her feet for a few long seconds. When she looked up, her eyes were wet with tears, and she looked terrified. "I'm... I'm not sure."

The teacher walked over and gave her a hug. "It's okay, Kailey. You'll be fine."

Peabo had no idea what was going on, but the other girls' thoughts gave it away.

"Will Executor Clara send her away?"

"Why'd she offer an answer when she wasn't sure?"

"Please please please don't send her out. She's going through the change and it probably confused her. I have the change coming next week. Nameless, save me from such a mistake."

Could a single mistake get a girl kicked out of this place?

From what Nicole had described, the selection process to enter the tower was brutal. It was probably easier to get into Harvard. And yet, for simply not knowing a single answer in a random class, you could lose it all?

Peabo had already seen what happened to girls who didn't make the cut: they were sold at auction.

He felt the girl's anguish as if it were his own, and it broke his heart. He wished he could protect her from what was going to happen. The answer she was missing was so simple. *The energy is probably too small to see,* he thought.

Kailey gasped, then turned and stared with bloodshot eyes at Peabo. When she spoke, her voice was trembling.

"Maybe... maybe the energy is too small to see?"

The teacher cupped Kailey's face and smiled. "Very good, young lady. Very good." She motioned to the girl's chair. "Have a seat."

The tension in the room suddenly vanished, and Peabo heard the thoughts of relief in the other girls.

"I've never seen someone get so close to getting kicked out before!"

"That was so scary to watch. Poor Kailey, she'll probably never answer another question voluntarily again."

Peabo stared at the poor girl, who was looking over at him curiously. Had she somehow heard him think the answer?

Apparently she had, for as she wiped the tears from her cheeks, she mouthed the words, *"Thank you."*

Peabo was stunned. Had he actually sent the girl his thoughts? He'd done that all the time with Nicole, but he was paired to her, which was like a psychic bond of sorts. But this girl was a complete stranger… and still she evidently had heard him. The more he replayed in his mind's eye what had just happened, the less doubt he had about it.

Peabo thought back to something that had happened a few months earlier. He and Nicole were in a forest, and he heard a warning from the semi-sentient trees. Nicole claimed that that shouldn't have been possible. But it had happened. And just now it had happened again, but in reverse—he'd sent the message.

Was this something to do with him being a plainswalker?

The teacher continued the lesson. "Kailey is correct: the energy is too small for us to see with our eyes. But it's there nonetheless." She turned to a chalkboard behind her and began drawing pictures—pictures that, to Peabo's surprise, were identical to ones he'd studied in chemistry classes back in school. She used words that he'd never heard before, but when she used them to label the pictures, Peabo knew exactly what she was talking about.

It was amazing. This was an entirely new world. In fact, it was supposed to be an entirely different universe. But Peabo had come to realize that many of the elements of science he was familiar with from back home still existed here. All he had to do was translate a few words, and everything the teacher was saying made sense.

"Everything you can see or touch, everything that exists, is ultimately made of atoms—the smallest units of matter. The different ways that these atoms are constructed give you different elements and therefore different amounts of energy.

Depending on their form, they help create everything in our world."

She didn't use the word "atom," but Peabo thought of it that way. And the drawing on the board consisted of the familiar shells surrounding a central nucleus. Basic chemistry.

She soon steered the discussion back to the concept of weaving energy. "Our bodies take energy from these tiny building blocks. When we eat, some of the energy stored in the food is taken to run our bodies, to keep us warm… and to manipulate weaving energies. We store that energy in our bodies for later use. But that's not the only place we can store weaving energies."

She held up a small crystal, about the size of a finger. "This is a weaving crystal." She then reached in her pocket and pulled out a second crystal, which looked much like the first—except this one was glowing brightly. "Class, the difference between these two crystals is that the glowing one has been infused with energy. A weaving crystal can capture and store the energy involved in the weaving process—so that it can be used at a later time."

Several hands shot up into the air, and the teacher pointed to one.

"How does the energy get into the crystal?" the girl asked.

"It takes a very specialized sort of weaver to route energy into a weaving crystal," the teacher said. "It's similar to the way a healer works, but instead of passing the energy from the healer to her target, a crystal weaver transfers that energy into the crystal."

Peabo raised his hand.

"Yes, Peabo."

"Does that mean if a healer wanted to heal an extraordinary amount of injuries, more than they'd normally be capable of, they could tap the energy from the crystal to assist them? Is that the idea?"

The teacher nodded. "Exactly right."

"And how common are crystal weavers?"

"Unfortunately, they are extremely rare. Healing weavers are the most common, with about three times as many healers as conductors. And with women that ratio is even larger: almost ninety percent of us have healing abilities, with only about ten percent being conductors. For men that ratio is a mere sixty-to-forty, though still in favor of healing abilities. The girls here already know that no one person has talent in both domains.

"But crystal weaving is quite specialized. In fact, we have only one crystal weaver in the entire tower complex. He spends most of his time in the southeast tower, infusing essences into forged items."

Peabo's eyes widened. She was talking about the old man who'd talked to him about Max, his sword.

The teacher continued. "You will find more in some of the larger cities, but it is estimated that there are no more than a few dozen crystal weavers in all of existence. Which makes these gems very rare—and very valuable."

Peabo raised his hand once again, and the teacher smiled. "Make this your last question, Peabo. We do have lessons to cover."

"Sorry. I was just wondering, how much energy can be

stored in a crystal? Is it an infinite amount? How can you tell how much energy the crystal has? Does it get brighter, or heavier or something, when it's charged more?"

"I can see that you have a natural interest in science, which pleases me. What you're asking about is still today being researched in the king's halls. But I can tell you it has to do with measuring the relationship of matter to energy."

She turned to the board and wrote out a long and complex equation. Then, smiling at the class, she said, "Don't worry, girls. You are not required to know this concept to pass on to the next phase of your education. But it may interest those of you who might want to enter the research field."

She opened a drawer in her desk and pulled out an ordinary pin. "Take this pin," she said. "It weighs very little. In the equation on the board, I've started with the approximate weight of this pin and converted it to another metric that you might be familiar with: the amount of power exerted by a horse. If any of you have ever tried to hold a horse back, you know they're very strong creatures. And yet, if we converted this tiny pin into pure energy, the result would be equivalent to the amount of energy required for a horse to pull a wagon for over three thousand years."

Several students in the class gasped, but Peabo's mind raced. What she'd just described, and the equation she'd written on the board, was very much akin to Einstein's most famous equation describing the relationship of energy to matter.

"So, Peabo, to answer your question, the amount of energy a single weaving crystal could hold is far, far more than you or

I could ever imagine. If there's a limit, it's one that nobody could ever run into. As to how to determine the amount of energy contained within a crystal, I'd have to research that. I can say that, theoretically at least, it would change weight as you suggest, but from a practical standpoint you're unlikely to be able to measure the difference. It would be much too small to detect."

Peabo's thoughts were racing as the teacher handed him a spare textbook from her desk and asked the class to open it up to a specific page.

If that gem could be used as a battery for magic, it seemed like something that would be crucial for critical situations.

The only time he'd ever used anything that resembled a weaving skill was when he'd hidden from Lord Dvorak's guards. Just that act alone had left him exhausted. He'd also seen how tired Nicole had become the various times she'd healed him. If a gem could be used to avoid that exhaustion and maybe even do way more than someone would normally be capable of, it could be a life saver.

As he opened the textbook, he shoved thoughts of magical batteries away for the moment. He had other things to worry about at the moment.

He put a hand to the back of his neck and grimaced. The soreness was coming back. That was the first sign he'd had before the headaches came, and then the inevitable nosebleeds. Whatever the executors had done to ease his pain, it was already beginning to wear off.

He needed to find a cure. Or this thing, whatever it was, would eventually kill him.

CHAPTER SIX

Peabo's head was throbbing and his neck felt stiff. He turned his head to the right until he felt a pop in his spine, then turned to the left and did the same. It helped loosen things a bit, but it sure didn't help with the anxiety. He was facing Executor Leena once again, and he'd come to dread these sessions of hers.

They were in the same empty room as always. Some unlucky maid must have been tasked with cleaning up each day, because somehow the white stone walls were unstained by his blood—of which he had shed more than he'd care to admit.

Though the woman was a foot shorter than him, and half his weight, her speed made all the difference. She could literally tell him that she was going to slap his left cheek and he wouldn't be able to bring his hand up fast enough to block the attack.

As for laying a hand on her… he couldn't do that if he

tried.

When Leena put her hand on his shoulder, it took every ounce of self-control he had to not flinch or back away.

"Peabo, it may seem like I'm doing this just to drive you crazy, but I assure you, I have a reason. You're subconsciously blocking your abilities from coming out, and we need to release them in order to cure you. How have you been feeling? Have the headaches started up again?"

Peabo nodded. A week ago, it had started with a sore neck, and since then things had gotten progressively worse. He knew that soon he'd be experiencing debilitating migraines that would sometimes affect his vision, and then the nosebleeds would start.

Leena patted him on the cheek, and this time he did flinch. "Unfortunately, pummeling you, while entertaining, hasn't unblocked your abilities. So let's take a different approach. I want you to attack me. Maybe if you're on the offensive, it will help you loosen whatever it is that's holding you back."

Peabo didn't need to be asked twice. He launched a punch directly at the woman's face, and to his surprise, he actually touched her nose—if only barely—as she pulled back.

She cackled with laughter and curled her finger at him. "Come on, big boy."

Peabo sent a kick at her, which of course missed. He continued to advance, using a barrage of punches, kicks, and leg sweeps. He even charged her, making an attempt to wrestle her to the ground.

He didn't touch her once. He always just barely missed, as if Leena didn't feel like it was worth the bother to move away from him any more than was necessary. It felt to Peabo like a taunt.

He continued attacking all the same, without Leena ever once making a counterattack. After about five minutes, Peabo was sweaty and breathless. He bent over at the waist, hands on his knees.

Leena walked closer. "You need to continue—"

Peabo lunged with an upper-cut that connected solidly with the woman's chin.

She staggered back several feet, and a trickle of blood coming from the side of her mouth.

He had hit her. And it felt good.

Leena didn't seem to agree. She wiped her face, looked at the blood on her fingertips, and howled with anger. Peabo felt her pound the side of his face before he'd even registered that she'd moved. His head rocked to the side, and before he could wind up for a return punch, she'd launched a kick to his jaw that made the room tilt. The next thing he knew he was staring up at the ceiling.

But Leena wasn't done. She launched another kick—this time between his legs. He convulsed from the sudden electric surge of pain, and when the next kick hit him in the face, he heard the bone crack.

The room turned gray. In time, he realized the attacks had stopped. Had he passed out? He must have, because he heard a woman's voice in the room, and it wasn't Leena's.

"Your tongue seems to be the only thing that got damaged. The healing should take full effect within an hour. Don't eat anything before then. How did he manage to hit you, anyway?"

"The animal attacked me when I wasn't looking," Leena growled.

Liar, Peabo thought. *I tagged you fair and square.*

"It looks like you taught him a lesson in response. Do you want him healed as well?"

A long moment of silence passed before Leena responded. "If it were up to me, I'd let him live out the rest of his days as a sterile, deformed freak. But Ariandelle thinks she can get something out of him, so do what you have to. But no more than that."

Her footsteps strode away and a door slammed shut, and then Peabo sensed someone kneeling beside him. A warm sensation bloomed below his waist, and he felt the full pain of his injury all over again. He cried out and curled up into a fetal position, his entire body breaking out with sweat.

That was when he opened his eyes and realized he couldn't see.

"Calm down," said the healer. "You'll be fine."

He felt her cool hand on his forehead, then a wave of heat flowed over his face. Flashes of light appeared in the gray, and he saw an older woman's face hovering over him.

Eileen.

She covered his mouth with her hand and motioned for him to be quiet.

"Hold still. I promise you'll be fine."

Her hand glowed white, and as he felt its warmth seep through his head all the way down the back of his neck, he both felt and heard the bones snap back into place.

Eileen worked on him for another ten minutes, checking

him from head to toe, making sure he had suffered no other injuries. Only when she was done did she allow him to rise to a seated position.

Healed or not, he was still in a great deal of pain. Just the act of sitting sent shooting pains racing from his groin in both directions, down his legs and up into his chest.

"What you're feeling is phantom pain from your injuries. Those will fade." Eileen handed him a moist towel. "Clean your face—you're a bloody mess. Then stand up and move around. I want to make sure I didn't miss anything."

Peabo wiped his face of the dried blood. A lot of it seemed to have come from his right ear. He knew enough about medicine to know that unless he had a punctured eardrum—which he didn't have, seeing as he'd been able to hear just fine—only cases that involved traumatic brain injury caused bleeding from the ears. The realization made him furious. That woman had come within a hair's breadth of killing him.

He pulled in a deep breath and let it out slowly, trying to calm his racing heart.

Eileen looked him in the eye. "Well? Do you have any other pains I need to know about?"

Peabo still felt the shooting pains from his nether region, but they were already less intense. "I think I'm okay," he said. He started to reach out to hug the older woman, then stopped and dropped his hands at his sides. "I heard what she said. About doing the bare minimum. Thank you, Eileen. I'll never forget your help."

Eileen's sour expression deepened. "I don't work for Leena. I work for the headmistress. But you're lucky it was me who was on duty. The best thanks you can give me would be for you not to need my services again." She motioned to the door. "Now get going. Given the severity of your injuries, the healing will require you to get some rest."

Peabo thanked her once more, then turned gingerly and left the sparring room. As he walked down the hallway, Leena's words sounded in his mind.

If it were up to me, I'd let him live out the rest of his days as a sterile, deformed freak.

Peabo couldn't think of anyone in his life that he'd ever hated. Even when he'd killed people during war, there was no strong emotion tied to his actions. Those kills were in defense of team members or country or both. It was never personal.

This was. He had a searing hatred for the woman who'd nearly killed him.

He knew it was an unhealthy emotion. And he had a looming dread when he thought of their next encounter. He had no idea how that would proceed, given what had happened today.

He was still on his way out of the tower when he heard the sound of a woman crying. The sound was close by, and Peabo stopped and scanned the hallway. When he spotted a door that had been left ajar, he poked his head in.

The door led to a training room similar to the one he'd just left. Standing in the far corner was a tall blonde girl, leaning her forehead against the wall and hugging herself.

She wasn't just crying. She was sobbing.

"Are you okay?" Peabo asked.

The girl spun to face him. Her nose was bloody and she had

the beginnings of a black eye. But he recognized her immediately. It was the bruised girl who'd sat with him in the cafeteria on that first day.

"Scarlett?" He walked toward her, concerned.

"I'm sorry," she said. "You shouldn't see me like this." But despite her words, she didn't turn away, and she didn't stop crying.

Without thinking, Peabo put his arms around her. She returned the embrace, buried her bloody face into his shirt, and bawled.

"Was this from training?" he asked when the sobs subsided a bit.

She nodded against his shoulder.

Nicole had told him that the tower training had been brutal, but she'd never talked about it other than in generalities. Now he was getting a clearer picture of what she'd been through— and why she didn't like to talk about it.

Scarlett pulled back and wiped her face. "Please don't tell anyone you saw me like this," she said. Then she grabbed a towel and ran out of the room.

Peabo looked at the empty doorway, trying to reconcile the value of what these kids were learning against the abuse they were taking. All in the name of becoming a so-called blood maiden.

He was no stranger to brutal training. He'd gone through the Q Course and all the associated hell that was required to make it into the Army's Special Forces. But that had been in the service of a lofty goal. More than that, it had always been a dream of his. To do something for his country. To make a difference. Was that how these girls felt? Was this a noble goal? And were they even old enough to make that sort of commitment?

They were practically killing themselves in pursuit of whatever this was. And with one simple mistake, they could have it all taken away from them.

Taking a deep breath, he left the room and headed once more for the stairs. As he walked, he once more felt the phantom pains from his groin. Phantom or not, they *hurt*. And the more he thought about what had happened, the more it affected him physically. He felt nauseated, and had to hold back a cry of pain when, for a moment, he felt as though his manhood was rupturing.

Was this what PTSD was like?

Two tours in Afghanistan and one in Iraq, and he'd never had an injury, nor had he suffered psychologically from the memories of some truly horrific scenes. But he suspected that the memories of today were going to linger with him for quite a while.

Worse, he'd have to face that woman again.

After lunch the next day—which he ate alone as always—he had a few hours' gap before his next class, and decided to use the time to explore. He hadn't yet been inside the northwest tower—the physical sciences building—so he went there first. He was relieved when he was able to turn the doorknob without receiving an electric shock.

Inside, a middle-aged man in glasses was sitting at a desk. "May I help you?"

Peabo wasn't sure what to say. He settled on the truth. "I don't know. I just... I had some free time and wanted to see what was in this tower. Am I allowed to do that?"

The man grinned. "I don't see why not. You must be the plainswalker. Peabo, yes?"

Peabo returned the man's smile. "Yes. That's me." He shook the man's hand. Though small, the man had a strong grip.

"I'm glad to finally meet you," the man said. "I've read about plainswalkers in the old texts, but until I heard about your arrival I had never imagined I'd meet one." He nodded at Peabo's arm. "You even have the lightning markers, just like the books say. Though they seem very faint."

Peabo was surprised to see that the markings were starting to come back. "Ah, well. They're not usually that faint. Before arriving here I took a potion that masked the markings. I guess it's wearing off."

The man nodded. "Of course, I understand. You wanted to travel without being recognized for who you are. Well, now that you're here, would you like me to show you around?"

"That would be great. That is, if you have time, Mister...?"

"Just call me Binary."

"Binary? That's an unusual name. Or at least, it is to me. Though I'm not from the mainland. Obviously."

"It's actually more of a nickname. Kind of a First Age joke."

Without explaining further, Binary led Peabo up to the

second floor, which looked very much like a museum exhibit. Tables were spread across the space, each holding an array of labeled objects.

"On this floor," said Binary, "are what the people of the First Age called 'household goods.'"

Peabo approached the closest table, upon which stood what looked remarkably like a stand mixer. In fact, it was almost identical to the KitchenAid model his mother had at home when he was growing up. What on earth?

He looked around at the other tables and spotted something else that caught his interest. "Why is that hook way over there?" he asked.

"What hook?" Binary looked confused. "I don't know what you mean."

"Let me show you." Peabo went over to the other table, retrieved the hook attachment, and brought it back to the mixer. "This attachment goes into here," he said, connecting the dough hook to the mixer.

"How did you know that would fit there?" Binary asked.

"Oh, I know what these were used for. I remember my mother—"

He stopped himself at Binary's look of wide-eyed amazement. It was probably best not to reveal too much about his unusual past.

"I mean to say, I remember hearing about such a thing from my mother. She knew a thing or two about history. This device was used in homes to help mix ingredients. And this hook attachment was used to knead dough. You know, to make bread."

The tiny man stared at the dough hook with a look that expressed nothing short of awe. "*Amazing.* I would never have guessed. Breadmaking! With that!" He shook his head and looked up at Peabo. "If you've heard tales such as these, you must tell me *everything.* Is there anything else in this room you recognize?"

Peabo laughed. He had been expecting this man to teach *him* about the First Age, and here Peabo was the teacher instead.

He walked between the rows of tables, and occasionally he'd recognize something simple: a rusted adjustable wrench, the remnants of some kind of engine, what might have been a broken motherboard. That word—*broken*—described a lot of the items here. And often they were just parts, remnants of something larger.

But it made no sense. The First Age was many thousands of years ago. How was it that they had technology that was far more advanced than what the present-day world possessed? Could a society really lose touch with everything they had known, to the extent that such simple everyday items had become no more than mysterious artifacts?

"Well?" said Binary with excitement. "Do you recognize anything else?"

Peabo decided once again to proceed with caution. "I'm afraid not," he lied. "Sorry. But maybe you can tell me what you know about these things. Where were they found?"

Binary looked disappointed, but perhaps more comfortable now that he was back to being the expert. "The items on this floor were found in an archaeological dig to the north. They come from a home that was somehow spared the great earthquakes and devastation at the end of the First Age. This is how we know they are household goods, even though in many cases we have not yet determined their use. Such as the breadmaking hook." He shook his head at that once again, then motioned for Peabo to follow him back to the stairs. "There's lots more to look at on the third floor. These items came from a shelter used to protect people from the attacks that caused the end of the First Age."

"Can you tell me more about that?" Peabo asked. "What exactly happened at the end of the First Age? I get that there was a war, but between whom?"

Binary tsked. "It's unfortunate that proper history is not covered in the schools like it should be. The First Age ended with what is sometimes called the War of the Gods. You're of course familiar with the Nameless One. Well back then there were other gods, specifically the twin gods known also as the Dark Ones. They and their faction launched an attack on those who were faithful to the Nameless One, and in so doing, they started the great war."

Peabo remembered what he'd learned about the twin gods in his history classes here in the tower, as well as what Nicole had told him long ago about the Dark Ones—namely that they were evil, and among the worst of their kind.

They arrived at the third floor, which looked to Peabo like a cross between a museum and an armory. The "artifacts" on display here were mostly weapons. Futuristic weapons, at least from Peabo's frame of reference. The one closest to him looked like a plasma rifle straight out of Buck Rogers. It had no magazine to hold bullets, but next to it was a battery pack of some kind. Or at least, Peabo thought that was what it was. Although it had long ago been ruined, it was undeniable that it would fit into the back of the weapon's buttstock.

Binary saw Peabo studying the rifle and joined him. "I've found some documentation from the First Age that called this an *ion pulse cannon*. I know not what that means, and its design is beyond our understanding, but the references in the archives suggest it was used to combat something called *electronics*."

Peabo had to suppress a smile. What the man was describing was tech that had been only theoretical back on Earth. An ion cannon was designed to send a beam of charged ions not at a person, but at an electronic object—a vehicle, computer, a power plant, or anything that might be damaged by having a surge of electricity run through it. Effectively, the cannon sent out a directional EMP—electromagnetic pulse—that disabled electronics.

Peabo was far from an expert on such things, but still this was undeniable proof that back in the day, the people on this planet had been at least as advanced as Earth was, if not more so.

Binary led Peabo across the room to a table that held two notebook-sizes devices. Next to them was a stack of yellowed paper with printing on it.

"Here we have something called a *computer*." Binary pointed at the two half-melted chunks of metal and plastic. "All we know of such things is that they were very powerful and controlled many things in the First Age." He motioned to the papers. "This is written in the language that computers speak. I've been working for many years to decipher it. In the First Age, the language was called... Binary." He winked.

Peabo smiled. "And thus your name."

"Exactly."

On the printout was an endless stream of zeroes and ones. Peabo had taken a couple of basic computer classes in college, just enough to know that at a very basic level, all of a computer's instructions were composed of on-and-off commands, represented by ones and zeroes.

As Binary looked at the printout, probably for the millionth time, Peabo wandered the rest of the room, scanning the rest of the artifacts. He stopped short when he saw the grenade.

It was a metal object the size of a baseball, and on one end it had what in the military he'd have called a spoon— a long piece of metal that acted as a safety lever. Attached to the top of the lever was a metal pin with a ring attached to it. Not only was this clearly a grenade, it was probably live.

And probably unstable.

The card on the table had no writing on it. Binary probably had no idea what it even was.

Peabo began backing away. "Binary, you don't try to *use* any of these things, do you?"

"Of course not. I only observe and read. I'm a curator. Why do you ask?"

"I guess I'm just worried that some of these things might be dangerous. I wouldn't want you to have an accident."

Binary laughed. "No need to worry. I've been studying First Age artifacts for many, many years. I know to approach them with caution. Though I'm always eager to learn more. If you've heard any more First Age stories like the one about the breadmaker…"

"I'll be sure to share. I really appreciate you taking the time to show me all this stuff."

"It was my pleasure. Please come back and visit any time."

"I'll definitely do that."

As Peabo went back down the stairs and departed the tower, he shook his head. He was more curious than ever about this planet's history. Back on Earth, there were examples of societies that had stagnated for centuries—like Europe during the Dark Ages—but Peabo couldn't think of a single example of a society where things went so drastically backwards, with so much being forgotten altogether. Maybe after the burning of the library at Alexandria? Peabo wasn't a historian, so he wasn't sure.

Just as surprising was the fact that this world, back in its First Age, had once been very much like Earth. Homes with appliances and electricity. Computers. Advanced weaponry.

He felt a sudden urge to find a library. This place must have one.

But that would have to wait. At the moment, he had some-where else he needed to be.

He had a meeting with the headmistress.

CHAPTER SEVEN

There was no doubt in Peabo's mind that he'd be dead if he hadn't come to the Sage's Tower. That he'd be dead if the headmistress hadn't known how to treat him. He owed her his life. But the woman still made him uneasy. Perhaps it was the white glow that emanated from her, like she was cloaked in a holy aura. Like an angel. But a dangerous one.

But despite his uneasiness, as the woman spoke to him, her voice wrapped him in a hazy cocoon, and he felt the strangest compulsion to agree with everything she was saying. If she had told him that up was down and down was up, he'd be very tempted to believe her.

"Peabo, you need to understand that you're here for your own safety. We're trying to help you."

Peabo felt goose bumps rise all over his body.

Accept what I'm saying. Believe me.

He was tempted to do just that. So he took a deep breath and focused on the throbbing pain in his head. "That woman. Leena. She almost killed me."

Ariandelle gave him an appraising look. "You don't look injured."

You're fine. Calm down. You are safe within these walls.

Peabo sensed the invisible waves of influence coming from the woman on the other side of the desk. It caused a hot anger to spark within him, and he focused on that, stoked that flame.

"I'm not injured now, but that's only thanks to the healing that I received afterwards."

Ariandelle graced him with a beneficent smile. "Leena is only doing the job that she's been asked to do—for your bene-fit. She's trying to help you break through your mental barriers. And she's very good at what she does. But if you're concerned with her approach, I'll talk with her. Perhaps we can find other ways. I promised the prelate of the Nameless One that you would remain healthy while under the care of the Sage's Tower, and I aim to keep that promise."

Trust me. Believe what I am saying.

Despite her soothing voice and warm smile, there was something about this woman that set off alarms in Peabo's head. She wasn't necessarily lying, but he felt certain she wasn't telling him the full truth, either. And yet he could see he wasn't going to get any more answers from her. Not today, anyway.

He stood. "Thank you for your time, headmistress. I appreciate you listening to me."

"Anytime, Peabo. Just remember, we're trying to help you."

As Peabo walked back to his room, he walked back through the conversation he'd just had. He hadn't sensed any deception when Ariandelle said they were trying to help him. And the truth was, he needed them to. His headaches were getting worse at a faster pace than the last time.

He just hoped they could find a cure for him soon. He didn't want to stay in this place any longer than absolutely necessary.

———

Peabo waited for Leena in the sparring room on the third floor, his head throbbing. He sat cross-legged, his eyes closed, trying to set aside the ache by focusing on his other senses.

He breathed in deeply but detected no odors. Just a sterile sense of nothingness. It was odd for a room not to have any smell to it at all. He was no geologist, but he knew that stone had some level of porosity, and that over time it should have absorbed some of the smells of people bleeding, sweating, and puking in this room. But maybe geology was different in this world. Peabo filed that question away for science class.

Suddenly he sensed something just outside the room, and he hopped to his feet as Leena walked into the room. She wasn't dressed in the normal shapeless woolen clothing that everyone wore in the tower complex. Instead, she was wearing a long shirt, leaving her legs bare up to mid-thigh, and she was barefoot. And as she approached him with a sly smile, he suspected she wasn't wearing anything beneath that shirt.

"I talked with Ariandelle," Leena said with a husky growl, "and there's been a change of plans." She walked up to him, placed a hand on his chest, and handed him a flask. "Drink this."

He took a cautious step back and sniffed at the unstoppered bottle. It smelled foul. "What is it?"

Leena once again closed the distance between them, and this time her hand didn't go to his chest. She gave him a light tap below the waist. "It's for you," she growled.

"Whoa there." Peabo set the bottle down on the floor. "Listen, I don't know what Ariandelle told you, but—"

Leena struck him with an open-handed slap, sending his head rocking sideways. "You think I *want* to do this, you lightning-marked freak?" She hit him with another slap that came out of nowhere. "Ariandelle thinks that maybe this will loosen your mental barrier." She pointed at the bottle. "Now drink that, you dog."

Peabo shook his head. "Absolutely not." He couldn't believe that his talk with Ariandelle had resulted in *this*.

With a blur of motion, Leena swept his feet out from under him, sending him onto his back, where he hit hard with a gasp of pain. Her face contorted with fury, she straddled his chest, wrapped her hands around his neck, and began choking him.

Peabo felt a surge of fear. He tried to fight back, but already his eyesight was dimming and he felt himself fading to black.

"You worthless piece of garbage," Leena snarled. "You're going to regret ever having insulted—"

It all happened in an instant. First Peabo felt something snap in his head. Then a pressure built in his chest, like he was about to explode.

He breathed in, but it wasn't air that filled his lungs.

All the light from the lanterns in the room rushed into him, and in his mind's eye he imagined a single blinding ball of white-hot energy.

He exhaled.

The ball of light streaked laser-like into Leena's mouth— and exploded out of her eyes.

She collapsed on top of Peabo, and the room was left in complete darkness.

Peabo scrambled out from under Leena and staggered to his feet. His heart raced as he ran through the dark and fumbled against the wall until he found the door.

For the first time that he could remember, he was in an absolute panic.

Ignoring the people in the hallway, he raced down the stairs and out of the tower, and headed north. Just as his mind began to clear, he felt an electric shock burst from the collar.

His muscles locked in place, and he face-planted, unconscious, into the dirt.

"Wake up, Peabo."

Peabo gasped as he bolted upright into a sitting position. His heart was threatening to beat out of his chest.

Eileen was at his bedside, her familiar sour expression focused on him. "How are you feeling?"

He rubbed his eyes. "I'm… okay, I think. What happened? Did I…?"

"It seems that you made a breakthrough last night."

That wasn't what Peabo had been asking. The image of Leena's contorted face with light shooting from her eye sockets was etched into his mind's eye. "Is she… dead?"

"Not anymore." A look of disdain appeared on Eileen's face. "She's being sent elsewhere, per the headmistress's instructions. For her safety as well as yours."

"Wait. What do you mean—not anymore?" Peabo swung his feet onto the floor to face the healer.

"The executor was resurrected," Eileen explained simply.

Peabo's jaw dropped open. It was one thing to accept magical healing. Wounds were just physical injuries, and magic or not, injuries could be fixed. But to return someone from the dead?

"Resurrected from the dead?" he said. "That's not possible."

"Why would you think that?" Eileen asked. "As long as one's life essence remains unclaimed, it can be coaxed back into the body."

"Were you the one who brought her back to life?"

Eileen nodded, her sour expression giving way to one of revulsion. "I did as I was instructed. Although in my view, Leena is lucky her life essence remained unclaimed. After hearing what she tried to do to you, I'm surprised you didn't take it."

Peabo shook his head. "I panicked and ran out of the room before I even saw the essence come out of her body."

"You're a good person," Eileen said, patting his cheek. "But even in a panic, I urge you not to try again to escape the tower complex. It looks like you only suffered some scrapes and bruises when you fell, but it could have been worse."

Peabo moved his arms back and forth. "I feel fine."

"How about your headache?"

Peabo tilted his head to the left and then to the right, and felt nothing. He smiled. "It's gone."

"That's excellent. You've made some real progress. Now tell me..." The healer leaned in and whispered. "What exactly did you do to that woman? I've never seen injuries like hers before."

"Honestly, I don't know. She was choking me. I remember everything seemed to grow dark. I thought I was passing out, but I guess that wasn't it. And then I felt something snap up here." He tapped the side of his head. "The light from the lanterns was snuffed out, and somehow I sent that light at Leena."

"That explains why there was no fuel left in that room's lanterns." The healer rested her chin on the palm of her hand and pursed her lips. "Though I've never heard of such a weaving before. The powers of a plainswalker, I suppose?"

Peabo shrugged. "Trust me, I'm as confused as you are."

"Well, for the sake of your treatment, this is something you'll need to try to understand. The headmistress has asked me to help see if you can reproduce the same action—in a less stressful situation."

"Less stressful would be good," Peabo said. He shuddered as he again pictured Leena's contorted face. She was evil, and the idea that she was still out there somewhere bothered him—a lot. "When do we start?"

"How about now?" She stood and motioned for him to follow. "The sooner you start, the faster you can go back to your normal life."

———

Eileen, lantern in hand, led Peabo to a darkened room on the fourth level of the tower. In the center of the chamber, a pig's carcass lay on the floor. Arrayed next to the animal were a series of unlit lanterns.

She set her lit lantern on the floor next to the others, then turned to Peabo. "I want you to try to do whatever it was that you did to Leena, but do it to this pig."

"And where are you going to be?"

"Don't worry about me. I'll be watching from a distance. Start whenever you like." Before Peabo could even respond, Eileen vanished with a loud *crack*.

He stared uneasily at the empty space where she'd been. That wasn't speed he'd just seen, like Leena's ability to slap him so fast he could barely see her hand move. The woman had literally vanished. From a scientific point of view, it made no sense, but it was clear that it had happened.

It occurred to him that the *crack* was probably the sound of air rushing in to fill the space where Eileen had been.

"Stop daydreaming."

That was Eileen's voice, and it wasn't in Peabo's head. She was here... sort of. Or perhaps she was both here and not here at the same time. Maybe invisible, somehow?

He turned his attention back to the task at hand. Clearing his mind, he focused on the lantern, imagining it dimming and coalescing into a floating ball of energy. But after a full two minutes of staring, shifting his body, imagining the lantern lighting the pig on fire, and everything else he could think of, he began to feel foolish.

"Eileen? Do you have any suggestions? I'm not a weaver. How do you even... turn your ability on?"

After several seconds of silence, the healer's disembodied voice returned. *"I know not of your abilities, but for healing skills, the source of one's abilities starts from within. Look inward. Tap whatever it is you think you're capable of. And then focus outward."*

Long ago, Peabo learned meditation from a fellow soldier who'd used it to deal with his PTSD. At the time it did nothing for him, but in subsequent years, he'd found that clearing his mind did help him to focus on his college studies. Perhaps it would also help him now.

He closed his eyes, willed his heart to slow, and focused on his breathing. Slowly the sounds of the tower faded away. Only then did he open his eyes once more. He decided to look not at the light, but at the pig.

It was a good two hundred pounds, and it had been gutted. It was probably taken from the cafeteria's larder and had been destined for a future meal.

He breathed in deeply... and the light wavered.

From the pit of his stomach to the top of his diaphragm, he breathed in, imagining himself drawing the energy from the world around him.

The lantern flared briefly, then dimmed. Peabo felt something building up in his chest. And then a faint glow appeared in the air, between him and the pig.

It was almost like... like he'd breathed using another set of lungs. A type of breathing that was more mental than physical. His skin tingled and the hairs on his body stood on end as he released this new set of lungs, directing his exhalation at the pig.

The light shot into the pig, and the room fell dark. The scent of burnt flesh filled the air.

"I did it!" Peabo cried.

A tiny glowing orb appeared, and then Eileen re-emerged with a *pop* from whatever hidden hocus-pocus dimension she'd put herself in. "Yes, it seems that you did." She looked amused.

He scrambled toward the pig to inspect it. The damage was more limited than he'd expected, more precise. He'd burned a hole in the creature's skin, but it was no wider than the tip of his index finger. It was as if he'd acted as a magnifying glass that focused the light from the sun into a small point. Except he'd done it with an artificial light source... and with no glass at all.

Eileen arranged the five lanterns in the room in a half circle on the far side of the pig's carcass. She then tried to turn on the lantern that had previously been lit, but though the flint sparked, the lantern refused to light.

"It's empty," she said, shaking it. "Just like what happened yesterday."

She lit one of the spare lanterns and adjusted the light so that it glowed more brightly than the previous lantern. "Now that you know how to replicate the action, our goal is to understand the nature of what we're dealing with. Unfortunately, the records from the First Age are very non-specific when it comes to weaving of any kind, and especially so when it comes to a plainswalker. The headmistress herself went through the archives and was unable to get much useful information. There are lots of stories of the powers of a plainswalker, but they're all vague and filled with warnings."

Peabo nodded. "I understand. I'm a big believer in the scientific method. What are you suggesting as the next step?"

"The first thing is to help you gain some control over your skill. Let's have you try that again, but this time I want you to hold back. Don't pull in *all* of the light from the lantern, take only a little. A sip, if you will. Then target the pig once again."

Peabo nodded, moved away from the pig, and sat cross-legged like he had before.

Eileen snuffed out the magical glowing orb, leaving the lantern as the only source of light. She vanished with another pop, and he heard her disembodied voice say, *"Go ahead."*

Instead of closing his eyes, which would be impractical in the real world, Peabo breathed slowly and calmed himself as he focused on the target. This time he felt the tingling on his skin almost immediately as he breathed in. The lantern sputtered and died, and a glowing ball of light streaked at the pig, leaving the room cloaked in darkness once again.

With a pop, Eileen returned.

"Sorry," Peabo said. "I tried to hold back."

Eileen lit another lantern and glanced at him. "That's fine, just try it again. Focus on minimal use."

When she vanished, Peabo focused on the pig once again.

It was exactly like taking a breath. Taking a slower or faster breath was easy, but taking a partial breath was not as simple as it seemed. And the result was the same over the next three attempts, leaving him frustrated—and leaving Eileen at a loss.

"You said it's like breathing in the light," she said. "Have you tried to slow your breathing and then stop midway?"

"I did," Peabo said, "but it's hard to explain. I guess it feels like trying to stop mid-blink. I haven't figured out how not to drain the lantern all the way."

Eileen frowned. "Let's try something different." She pointed up at the magical glowing orb that reappeared every time she did. "Let's see if your ability can deal with other forms of light."

Peabo was uncertain. "I don't want to accidentally…"

"I'll be fine. Trust me, I'll be beyond your ability to touch."

"And you'll still be able to leave the light on?"

The healer looked up at the orb. "Actually, I've never tried. Let's see." She vanished with a pop.

"The orb is still here," Peabo said.

"I know, I can see it too. Now try to use your ability on it. Let's see what happens."

Clearing his mind, he focused once more on his target and breathed in. The effect was stunning. He felt as though a thousand ants were crawling all over his skin, and the room lit up with an explosion of bluish-white light. A beam of destruction slammed into the pig carcass, sending smoking gobbets of flesh in every direction.

And in an instant, all was dark.

Peabo's hands shook. "What the hell?"

In the darkness he heard the now-familiar *pop* of Eileen's return, followed by the thud of a body hitting the floor.

"Eileen!" Peabo scrambled in the direction of the noise. "Eileen! Are you okay?"

She groaned. "I think so…"

Feeling around blindly, he touched something soft. She slapped his hand away and said with a weak voice, "Light the other lantern."

He felt his way over to the lanterns, found one, pressed its starter button, and nothing happened. He found and tried two more lanterns before finding the one that still had oil in it. When it bathed the room in its warm glow, he hurried back to Eileen, who was now sitting up, looking nauseated.

"Eileen, I'm so sorry. I didn't—"

"Don't apologize, you dangerous, dangerous man." She smiled weakly. "You didn't know, and neither did I."

"What happened?" Peabo said. "Your light wasn't even that bright."

Eileen grumbled and shook her head. "I should have known better. That was stupid."

Suddenly Peabo understood. "Oh crap. Just like I drained the lanterns. Did I end up—"

"Draining me of energy? Yes."

"Are you going to be okay?"

"Let's just say that I'm done for today. I need to rest." Seeing Peabo's look of concern, she wagged her finger at him. "Stop that. Don't give me that look, or blame yourself for this. I'll be fine. We just pushed a little too much today."

Now that his heart wasn't beating a million times a minute, Peabo's own fatigue began to set in. Whatever he'd done, it had taken its toll on him too.

"Well, we've learned two things," Eileen said, standing gingerly, with Peabo's help.

"Whatever it is that I'm doing, it works on more than just lantern light," Peabo said.

"Yes, that's one thing. And the other is that you have trouble with nuance."

Peabo chuckled. "That's a polite way of putting it. I think I'd have said I'm completely out of control." He held out his arm to help Eileen steady herself, and she took it.

"Well, yes. And that's a really serious issue given that you seem to be able to apply this skill to *any* light source. Consider —what if you were outside on a sunny day and you tried to do this?"

Peabo swallowed hard at the implications. As he helped Eileen out of the room and down the stairs, it was all he could think about. None of this made sense to the science half of his mind, but he knew the truth of what he'd just experienced. It was real. And he needed to be able to control it.

Eileen patted his arm. "I'll talk to the headmistress and give her an update. She might have some suggestions. In the mean-time, get some rest, and for the sake of us all, don't experiment with your newfound ability until we can set up some safety protocols."

Peabo nodded. He tried to look calm and confident, but inside he was panicking. If he didn't use his abilities, they would eventually kill him. And yet using them had nearly killed someone else. He was stuck between a rock and a hard place, and all he wanted to do at the moment was throw up.

CHAPTER EIGHT

Peabo sat in Ariandelle's office with Eileen and the headmistress, scanning a sheet of paper filled with Ariandelle's handwritten notes.

"Is this true?" he said, turning to Eileen.

Eileen's haggard expression illustrated her continued exhaustion. Neither of them had gotten any rest before the headmistress called them in. But her voice was firm as she spoke.

"The headmistress is a scholar of First Age history and writing. I'm sure her notes are accurate."

Peabo read the page again.

As was foretold by the first plainswalker, the chaos that rules within a plainswalker may be controlled by an outside moderator. Only a moderator can rein in that which a plainswalker cannot. The Sage left instructions, given by those she had communed with, on how a future plainswalker could be mated to a moderator. It is the only way to prevent the disaster that the Sage feared might occur when facing her enemy.

"The Sage—she's the first plainswalker?"

Ariandelle nodded. "And the founder of this institution."

"Have there been any plainswalkers since then?"

"No true plainswalkers. There have been ghost-like images of plainswalkers known to walk the Desolate Plains, but as far as I'm aware, you are the first corporeal plainswalker since the end of the First Age. That passage came from the First Age archives in the basement." She patted a thick tome with gold binding. "Specifically, this book, though I had to translate it. This is one of the few intact records we have of the time just after the collapse of the First Age."

Eileen looked upon the book with reverence. "The scholars who wrote that book were alive when the Sage walked this land."

"So I need a moderator to help me control my ability," Peabo said. "But it's obvious that the first plainswalker didn't take advantage of this. So I'm supposed to be the first to test out this secret method?"

"Oh, it's not a secret." Ariandelle let out a genuine laugh. "The process has been used for millennia, with quite a bit of success."

Peabo didn't understand. He pointed at the golden tome. "Can I see where this is written in that book?"

Eileen's expression soured even more than normal. "Peabo, it's written in an ancient language. You just heard the headmistress say she had to translate it."

"No, it's okay," said Ariandelle. She pulled on a pair of white linen gloves, opened the book, and carefully flipped several of the stiff pages. It seemed the pages weren't made of paper, but rather, thick golden sheets. No wonder it had survived thousands upon thousands of years. Gold was one of the few elements that didn't decay over the years. Of course, the book probably weighed fifty pounds as a result.

When the headmistress found the passage, she turned the book so it was facing Peabo. "Please try not to breathe directly on this, plainswalker. There are no copies."

Peabo stood and leaned over Ariandelle's desk. When he looked at the text on the page, it took every ounce of self-control he had to not begin laughing nervously.

He'd expected some arcane predecessor to the runic language that was the common form of writing in this world. But this... this text was written in English. *Earth* English. The language he'd grown up with.

How was that possible? This world wasn't even in the same universe as Earth. English should be an impossibility here. Yet then again, this wasn't the first time he'd encountered unexpected remnants of English in this world. And to be fair, not all of the text was in English. Some of it was in some runic writing system that resembled nothing he was familiar with.

Ariandelle pointed to the passage she'd translated, and Peabo took it in. The headmistress's translation wasn't exact, but she'd gotten the gist:

. . .

The first plainswalker predicted that she needed something to temper the power blooming within her, but it was too late. The ability to rein in the chaos that seemed endemic to being a plainswalker could be achieved only by pairing with another who showed the ability to weave the elements around them. She was given instructions on how a future plainswalker could be paired to a moderator.

It's the only way to prevent disaster, if there truly is a next time.

At the mention of pairing, Peabo pictured Nicole's face, and he felt a yearning that made his throat tighten with emotion.

He scanned the rest of the page, picking out the other paragraphs written in English. The writing was strangely modern-sounding. It was much the same language Peabo would once have used when writing an email.

It's been confirmed that the plainswalker has vanished from this plane of existence. The clerics of both the Nameless One and the Dark Ones have lost their minds.

The plainswalker, she predicted all of this. She saw the disaster coming. She knew that once she attacked, she wouldn't be able to control things.

.   .   .

The prelate of the Nameless One claims that his master isn't dead. He's communed with the Nameless One, and evidently his master claims that the time of reckoning will come when the next plainswalker arrives. So the Church of the Nameless One has taken it upon itself to set watch over the Desolate Plains.

The Dark Ones' prelate has gone insane. She speaks of the coming of the True Darkness. None of us know what that means. We suspect that the Dark Ones' church knows what this so-called True Darkness is, but they refuse to speak to any of us about that. Before everything blew up and communications were cut off with the Dark Ones, they also predicted the coming of another plainswalker. They seem to be preparing something for his arrival. They claim with certainty it will be a male this time. The Dark Ones' prelate did give us a warning during one of her rants: if the plainswalker doesn't succeed in his destiny —none of us know what destiny she's speaking of—within a generation of his arrival, the True Darkness will again walk the land. We presume that to be a bad thing.

The prelate has given direction to what remains of her order. They are to prepare "the Seeker." We don't yet know what that means. However, this Seeker is to be ready for when the plainswalker returns.

.   .   .

That was all the English on the two pages Peabo could see.

Ariandelle looked at him curiously. "The way you're studying the text… can you read it?"

"Some of it," Peabo said, and instantly regretted it. He didn't want this woman to know anything more about him than she needed to.

Her eyebrows shot up. "Fascinating."

Peabo quickly clarified. "I mean to say, some of the runes look familiar. I was just trying to understand what they meant."

"Ah." The headmistress nodded. "Well, perhaps I can see about getting you a translation of other passages. But for now, I'd like to focus on resolving your issue."

"I would too," said Peabo. "This 'mating' to a moderator… what does the procedure entail?"

The headmistress opened a drawer in her desk and pulled out a tube not unlike a Chinese finger trap. Peabo immediately recognized what it was—and thus what all of this meant. He once again remembered Nicole's final warning message to him. *"Don't admit to being paired with me. It'll keep you safer in there."*

Ariandelle held up the tube. "Your finger goes in one end of this device, and the moderator puts her finger in the other end. It will then link the two of you with an everlasting bond."

Everything she'd said was true. That was just how the process had worked with him and Nicole. He'd had no idea what he was doing at the time, but it had caused no harm. Aside from them being able to sense each other's location and having a strong telepathic bond, it had caused no other effects.

But at least he liked Nicole. He didn't particularly want to be paired with someone else too. He wondered, though: Did he have any choice in the matter?

He looked to Eileen. "Would you be my moderator, then?"

Eileen shook her head quickly. "No. I am already paired to another. I can't be paired to multiple people."

That was going to be a problem. If he was already paired to Nicole, this procedure couldn't possibly work.

"Are you sure about that?" he asked.

Ariandelle answered. "We're sure. When you're paired with someone, the bond you share erodes the emotional boundaries between the two individuals, until over time they become like one joint identity. I've seen my fair share of blood maidens who have lost their paired partner, and believe me, the mental trauma is devastating. But we can find you another who isn't yet paired. Maybe someone in the upper class? They're already prepared for such a pairing."

"How about Scarlett?" Peabo blurted the name out before he even knew he'd done it.

Eileen's eyes widened.

A sudden flush of heat flowed up Peabo's neck. "Actually, maybe not—"

"That's an excellent choice," Ariandelle announced. "Eileen, can you go collect her? She should be in the southwest tower assisting Joanna with her class."

Eileen departed with a nod, and Peabo turned back to Ariandelle.

"You said this has been done before. You mean the mating, or did you mean there have been other moderators?"

"I mean both," Ariandelle explained. "You aren't the first

person to be unable to control your weaving skills—though you create a much greater danger than sending sparks in all directions when you sneeze. Blood maidens are typically paired with people who are in need of moderation. Sometimes it's a weaving issue, other times it might be a compulsion to drink, or even to hurt people. Blood maidens help dampen what would otherwise be a harmful attribute."

She made it sound as though a blood maiden watched over a person's thoughts, and calmed those thoughts before they became actions. Peabo wondered if Nicole had ever done that to him.

It wasn't long before the office door opened, and Scarlett stepped in alone. Apparently Eileen felt her own presence was no longer needed. The girl looked nervous at just being in the mere presence of the headmistress.

"Scarlett," said Ariandelle, "please have a seat. I have some news that I think you'll be pleased with."

Scarlett looked up at Peabo only briefly before shyly looking back at the device the headmistress had handed her. She studied it, turning it end over end before at last putting her index finger into one end. Then she pressed her lips together and looked Peabo in the eye as she offered the other end of the tube to him.

He could tell she was nervous—and with good reason. They both knew the consequences of this action. He was about to create a lifelong connection with this girl, and he was annoyed that the headmistress had never even given the poor girl a choice.

He was nervous for another reason. How was his pairing with Nicole going to affect the process? The headmistress and Eileen had said it wouldn't work... but what would happen instead?

But there was no going back at this stage. Not without revealing his pairing to Nicole—and she had explicitly told him never to do that.

Taking a deep breath, Peabo stuck his index finger into the other end of the tube.

It clamped down with a click, pricking the tip of his finger. The tube brightened, and he felt a warmth spread from his finger, into his hand, and up his arm.

Scarlett gasped, pulled her finger out of the tube, and licked the dot of blood off its tip. Peabo removed his finger as well, and Scarlett grabbed his hand, licked the tip of his index finger, and hugged his hand to her chest.

"Thank you," she said.

Peabo could only smile back awkwardly.

"Well, I suppose congratulations are in order," Ariandelle said, sounding pleased. "Scarlett, you may move your things into Peabo's quarters if you like, since he has a spare bed."

Peabo tried not to show his surprise. He knew that being paired wasn't like being married; he'd been paired to Nicole for many months and had never hugged or kissed her—though ironically he'd shared a bed with her the entire time. He wondered why it was necessary for him and Scarlett to now share quarters.

Scarlett looked uncertainly at the headmistress. "I'm supposed to help Executor Ivanka with her advanced weaving class." She held Peabo's hand with a tight, almost desperate grip.

Ariandelle waved dismissively. "Not anymore. I'll talk to her about it. And from now on, whenever you're busy helping Peabo with the problem as I explained it to you, just let me know and I'll make sure you get credit for any class that you might miss."

She waved toward the door, and apparently that was that. The newly paired couple was being sent on their way.

As they stood and left the headmistress's office, Scarlett wrapped her arm around Peabo's.

"Let's go to our room so you can get some rest," she said. "While you're sleeping, I'll bring my things over."

"I can help with that."

Scarlett laughed, a laugh that reminded him of wind chimes. Bright and airy.

"Don't be ridiculous. I don't think my roommate would appreciate you being in her room." She hugged his arm tightly and looked up at him. "And besides, my roommate is probably taking a nap right now. I wouldn't want you to accidentally see any other girl naked."

Peabo's stomach squirmed. He wasn't sure how he'd managed to get into this situation, but he knew that at some point, he'd have a lot of explaining to do. To both Scarlett *and* Nicole.

CHAPTER NINE

Peabo startled awake and felt Scarlett shift slightly as she draped her arm over his chest.

"It's the middle of the night," she said. "Go back to sleep."

His heart raced as he became much more aware of Scarlett's warm body pressed against his.

Peabo looked at the other bed. She'd lain her folded sheets on top of the mattress, but had clearly not slept there.

His mind flashed back to the first night with Nicole after they'd been paired. Similar to this, there wasn't even a discussion—she'd just gotten undressed and lain next to him. And that was simply the way it was. It had taken him some time to get used to the idea of a naked woman in his bed that wasn't a girlfriend. But this was different. In the place where he and Nicole had stayed, there had been only one bed. Here, there was another bed available. But Scarlett had other plans in mind.

She'd managed to wriggle her way into the crook of his left arm and her head was resting on his shoulder. "Are you okay?" she said. She reached across his chest and gave him a light one-armed hug.

"I'm okay. I guess I was asleep when you came back in the room."

She hushed him and spoke with a tired voice. "We both need some sleep; it'll be morning soon." The girl buried her face in the side of his chest, and he felt her body relax against his.

Peabo rested his head on the pillow, and within a minute, she was quietly snoring.

This was not how he'd anticipated his life unfolding. Stranded in some universe other than his own, his mind stuck in the body of a race that hadn't been seen since ancient history, and paired to not one but two women who didn't know anything of each other. He chuckled as he imagined the disappointed look his mother might have given him, while his father, had he been alive, would have secretly given him a thumbs-up signal behind his mother's back.

Despite his military background, he took more after his mother than his father when it came to some things. Peabo was disappointed in himself that this had come to pass. He'd like to think that Nicole would be upset, but he wasn't actually sure she would be. She was an enigma in many ways. Scarlett, on the other hand… she was younger, seemed to be more prone to showing her emotions, and seemed unusually touchy-feely— which wasn't an attribute of Nicole's.

He closed his eyes and sighed. No matter what, one or both

of these women were going to be upset, and Peabo wasn't sure how he could have avoided any of this.

He focused on clearing his mind. These middle-of-the-night worries weren't doing him any good. And as he focused on his breathing, darkness claimed him for the remainder of the night.

Peabo felt a sense of déjà vu as he sat cross-legged on the fourth floor of the main tower, facing another gutted pig. With five lanterns in total, and only one lit, this was going to either be a really awkward mistake or a fascinating turn of events. He turned to Scarlett, who was sitting next to him. "It seems weird that I don't know, but are you a healer?"

Scarlett shook her head. "I'm one of the few in the tower that isn't a healer." She smiled, leaned over, and bumped her shoulder against his. "So don't do anything too damaging, because I'm not good at the healing thing. Okay?"

"I'll try not to. But unless we make some kind of break-through, the room will probably get completely dark." He pointed to the stone ceiling. "Can you wiggle your fingers and bring up some light if we need it? I know it might seem surprising, but I'm totally clueless about weaving and the specifics of who can do what."

"Aw, that's okay if you don't know. And yes, I can bring forth light if we need it. Also, don't worry about not knowing something, especially when it comes to weaving. That's one of the few things I'm particularly good at." She put her hand on his shoulder and gave it a light squeeze. "And besides, we're a team. You can ask me anything."

Peabo was struck by Scarlett's sincere expression. The lantern's light bathed her in a warm glow that gave her an angelic look. It made his stomach squirm as a feeling of guilt washed over him. The memory of his mother popped up in his mind's eye, shaking her head, reminding him that he wasn't being truthful with the girl.

Wrenching his gaze from Scarlett, he focused on the pig's carcass. "I know what I need to do when it comes to breathing in the energy from the light, but how does this moderator thing work? Do I have to do anything different?"

Scarlett placed her hand on his knee. "Just tell me when you're about to start, and I'll see what I can do about getting our minds in sync with each other. I've never done this either, but from what I've been taught, I should be able to sense your weaving and either stop it or maybe slow it down."

He noticed that she'd closed her eyes and was looking down almost as if she was praying. "What did they teach you about this? I mean, why are the blood maidens paired at all?"

"It's to help our partner, I suppose. The example the executors talk about in class was from long ago. There was a powerful conductor of some of the most dangerous elements. He could call down lightning when there was barely a cloud in the sky, or force fire to bloom up out of the ground almost at will. The problem was, once he started, he couldn't stop. It was like what you described to me with you and the lantern. This was centuries ago, but from what I was told, they paired him with a maiden who was able to help him control what was a runaway use of his skills. I suppose that's what I'm about to try and do with you."

Peabo nodded. Her story matched the general tenor of what the headmistress had said. "Okay, I'm about to start. Are you ready?"

"Yes." Her voice trembled a bit and she tightened her grip on his knee.

He put his hand on top of hers, focused on his target, and breathed in.

The light from the lantern flickered, and he immediately felt something very different. There was a weird sensation up in his head—a bit of pressure—but it wasn't uncomfortable. It was just a noticeable difference.

Previously, breathing in the energy wasn't that different from breathing in the air. It was an unobstructed flow from the lantern to him. But now, things felt strained. Almost like he was pulling a breath in through a thin straw—and suddenly he couldn't pull in any more.

A small, fingernail-sized ball of light hovered in the air and Peabo released the breath.

A needle-like spear of light slammed into the pig, and for the first time, Peabo saw a small puff of smoke come up from the pig's skin.

He smiled as the light from the lantern continued pouring forth. "You did it!"

Scarlett opened her eyes and squealed with delight. She hopped into his lap and gave him a big hug. "It worked! Just like they said it would."

Peabo couldn't believe it had actually worked the way he'd

hoped it would on the first try. "Let's do it again."

"Okay," Scarlett said, with youthful exuberance. Still sitting in his lap, she leaned sideways against his chest and rested her head on his shoulder. "Just go ahead when you're ready. Don't give me any warning."

Peabo chuckled and adjusted his sitting position to try and make himself more comfortable with her sitting on him. He focused on the target and felt the same pressure in his head. Whatever Scarlett was doing was more present than the previous time. There was no doubt that that she was up there somewhere doing something.

For a second, he worried about whether she'd be able to read his thoughts, but then he wiped the concern from his mind. Nicole had said repeatedly that she couldn't read what he was thinking, just his emotions or moods.

Then again, he had never felt Nicole wading into his head the way Scarlett was doing at the moment.

Setting aside the concern, he cleared his thoughts and breathed in. The light from the lamp flickered, and immediately his energy-absorbing breath halted.

Where previously he'd been sucking through a thin straw, suddenly that straw had been plugged with something. Scarlett had cut him off. There was a small pinprick of light hovering in the air, and Peabo stared at it with fascination. It was probably no larger than a grain of rice.

And then he exhaled.

The tiny white blur shot into the pig, and it didn't even raise a puff of smoke.

Scarlett wrapped her arms around him and squeezed. "It's

working."

"Better than I could have hoped," Peabo agreed. "Do you mind if we practice with more than one lantern?"

"Sure, let's do that."

"We'll eventually have to upgrade this experiment and maybe even go outside, but if we get this totally under control, that means we can get out of here."

Scarlett's back stiffened. "I have three more months until I can graduate."

Peabo felt a surge of mixed emotions as she looked him in the eyes with a worried expression. He wanted out of this place, but he owed Scarlett—he couldn't leave without her. He returned her a hug and whispered, "Of course. There's plenty of things I still want to learn while I'm here. Three months sounds like just enough time."

Scarlett leaned against his chest and whispered, "Thank you."

She then hopped up from his lap and began turning on all of the lanterns, flooding the room with light. "Let's get to practicing."

As soon as she'd lit the last of the lanterns, Peabo patted the ground next to him. Scarlett duly ignored him and settled back into his lap.

Peabo grinned and gave the girl a one-armed hug around her waist. She was definitely very different than Nicole.

"Don't you have classes that you have to attend?" Peabo asked.

"I do," Scarlett huffed, "but what if you need my help?"

Peabo shook his head and gave her a smile. "I'm pretty sure I don't need any help to take a look at some of the First Age stuff in the northwest tower."

She grabbed his hand and held on to it. "I know you don't need help with—"

"Listen, you have classes you need to finish. You said so yourself. And I don't want to stay here any longer than we have to. Is there a reason you have to finish classes? Why don't we just leave now?"

Scarlett's eyes widened and she shook her head. "No, I guess you're right. I'm just being silly." Her face flushed red. "I'm sorry—"

"No, seriously. What's preventing you from telling the headmistress you want to leave?"

Scarlett took on a panicked expression. "There's more lessons I need to finish, and I still haven't hit level seven yet. But I also want to spend time with you. I can't..."

Her chin began quivering, and Peabo pulled her into a hug. "Forget that I asked. It's okay. We can be here as long as it takes." He cupped her face in his hands and smiled. "Let's just do what we have to and then we have the rest of our lives to figure out what's next. Okay?"

"Okay." Scarlett tilted her head down slightly and looked up at him. "I'll try not to be so... I don't know, possessive of your time." She turned away and fast-walked toward the stairs.

Peabo stared after her and felt ill at ease. Scarlett was a living, breathing bundle of ever-changing emotions. It was exhausting. But she was young, barely eighteen, and maybe he had been like that as a teenager, too. He'd been paired with her for less than a day and already he needed some room to breathe. Her youthful intensity was a bit much for him to take all at once.

He turned and walked out of the main tower, and instead of heading northwest, he aimed for the southeast tower. As he neared the fifty-foot-tall building he caught sight of the short white-haired man he'd wanted to see.

The man was approaching from the east, which made Peabo again conscious of the metal collar around his neck. He'd played with it earlier and it seemed like a seamless loop of metal with no obvious way of taking it off. But somewhere between where Peabo was standing and the older man was an invisible line he couldn't cross. He was effectively a prisoner, and that really irked him, especially since the reason he'd initially come here was no longer valid. He was pretty sure that he now knew how to keep the headaches at bay.

If Scarlett could help him tame the use of his skill, couldn't Nicole?

He closed his eyes and sensed the connection he had with both Scarlett and Nicole. It was one of the only obvious signs he'd encountered from the pairing process. If he closed his eyes and focused, he could sense their hearts beating. One was behind him somewhere, nearby in the main tower. The other one was far away... somewhere underground, likely in Myrkheim.

His pairing to Scarlett had seemingly done nothing to his connection with Nicole. He was paired to both, and that was a separate sort of prison—one of his own construction.

"Plainswalker!" The old man waved as he got within yelling distance, never increasing his pace, but shuffling slowly like many men in their later years.

Peabo waved. "How are you doing?"

They clasped forearms.

"As well as can be expected for someone with eighty turns of the seasons under his belt." The old man motioned in the direction of the tower entrance. "Were you here to see me?"

"I was."

He looked at Peabo from head to toe and raised one of his thick eyebrows. "I don't see your sword."

"I didn't bring it." Peabo looked over his shoulder, saw nobody walking around, and turned back to the old man. "I heard a rumor that there's a crystal weaver working in the southeast tower."

"You did, eh?" The old man grinned. "I've heard that old Grundle is wandering about at times. What did you want from that old fraud?"

Peabo lowered his voice to a whisper. "One of the teachers taught us about... I don't know what they call it, but the kind of crystal that can store—"

"They're called power crystals."

"Yes, well, I've been thinking about those power crystals, and I had some questions for the crystal weaver."

The old man extended his arm and bowed. "Grundle, the crystal weaver at your service." He put his hand on Peabo's arm, panned his gaze across the tower complex, and whispered, "I'm glad you're here. You and I need to talk. Follow me."

CHAPTER TEN

Peabo followed Grundle up the stairs to the third floor, weaved through the stacks of half-finished armor, past the work desk where the man had examined Max, and into an alcove with a door. The old man unlocked the door, motioned Peabo to enter, and locked the door behind them. They were at yet another set of stairs, and Peabo followed the eighty-year-old, who was moving at a pretty decent clip for a man of his age. At the fourth floor of the tower they entered a room that was lit only by a single window with metal slats that let in the sunlight.

"I didn't think—" Peabo began.

"Hush!" Grundle barked. He grabbed Peabo by his arms and moved him into the center of the room. The old man rolled up his sleeves, and his hands began glowing. He made circular motions along the walls, almost as if he were Danny LaRusso practicing his wax-on and wax-off technique.

All Peabo saw was an old man seemingly wiping a section

of the wall and then moving to the next section. But as Grundle moved from one section to the next, the prior section seemed to grow hazy somehow. Almost as if Peabo's eyes couldn't focus when he looked at that part of the wall.

Grundle continued wiping the walls until he'd placed the hazy effect in every direction. Even the stairway they'd come from was blocked by the haze. Finally the old man walked back to the center where he'd left Peabo, but now his arms were glowing from the tips of his fingers to his elbows.

He touched his palms to each other, and Peabo heard a buzzing, staticky noise. Grundle breathed deeply and made a dramatic outward motion with both hands. The glow drained from his arms, sprinkling tiny glowing dots all around the edge of the room, and the static vanished.

He turned to Peabo and grinned. "And now, you and I can talk without those women seeing or hearing what we're doing."

Peabo stared wide-eyed at what the man had just done. He'd seen another person do something like this before, but it was to block out anyone from overhearing a conversation. Whatever that hazy effect was, that was something Peabo had never seen before. "Are you worried about the headmistress spying on us?"

"She's the least of our worries in this place." Grundle sat cross-legged on the floor and motioned for Peabo to join him. "No, to be honest I think that woman is trying to do the right thing for those around her, but she's blind to the others. It's a shame—I've been here over fifty years, and it wasn't like this before. It's almost as if a darkness has come over some of these women. I don't trust any one of them." He wagged his finger at

Peabo. "And you shouldn't either. That's why I'm glad you came. Ever since you left, I've regretted not warning you of the dangers that are in this nest of vipers. You can't trust a one of these so-called Executors. You should leave this place."

He pointed at the metal collar around Peabo's neck. "Unfortunately, I don't have the right type of weaving skill to remove that thing from your neck. You'll need a conductor for such a thing, and one whose skill is sufficient to slice the metal without slicing your head off. Ariandelle could do it, but I'm assuming she's the reason you're wearing that thing to begin with. I'd find someone for you, but there are few in this world who would make enemies of those from the Sage's Tower. Their enemies tend to vanish, never to be seen again."

Peabo nodded. "Isn't that why they're called blood maidens?"

"Aye, that's the truth of it. Assassins, all of them. Even the most innocent-looking of those blonde girls will kill you and never think about you again." He leaned forward and patted Peabo's knee. "I've removed my burden of conscience by giving you a fair warning. Now, what was it you want to know from this old crystal weaver?"

Peabo furrowed his eyebrows. "I guess it's sort of complicated."

Grundle smiled. "Then start at the beginning. That's how most good tales start."

Peabo returned the smile. "I guess it started when I was almost dead and I was brought to the Sage's Tower..."

The old man fidgeted with a leather pouch tied to his waist. "Damned thing always gives me trouble," he muttered. He fumbled with the knot and finally loosened it enough to pull out two crystals, each the size of Peabo's thumb. "I happen to have a pair of power crystals handy."

Peabo pointed at the one that glowed dimly with a white light. "Does the glowing one mean it has some energy stored in it?"

"That it does." Grundle nodded. "So, from what you've told me, your skill is somehow related to manipulating the energy associated with light. Is that a fair summary?"

Peabo nodded. "It is, but I'm wondering... for the future, what if I find myself in a situation where I'm in a dark cave? Let's say I'm somewhere underground, like in Myrkheim, and there's no source of light. Would I be able to use a power crystal instead of a light source?"

"I have absolutely no idea," Grundle said with a shrug. "Let's find out." He set both crystals on the floor, stood, and sealed the window's shutters.

The room was plunged into darkness. The only light was the faint glow of one of the crystals, and it was barely enough light to even reveal Grundle's shadowy outline as it settled back onto the floor.

"You can see both of the crystals, right?" the old man asked.

Peabo nodded.

"Speak up, I can't see if you're nodding."

"Yes."

Grundle cleared his throat. "Just to be clear, your target is the crystal that *isn't* glowing."

"One second—I guess I'm a bit confused. Normally when I send energy at something, it damages it. Are you going to do something that changes the effect I'll have on the crystal, or is it the crystal itself that's unusual?"

"Good question. It's a little of both, my young friend. The crystal is needed because its structure allows for the energy to be applied in an orderly way within its lattice structure, and that energy remains available until called forth. But I also have to convert the energy coming from you into a structured form that the crystal can accept without being damaged." The old man nudged the glowing crystal toward Peabo. "Go ahead and take that into your hand."

Peabo picked it up and studied it. The idea that a substance could be charged with some amount of energy made a lot of sense to his science-based mind. It was the same concept as a battery. But the specifics of the hokum that Grundle was doing... that part was beyond him. He'd give just about anything to have an oscilloscope or some other way of analyzing what was actually going on with these so-called streams of energy. But the nearest oscilloscope was probably in another universe somewhere. This was yet another thing he was going to have to take on faith, not completely understanding how it worked.

"Okay. So normally I kind of breathe in the light from wherever it is I'm getting it from. I don't suppose that's how a gem is used, though? Remember, I've never even seen a charged gem get used before."

The old man made a clicking sound with his tongue. "I can route someone's use of energy into a gem, but I can't extract it. I've heard others describe it in a similar way as you did, breathing the energy in. The way it's been described to me is that when a conductor pulls energy from his surroundings, he is willing it in a similar way that you'd pull something physically —but for them, it's a non-physical act. Does that make sense?"

"I think so. For me it's like taking a breath with a different set of lungs. I guess all I can do is try it and see."

"I'm ready when you are, young plainswalker."

"Okay, here I go."

Peabo held the glowing crystal in his hand and focused on the darkened gem on the floor. He breathed in, and the hairs on his arm stood on end as he felt a rush of energy flow into him from the crystal in his hand. But instead of that energy accumulating as a glowing ball of light, a glowing fog erupted from him and fell onto the empty crystal—which began to glow just as the glow from the one in his hand was snuffed out.

"It worked!" Peabo said with amazement.

"Did you expect otherwise?" Grundle asked.

Peabo gasped as a new thought popped into his head. "If you can take the energy coming from me and route it into a gem... oh, wow!" He glanced at the window with the metal slats. "If we open that window and I try that again, and then we close it, do you think that would work?"

"I don't see why it wouldn't. Is that something you're capable of doing? Taking raw light from the outside and directing it?"

"I don't know." Peabo winced. This was a stupid idea

without Scarlett to prevent a possible disaster. "It might be too dangerous."

Grundle hopped up, walked over to the window, and adjusted the window's slats. The room was suddenly bathed in light. "Let's try. I'm old and probably won't get another opportunity to see such a thing. I can always close the slats if there's a problem."

Peabo's heart raced, and a voice in him screamed not to do this.

"Go ahead and use the empty crystal as your target," Grundle said excitedly. "That way I can measure the amount of energy you pulled in. I'll close the slats after one heartbeat's worth." He stepped away from the window, giving the light unobstructed access to the room.

Peabo's heart felt like it was about to beat its way out of his chest. "Realize that my problem is that I can't seem to stop when I start…"

"I told you." Grundle pushed a lever, and the slats closed with a loud slapping sound. He pulled the lever and the light poured into the room again. "I can close it very quickly. Don't worry."

Peabo clenched his jaw and nodded. "I guess I'm ready."

Grundle smiled. "As am I. Go ahead. Let's see what a plainswalker can do."

Peabo set the empty crystal on the floor and took several steps back. It took him a moment to clear his head and concentrate on the crystal… and then the light faded from his focus until only the crystal was there.

He breathed in.

Everything seemed to move at a snail's pace as a rainbow of different colored lights poured into the room. A phantom music played in his head, and he heard voices in the air. Somewhere out there, he sensed Nicole's voice.

I can still feel him. He's alive. They haven't destroyed him yet. Brodie, what are we going to do? Do you think they'll ever let him go?

The world turned white, and the last thing he remembered was the old man gasping with shock.

Peabo felt a cool hand on his forehead and jolted upright. Grundle was beside him, grinning from ear to ear. All Peabo could remember was a bright light.

"What happened?" he asked, blinking.

"Well, one moment it was just the two of us on the fourth floor of the tower, and then the next moment, I couldn't see a thing because the sun was temporarily occupying residence in here with us. Luckily I closed the slats just as you passed out." The man patted him on the shoulder, still grinning widely. "It was a light show I'll never forget."

Peabo scanned the room. "What happened to the crystal? Was it destroyed?"

The old man held up his leather pouch. He was about to open it, then instead handed it to Peabo. "You open it. But I warn you, you'll want to shield your eyes. I've never in my eighty years seen such a thing."

Peabo shielded his eyes as he loosened the drawstring on

the pouch. The moment he cracked open the top of the pouch, a blinding light shot from within. He reached inside, touched the gem, and the world stopped.

A surge of energy raced up his arm, into his chest, and throughout his body. The world wavered as he shuddered with the familiar euphoric sensation.

And suddenly everything snapped back into place.

Time moved forward at normal speed, and he felt completely invigorated.

He'd just leveled.

Normally leveling was triggered after capturing a lot of essences from things he'd killed, but he'd learned that occasionally it was possible to level from other actions. Like the time he first wrapped his hands around Max's hilt, and leveled up immediately.

Grundle grinned. "Congratulations. That's an unexpected treat for you, I'd imagine."

Peabo looked at him with surprise. "Was it that obvious?"

The old man chuckled. "When you've lived as long as I have, you can see the signs. What level are you now?"

"Six."

The man raked his hand through his unruly mop of white hair. "I remember when I was your level. That was back when my hair was black. I long ago stopped adventuring, though, so I'm only level ten."

"Only?" Peabo laughed.

The old man shrugged. "You came from Dvorak Island where most people spend their time digging in the dirt and producing food. Things are different here on the mainland.

There's a lot of frontier and wilderness that's still unexplored, and there's a great demand for souls with a more adventurous bent to them. Having higher levels than your typical farmer isn't uncommon here."

Nicole had said something to that effect as well.

Peabo pulled the gem from its pouch, finding he was forced to squint to even look in its general direction. The light reminded him of the brightness coming off of an arc welder, or from looking directly into the sun. "How long was the window open for?" he asked.

"Just a heartbeat, like I said."

Peabo put the gem back into the pouch and handed it back to Grundle, who immediately waved it away.

"Keep that hidden for yourself. I have no adventuring in my future, but you might find a need for such a thing."

Peabo's eyes widened. "Are you sure? I don't have a way to repay—"

"Bah!" Grundle waved dismissively. "I forced you into doing something you weren't ready to do. That was poor form on my part. You're young yet, and probably not ready for whatever it is you're destined for. You're certainly not ready for the full use of your skills, though I'm sure you'll grow into that. I consider my being able to see even a young plainswalker's abilities in action more than payment enough. I now have an inkling of what those in the First Age must have feared. But I sense a goodness in you, Peabo. Don't let yourself stray or be unduly influenced by those who don't have your best interests in mind."

Peabo tucked the pouch into an inner pocket of his shirt and clasped forearms with Grundle. "Thank you so much for the information you've shared." He patted at the pouch under his shirt. "And also for this. I'm sure I'll have a need to use it at some point."

"Plainswalker, it's been a joy meeting with you." The old man patted him on his chest. "If you forget everything else anyone has ever said, remember this: you are the light within the darkness; don't allow the darkness to spoil your light."

CHAPTER ELEVEN

Peabo felt a sense of anxiety as he and Scarlett walked out of the main tower at night. It was dark, and there were no lights from any of the towers, mostly because the main tower had no windows and the other towers were only occupied during the day. This was a natural next step in their testing, but nonetheless he felt a bit nervous as he placed the large chunk of roughly hewn wood onto the ground in the middle of the courtyard.

Scarlett sat on the ground, her eyes flashing almost cat-like in the darkness as she looked up at him and grinned. "This is going to be really interesting, don't you think?"

Peabo motioned for her to scoot back. "Don't sit so close. We don't know what might happen." He settled on the ground about twenty feet from the wooden target as his mind replayed the explosion of power he'd witnessed at the top of Grundle's tower.

"Don't be so nervous." She scooted close enough for their knees to touch and laid her hand on top of his. "I'll be right here to make sure nothing gets out of control. And besides, it's pretty dark, so I wouldn't imagine it would be too crazy."

They were a few hundred feet from the nearest tower and there was no sign of people anywhere. He looked up at the night sky. There were a few stars, and a crescent moon rising, but otherwise the night was fairly dark.

He'd felt nervous having the charged crystal on him, so he'd hidden it in his room. It and its leather pouch were just small enough to go inside Max's scabbard, which he already knew was going to zap anyone who tried touching it. He hoped that would keep it safe from most prying eyes.

Peabo rolled his shoulders and stretched his neck as he prepared for the experiment. "Okay, let's start off with something very safe. If you can do that straw-narrowing thing for me and cut me off after a second, we'll start with that and see what happens. Does that work for you?"

She looked at him with a thoughtful expression. "Straw-narrowing? I assume you mean slow down your uptake of the light, right?"

He nodded.

Peabo felt that strange pressure in his head as Scarlett wriggled her way in there to get ready. At first it was just a pressure, but then he could almost feel the tendrils of something stroking his mind. It was a mildly unpleasant sensation.

"Okay," said Scarlett. "I'm ready when you are."

Peabo stared across the ground at the large chunk of firewood. "Here we go."

As he cleared his mind, he sensed a few dozen tiny flickers of light that hadn't been there before. Lightning bugs. He focused on his target, and his senses expanded even further—now he not only felt those tiny sources of light flickering on and off all around him, but high above him loomed a much deeper and greater pool of something he couldn't see. It wasn't the reflected light coming from the crescent moon, or even the stars. Somewhere up there he sensed... something else.

"Are you going to start?" Scarlett asked, giving his knee a light squeeze.

Peabo nodded. He breathed in, and everything slowed. A few dozen barely perceptible streaks of light jetted toward him from all directions, but they were nothing compared to the blooming pressure within his chest. It was almost like a deluge from above as he sensed, but couldn't see, a flood of energy coming down.

His mind filled with noise that reminded him of the squeal of a modem's static. And buried within the cacophony he heard a synthetic voice.

"Timecode reactivation initiated. Relativistic elapsed time since last communication: two million five hundred forty-three thousand and twelve solar cycles."

A dark mass hovered in the air, and tiny sparks of light flickered randomly. Peabo's heart raced as he felt a growing vibration from the mass, which was increasing in size. It felt like ants all over his skin.

The power pouring from above intensified. He glanced over at Scarlett, whose eyes were as wide as he'd ever seen them.

Even though he couldn't see it, he knew that too much power had already accumulated for him to strike out at anything as close as the log. Peabo shifted his attention past the towers, past the forest. There, off in the distance, was the shadowy outline of a craggy mountain peak.

Without thinking, he aimed and exhaled.

At that moment he felt Scarlett's abilities clamp down on his.

It was too late.

Peabo felt more than saw the mass of accumulated power streak off into the distance. The tops of a few nearby trees burst into flame, and then, from much farther off, came a massive flash.

Peabo stared into the darkness, not fully comprehending what had just happened.

"Peabo? I don't underst—"

The ground vibrated beneath them, and suddenly a huge booming sound hit them. Scarlett gasped, and Peabo felt the blood drain from his face.

Had he released that attack anywhere within these grounds, he would probably have leveled the entire area.

He gave Scarlett an accusatory look. "You said you were going to cut me off right away!"

"I did!" Scarlett responded with a tinge of anger. "You took a long time to start, I touched your knee, and the next thing I knew there was something going on that was sending vibrations through my body. I stopped you instantly."

The door to the main tower opened, and Ariandelle's glowing form appeared outlined in the doorway. She cupped her hands to her mouth and yelled, "Stop whatever you're doing. We need to talk."

Scarlett frowned as she stood, offering Peabo her tiny hand.

Leaving the wood behind, they both walked toward the tower. With adrenaline rushing through his bloodstream, Peabo felt like he'd just been involved in a firefight. He'd released an enormous amount of destruction and his mind raced with the consequences. As he looked at the simmering expression of the headmistress, he couldn't avoid thinking that he was going to the principal's office—which wasn't exactly inaccurate. This was probably going to put a crimp in his plans. The last thing he wanted was to delay his departure from here.

If Scarlett couldn't help him control the use of his powers outside, was that a problem? He could certainly survive knowing how to use his powers in a controlled environment, but he was probably at some point going to need to do more than just survive. There wouldn't always be a mountain a few miles away to send a runaway amount of energy to.

As they approached the main entrance, the headmistress was looking toward the mountain. There were now signs of a fire at the base of the rocky formation. Peabo prayed there was nobody in that area.

Ariandelle motioned for both of them to enter. "Let's discuss what just happened."

The meeting with Ariandelle wasn't as bad as he'd feared. The headmistress was going to do more research in the basement archives, and until then, Peabo and Scarlett were forbidden from experimenting outside. That all made perfect sense to Peabo. He just hoped it didn't take too long for that research to complete.

But Scarlett took the whole thing rather poorly. She felt she'd failed him, even though he tried to tell her otherwise. Even as they went to bed, with her face nestled in the crook of his neck, her arm draped over his chest, she was inconsolable. And the more emotional Scarlett got, the more Peabo longed for Nicole's level-headed personality. Thankfully it didn't take too long for her to cry herself to sleep.

Lying in bed, staring up at the ceiling, Peabo replayed the night's experiment and tried to make sense of it.

As far as he knew, there had been very little to tap into with regard to visible light, but it was obvious that there was a lot of *something* he'd retrieved. Could it have been something outside the visible light spectrum? Most people didn't think of light as having a range beyond the rainbow colors, but light, which was nothing more than a packet of energy, had wave-lengths that were much longer than red and much shorter than violet.

Maybe there were strong sources of ultraviolet waves up there. Hell, if this place used to have a much higher level of technology, there might even be radio or even TV broadcasting satellites up there—

Peabo stopped himself short as a memory from the evening flashed in his head. It had barely registered at the time; so much was going on at once. But there had been a voice…

"Timecode reactivation initiated. Relativistic elapsed time

since last communication: two million five hundred forty-three thousand and twelve solar cycles."

A chill washed over him as he internalized what he'd sensed. How he'd heard it, he had no idea. Had he sucked down some broadcast frequency from way up in orbit and it somehow translated in his head?

Maybe.

But could it actually mean what it said?

It seemed like his breathing in the signals from above had registered as a communication of some kind to the satellite. He presumed it was a satellite up there... maybe?

He couldn't be sure of anything anymore.

But the rest of that message. It implied that the last time it had received a signal was over two million years ago.

The timeline for this world was very fuzzy in his head.

He had been half-conscious when he was first brought to the Sage's Tower with Nicole and Brodie, but he remembered asking how old the Sage's Tower was—and that the high priest's response was startling yet vague.

"I can't really say. It's a construction from the First Age, so at least one hundred thousand turns of the season."

So... if there actually *was* a satellite above, one that had last heard from someone two million years ago, that would mean the First Age ended somewhere between one hundred thousand and two million years ago.

Quite a span.

He had no idea what any of this meant, but fatigue was finally setting in. Peabo's last thought as darkness claimed him was to wonder if he'd be allowed to do his own research in those archives.

It felt like snakes were wriggling around in his head. They poked and prodded, searching for something. They were hungry, and they needed to eat...

Peabo lurched up into a sitting position. He felt the all-too-familiar pressure from Scarlett's mental probing ease off and vanish.

He looked down at the wide-eyed expression on her face and felt the heat of anger rising up his neck. "What were you doing?"

"Nothing." She trailed her fingers across his back. "You must have had a nightmare. It's a few hours before dawn. Come back down and lie here with me."

She pulled lightly at his arm and he lay back down, feeling the rush of adrenaline and a tingling sensation from head to toe.

Scarlett leaned the front of her body against his side and nuzzled his neck. "I'm sorry I was such a mess last night." Lightly trailing her fingers across his chest, she whispered, "Do you forgive me?"

"I told you there was nothing for me to forgive or for you to be sorry about. Not everything works the first time." Peabo tried pushing aside the feeling he'd had with her traipsing through his head. He shuddered at the sensation of snakes searching for something.

"Are you cold?" Scarlett scooted even closer against him and kissed the side of his neck.

"Let's get some sleep," he whispered, knowing full well that he wasn't going to get any more sleep tonight.

With an almost purring sound, Scarlett spoke softly with a husky tone. "We don't have to sleep, you know." Her fingers wandered down from his chest to his stomach. But just as she reached his waistline, Peabo grabbed her hand.

"No," he blurted, louder than he'd intended. "Not now... I just can't."

Scarlett looked concerned as she levered herself up on her elbow. "Why? Is it those phantom pains?"

Peabo frowned. "What do you mean?" She knew about what Leena had done to him, but he'd never mentioned the phantom pains to her.

Scarlett shifted her gaze away from his face and down to his chest. "Well, I'd heard that such injuries could cause such pains."

She was lying.

Peabo clenched his jaw and closed his eyes. He'd seen people lie a thousand times. He'd been trained to spot such things while in the military. But *why* was she lying? Had she plucked that memory from his head? He had no idea if that was possible.

He opened his eyes and felt nothing but disappointment as he looked at her. "Yes, it's because of the pains," he lied. "I'm sure it'll go away soon enough." He swung his legs off the bed.

"What are you doing?" Scarlett asked.

"I'm too awake—I need to exercise. I'm going to run laps around the courtyard."

"Do you want me to come?"

Peabo shook his head as he got dressed. "No, you go ahead and sleep. Also, I'll be out there for a while. I'm planning on studying some stuff in the northwest tower. You might as well get some of your classes done."

Scarlett nodded. "Okay. I'll miss you."

Peabo waved and left the room.

As he exited the main tower and began jogging, he couldn't forget the sensation of snakes crawling around in his head. He had no idea what she had been trying to do. She was more than likely just curious. Maybe her action was this world's equivalent of peeking in someone's diary. But it was still a betrayal, and it was going to take time for him to stop being mad about it.

Shifting his thoughts away from what had just happened, he looked back at the failed experiment. How was it possible that so much energy could have been pulled in an instant? He already knew that his perception of time when he did this stuff was all out of whack, but Grundle had managed to close the slats on the window fast enough to prevent disaster.

Admittedly, that was different. Grundle was targeting that crystal, and the crystal looked like he'd captured a piece of the sun. So maybe Scarlett had actually cut him off as quickly as she could.

He sighed as he finished the first lap around the inside border of the tower complex.

Knowing she'd lied to him set him on edge. It put every-thing else in doubt.

But she was young. She'd just turned eighteen.

He'd done stupid things at eighteen as well.

Peabo felt a growing sense of dread. He knew he was going to have to confront her and get the lie out onto the table so they could discuss it. It was the only way. He was going to have to deal with a lot of crying.

But maybe after it was all out in the open, things would be better.

A thin glow had appeared along the horizon to the east, indicating dawn wasn't far away. He decided he wouldn't unroll the rest of today's plan until he knew Scarlett was in her class. That would give him some definite alone time.

And given what he had planned, he would need it.

CHAPTER TWELVE

During his morning run, he'd found a single weather-worn glove near one of the flower beds, and it had given him an idea. He'd just barely managed to squeeze his hand into the stiff glove and tested it on one of the bedroom doors he wasn't allowed to enter. As he touched the doorknob, he didn't feel even a tingle through the leather, which was exactly what he'd hoped for.

Now he looked down the hall and felt a wave of apprehension. At the end of the hall was the headmistress's office. The last thing he wanted was to give her a reason to turn him into a frog, slice him in half, or whatever that woman was capable of.

He walked down the hall and knocked on her door.

After a few seconds of silence, he knocked again, and was about to scrap his plans when an executor walked past him and said over her shoulder, "The headmistress is out for the day. You'll need to come back tomorrow."

Peabo smiled. "Perfect."

He walked back the way he had come, past several class-rooms toward the main tower's entrance.

Over the last couple of weeks he'd learned that he wasn't required to attend his classes. They'd only assigned the classes to him so he'd have something to do. If he preferred, he was free to explore instead—as long as he remained within the confines of the tower complex. And he had a particular target in mind.

When he reached the tower's entrance, he turned and faced the halls that led to other parts of the first floor. Under normal circumstances, he'd employ a grid pattern to search for some-thing hidden in a confined location, but that would be impos-sible in this maze-filled tower with hallways that sometimes doubled back on themselves. He did his best to be methodical, however, starting with the hallway to his left.

He was looking for doors that didn't lead to either class-rooms or student quarters. The classrooms were easy to spot, since they always had a high window cut into their doors, and the students' quarters were clearly marked with numbers. After about twenty minutes of exploring what he thought was the entirety of the first floor, he'd managed to narrow his target to one of a handful of doors. One of those was the headmistress's office, which he dismissed entirely. There was no way he was going to poke his head in there. For all he knew she had a medusa hidden in there, ready to turn to stone anyone brazen enough to enter.

The first couple of doors he opened led to supply rooms

filled with bags of dry goods for the kitchen. Another room was filled with barrels that smelled strongly of flower petals, an omnipresent scent throughout the tower. And that left one door that was different from all the others. Instead of a smooth doorknob, this one had a lever handle and a keyhole.

He'd never previously seen a door with a lock in this world. The only thing that kept people out of a home in this world was a bar on the door from the inside. And in the tower complex, even the bar was unnecessary. Given the blood maidens' reputation for being bloodthirsty killers, nobody in their right mind would break into this place.

Of course, the door was locked. That left him with a couple of choices. One was trying to force the door open. But that might make a huge amount of sound, and he didn't want to draw the ire of Ariandelle or the rest of the women working here. And even if he was silent, Grundle had implied that there were eyes and ears everywhere. There were probably high-level blood maidens wandering about as guards. The fact that he saw no such guards meant nothing. Eileen had demonstrated that with her trick of being able to vanish but still be there at the same time. If she could do it, there were most certainly others that could. For all he knew, someone was staring at him right now, wondering why he was so interested in this door.

He stood and fast-walked toward the main hallway. He had an idea.

In the six or so weeks that he'd been there, he'd been zapped by his fair share of doors. None of the classrooms had a charge to them, which made sense, but the bedrooms all did—

though it was only him and the girls who got zapped—because it was only him and the girls who wore collars. The teachers, who wore no collar, had no problems with any of the doors.

And that raised a question. If the collars could keep students out of any given door in the complex, why would this one particular door also need a lock?

The answer was clear. The lock wasn't there for the students, who could already be denied entry with a zap. The lock was there to keep others out, too. Even the executors.

It was the only thing that made sense.

Peabo entered the cafeteria. It was an hour after breakfast, and the kitchen staff were all busy cleaning and preparing for the next meal. He grabbed two forks from a bin, turned around, and went back to the door with the lever handle.

Along the way he bent the prongs of the two-tined forks so that he had what amounted to two thin metal rods.

Using his gloved hand, he inserted one of the metal rods into the hole and slowly explored the inner workings of the lock mechanism. Soon he felt something metallic at the end of the hole push inward. Not wanting to get electrocuted, he awkwardly shifted his body so that he held the tension with his hand as he pressed up with his knee on the lever.

The lever moved up—and the door opened wide.

Peabo grinned. That was entirely too easy.

He peered through the doorway, feeling a small sense of victory. A set of stairs led down into darkness, and an unlit lantern hung on the wall.

"Bingo."

He lit the lantern, closed the door behind him, and started

down the stairs. The scent coming from below reminded him of the back of his grandparents' storage shed. It was the smell of age. The air was stale, as if what lay in this dark cellar had been lying undisturbed for a very long time.

But as he made his way further down the stairs, the smell began to change. It still had the smell from the back of the storage shed, but mixed in there was the scent of old books. More specifically, he was reminded of the smell from the Carnegie Library in DC. That old building and the books within had created a distinct and unforgettable miasma of scents.

He reached the bottom of the stairs and held the lantern aloft. He was at the entrance to a large room filled with wooden crates as far as the light penetrated. The crates all had markings, indicating some type of organization. Some of the symbols were of the runic alphabet that was common in this world, but others were stylized versions of three or four English characters.

And there were just so *many* crates here. Long corridors led through the crates, which were stacked ten feet high. And as he stepped forward through them, he was reminded of the last scene from *Raiders of the Lost Ark*, where the crated ark was being wheeled into a seemingly endless warehouse where it would likely never be found again.

But Peabo's challenge was even harder than finding the ark. Because he didn't even know what exactly he was looking for.

He crisscrossed through the aisles, looking for any sign of previous foot traffic, scanning for anything that had been opened or disturbed. "Where did she get that golden tome from?" he asked himself aloud.

After about ten minutes of searching, he reached a part of the basement that contain crates that seemed older than the rest. These boxes had gained a dark patina from exposure to the air for unknown millennia. And each was marked with a clear alphanumeric code.

Although the codes meant nothing to him, the aisles were at least organized in a descending order. Box FB01 was followed by FB02 and so on. The next aisle had the FA's, and the pattern continued.

As he turned into a new aisle, the lantern's light reflected off a metal object. He walked closer, and discovered a claw hammer lying atop a box that had been partially pried open.

Peabo set the lantern down and used the claw hammer to pry the box's lid off all the way. And when he looked inside the crate, his eyes grew wide.

It was filled with gold-covered tomes.

He picked one up with a grunt. It had to weigh a good forty pounds. He set it on top of another crate, opened the cover, and looked at the first etched gold page. It was a title page, written in English.

The Politics of Religion

·   ·   ·

The subject wasn't interesting, but the language was. *English.* A language entirely familiar to him but which no longer existed in this world.

On the next page, a few words were written using the runes of this world: *"Archived on gold leaf from the original paper."*

Peabo understood. Someone long ago had transcribed what was probably a deteriorating original document onto something that would last through the ages.

He turned another page. Each gold leaf was the thickness of maybe ten sheets of aluminum foil. No wonder the book weighed a ton.

Knowing that he was probably going to be prevented from coming here again, he began skimming the contents of the book as quickly as he could.

Peabo skimmed books written about political factions that had disappeared ages ago, farming techniques, and other mundane topics that all seemed to be appropriate for a largely agrarian society. It wasn't until he came across a book titled *Society in Decline* that he knew that what he was reading had come from a time just after a world-changing event.

One particular passage struck him as heartbreaking.

The society I was born into is now truly gone. The cities were destroyed during the Great Bombardment. Nothing escaped the destruction. The only survivors were those of us who'd seen the strife between the factions and had chosen to leave polite society.

The maniacs have finally killed each other, and even the gods have turned silent, ashamed of what has been done in their names.

At this point, whether you're a follower of the Nameless One or of the Twins, we're all dying in a world that is hostile to us.

Diseases run rampant, and the medicines have long ago either been destroyed in the fires, consumed, or rendered useless.

Society has fallen back to its baser instincts.

The ruined cities have been picked clean of anything useful. Only bandits and unimaginable creatures created from the poisons of the underworld are seen in those desperate places that we used to call home.

Hunting for game is the only way to survive. People are eating rats, grubbing through the dirt looking for edible roots, and if someone finds clean water, they might kill you before sharing it with one who isn't familiar to them.

Even the forest has grown hostile to us. I heard the other day of a hunter who became entangled in the roots of the forest floor. The lower half of his body was consumed, and the man, who somehow managed to not bleed to death, claimed it was a tree that had trapped and eaten him.

Nobody knows what to believe anymore.

The world is dying, and I doubt anyone will ever see these words I write. If anyone does read this, just know that Harold Cartwright did his best. And to the God who seems to have *abandoned his people… I still believe you're out there watching. Please send help. We're desperate and at the end of our rope.*

The testimony sent chills up Peabo's spine. He pictured what the end of the world must have seemed like to the person who'd written that.

The folks back home on Earth would probably have had a similar reaction when faced with suddenly losing everything they had known. Peabo had had training in the military and had been a Boy Scout as a kid, so he knew how to survive in the woods if he had to, but most of the civilized world was used to everything coming in nicely packaged bundles for them. The idea of Joe or Joanne Six-Pack having to process their own deer, preserve meat, and make their own clothes was almost unfathomable.

It must have been like that for the people of this world.

Peabo felt a tickle on the back of his neck and a sudden pressure building in his head. Grabbing the lantern, he walked into the main aisle and saw another light at the far end of the floor.

"Peabo?" a voice yelled across the basement.

It was Scarlett.

He began walking in her direction. "Yes? Aren't you supposed to be in class?"

"Why are you down here?" she called out across the darkness.

He felt that same uncomfortable feeling of snakes in his

head. She was up there, probing. The heat of anger flushed through him as he yelled, "Get out of my head!"

"What do you mean?"

His entire body tensed as he felt her pushing and prodding in his head. "I can feel you up there. Stop it!"

She was now close enough for him to see clearly. Her eyes had a predatory stare. "I'm doing this for your own good," she said. "You're not supposed to be down here."

For the first time that he could remember, Peabo exploded with anger. *"Get out of my head—now!"* He yelled it through their telepathic link. One he'd never used with her before.

Scarlett's eyes widened as she took two steps back. A shimmer flashed all around her, her skin glowed, and her youthful face morphed into someone else's. But just as quickly as it had happened, Scarlett's face snapped back into place and her skin returned to normal.

The pressure eased in Peabo's head. "Who the hell *are* you?" he growled.

"What do you mean?" Scarlett tilted her head and blinked innocently.

Peabo breathed in, but Scarlett instantly clamped down on his ability. "I saw through your... your illusion," he said. "You're no student."

"You aren't supposed to be down here," she repeated... and then she dropped the illusion. Scarlett vanished, and before Peabo now stood a middle-aged woman with a glow similar to Ariandelle's. She smiled and shook her head, and when she spoke, she sounded amused. "What are we going to do with you?"

Peabo felt a fury of betrayal flooding through him. He cleared his mind and said through their mutual link, *"You're going to do nothing."*

He strained against the hold she had on his abilities, and as he did so, he felt something snap in his head. The two lantern lights that he'd been trying to draw energy from suddenly *changed*—separating into a rainbow-like pattern. The pressure in his head grew, and now even the crates all around him glowed with internal light, each with its own pattern, its own fingerprint of colors that he instinctively knew reflected the contents within.

He realized, with a startling epiphany, that *everything* around him had its own distinct color pattern. It felt like he was looking at the world through a thermal camera. But this was much more than heat signatures. This was...

This was a new ability. He'd broken through some kind of barrier and had discovered another world on the other side.

The pressure in his head continued to build, and it was now obvious that the woman was behind it. Her brow was furrowed in concentration, and any pretense of friendliness was gone. He stepped closer to her, straining at the lock she had on his abilities, and it was then that he noticed two golden threads projecting from his chest. One shimmering tendril connected directly with Scarlett's chest. The other extended somewhere far to the north.

"You're going to come upstairs with me," Scarlett said, her tone authoritative.

The pressure around Peabo's head was like a tightening

iron band. Whatever she was doing, it was sending shooting pains down his neck and into his shoulders.

Struggling against the pain, he focused on Scarlett and exhaled what little bit of energy he'd grabbed before she clamped down. It was a relatively harmless speck, but she gasped as it slammed into her.

The pressure released for just a moment.

Peabo inhaled as hard and as deeply as he could.

The lanterns flickered for only the blink of an eye before she slammed his connection shut. But it was enough. Now he had a larger ball of energy.

He stepped closer to Scarlett, whose face was contorted with effort. His knees almost buckled. He felt and then tasted a drop of blood coming down from his nose.

Focusing as hard as he could, he put his finger under his metal collar, pulled on it as hard as he could, and exhaled.

With a flash of heat and an explosion of light the collar snapped. Half of it launched over the nearest stack of crates. The other half fell to the stone floor with a heavy metallic clank.

He inhaled again before Scarlett could clamp down on him yet again.

"You're wasting your time," she said, grimacing, her face red with effort. "You won't be needing that collar anyway. There's a place where we'll keep you safe. You'll never see daylight again."

Peabo fell to one knee, her grip on his mind tightening.

She smiled and took a step forward.

Peabo knew he had only a few seconds before it would all be over for him. He had one last move.

Focusing on the shimmering golden thread connecting him to Scarlett, he exhaled the last of his energy. The tiny dot struck the otherworldly connection with an explosion of rainbow-colored sparks, and the connection was severed.

With a scream, Scarlett fell to the floor, unconscious.

The pressure in Peabo's head vanished instantly. But his heart was still racing and his fury was unabated. He howled, breathing in every bit of light the two lanterns could produce, until the basement fell into utter darkness.

Or what would be darkness to anyone else. To Peabo, every object around him—the crates, the floor, the ceiling—gave off a multi-colored glow. Each item with its own unique signature.

He looked down at Scarlett's unconscious body. One kick was all it would take to eliminate her as a threat. He already had another blood maiden out there who wanted him dead. Leena. Could he afford to have another?

Grundle's words played in his head. *"You are the light within the darkness; don't allow the darkness to spoil your light."*

He spit at the woman and ran to the stairs, leaving her behind in the dark. The energy he was holding crackled, waiting for him to release it, and only then did he realize that the lightning-like markings all over his skin had begun to glow.

Was this what those markings were all about? An indicator of whether a plainswalker was holding power within him?

As he climbed the stairs and returned to the tower proper, he left the door ajar. He didn't care anymore who saw him or what they had to say. The few students he passed gave him a wide berth as he fast-walked past them.

He stopped at his room, strapped Max's scabbard to his waist, and drew the sword.

"It's about damn time, pea brain. Are we done with this place?"

"Abso-freaking-lutely."

Peabo retrieved the pouch with the crystal from within the scabbard, put it in his tunic's inner pocket, and left his room for the last time.

An executor approached him in the hallway coming from the opposite direction. Her eyes widened, and she bowed her head. "In the name of the Twins and those who've fallen before them, I wish you peace and harmony, plainswalker."

Peabo continued marching toward the tower's main entrance. As he approached the doors, they opened, and the glowing form of Ariandelle walked into the tower.

He stopped in his tracks and stared. She'd always had a white glow emanating from her skin, but now, with his new sight, he saw her in a completely different manner. The white glow held coruscating streaks of pulsing red and black that churned and twisted all around her.

It struck him as a shield of sorts.

And there was more. Hovering around her head was a colorful pattern that reminded him of the boxes. It was a unique signature that spelled out who and what she was. He had the feeling that these patterns all meant something—that if he understood them, he'd be able to glean information about her. But he had no idea what any of it meant.

Ariandelle pressed her lips together into a thin line. Her gaze shifted to the sword he was holding, then she grinned and met his eye.

"She wants to kill me!" Max yelled in his mind. *"Let me gut her! I'll chop up those glowing entrails of hers so small we can leave a trail of them from here to the mess hall."*

"Plainswalker." Ariandelle's voice projected loudly as if she were holding an invisible loudspeaker. She breathed in deeply and stepped away from the doors, which remained open. "I see that you've removed your collar." She nodded. "We *will* meet again." Then she turned and walked toward her office, leaving him standing alone before the entryway.

"That lady doesn't like you very much. Did you piss in her Cheerios or something?"

"Shut up, Max."

Peabo stepped outside. There were colors everywhere. It was almost overwhelming in its power and beauty. Yet it was not his sight, but another sense that he focused on now. He reached out until he felt the familiar heartbeat that wasn't his own.

His throat tightened with emotion.

She was out there, and alive.

He shifted his direction, aiming for where her signal was the strongest.

As he approached the edge of the tower complex's property, he saw a dark shimmering line on the ground. It probably had something to do with whatever had zapped him before. But now, collar-less, he simply stepped over the line.

Relief washed over him, and with a smile, he began jogging to the north.

Nicole, the one person who mattered to him in this world, was out there somewhere, and he was going to find her.

He knew roughly where she was, but if his bearing was right, she was deep underground. The real trick would be finding the entrance to the underground world the dwarves called Myrkheim.

CHAPTER THIRTEEN

He had been stuck in the Sage's Tower with those women for just over two months, and though he'd gained some knowledge that he might not have gotten elsewhere, he felt like a heavy weight had been lifted from his shoulders. That Nicole, or any of those women, could survive growing up in such an oppressive environment was a testament to their fortitude. His only regret was leaving the contents of that basement to those people. He would have loved to have spent the entirety of his stay there just reading and learning about what had really happened in the distant past.

But for now, he had only one goal, and that was to find Nicole. Together they would figure things out from there.

After almost six hours of trudging north, he couldn't tell if Nicole's signal had gotten stronger or not. This link that the pairing process had established between them wasn't exactly precise. He had only a general feel for direction and distance.

It was getting dark in the woods, and though his night vision was very good—in fact it had improved yet again when he gained another level, and perhaps also because of whatever had been unlocked up in that head of his—he knew that falling asleep in the woods could be dangerous. At the same time, he was going to be very conspicuous if he entered any of the cities with the tattoo-like lightning markings all over his body. The last time he'd been out and about, some alchemist's potion had masked those markings, but it had now worn off, and the markings had returned. Worse, the energy from the lanterns, which he still held inside him, made those markings *glow*. Only a blind person wouldn't do a double-take if he passed them on a street.

Yet he wasn't about to release that energy without a good reason. It was like having a gun with a single bullet in the chamber. And that one bullet could be the thing that might save his life. For all he knew, the tower might be sending someone to track him down. Ariandelle's parting comment certainly promised that their interactions weren't over, and the last thing he wanted was to deal with those women again.

Which meant he had to avoid prying eyes, first and foremost. Leaving the woods as his only option.

The wind blew through the boughs of the trees high above, and Peabo looked up at the pines stretching a good two hundred feet straight up. He patted the nearest one on its rough trunk. "I'd consider it a favor if you could warn me about approaching danger."

He heard the low rumble of the trees and wished that he

knew what they were saying. Nicole and Brodie were both able to talk to the trees, yet…

Peabo put his hand on Max's hilt, and the sword yelled at him immediately. *"Get your ass moving! We've got incoming!"*

With his heart racing, Peabo expanded his senses, looking for the source of the danger. His ears detected something off to the northeast—a series of barks, a tremendous crash, and a yowl of pain.

There was more rumbling and the sound of snapping twigs. Then more barking.

"Damn it, pea brain, get your candied ass into hiding, now! Don't you sprechen their language or what?"

The boughs groaned again, and a giant pine next to Peabo shifted slightly. Its bark cracked open, revealing an opening that descended into the ground.

"Move it, move it, move it, you lazy greenhorn! Get your ass moving!"

Peabo scrambled into the passage. The entrance sealed itself shut behind him, leaving him in utter darkness.

As he focused on slowing his heartbeat, Peabo listened to the growling and scratching of dogs somewhere nearby. One of the dogs howled with pain as something heavy crashed to the ground, and a man's voice yelled, *"Damn it, kill that wolf before it attracts even worse things to us."*

"Watch out!" shouted a man from a different direction, and the ground shook with another heavy thud.

"Razer! Ah, crap, I hate this place after sundown. The damned place is haunted!"

Peabo listened intently as the forest came alive. The trees

all around him groaned and creaked ominously. He couldn't see what was going on, but he could hear it as clearly as if he were standing aboveground, a witness to it all.

Another voice farther away yelled, *"The wolves have tracked the plainswalker to that tree!"*

"I don't give a damn what that witch in the tower said." This voice, low and gravelly, sounded like it was within arm's reach. *"Two of my wolves are dead, and that plainswalker sure as hell hasn't gone invisible. He's slipped the noose somehow."*

One more loud crash, and yet another voice cried out. *"That thing almost hit me in the head! I don't care what that witch said she'd pay. If we stand around looking at each other for much longer, we won't be alive to spend any of it."*

"Enough!" This voice was new, booming, and had the sound of practiced authority. Someone who was used to getting his way. *"Let's go. I'll report to her we couldn't catch his trail."*

"What about their pelts? We can get ten gold royals for each—"

A loud crash sounded within a few feet of Peabo's hiding place.

"What in the Nameless One are you thinking?" the commanding voice yelled. *"Leave the damned things. This was all a waste of time. Maybe the king's men will help with this."*

As Peabo listened to the rapidly receding footsteps, he pressed his hand against the inside of the tree. "Thank you, my friend. I wish I knew how to repay you."

He both felt and heard the rumbles from the giant pine, and put his hand on Max's hilt so the sword could translate.

"Woody over here is saying there's others looking for you," Max said. *"He and his buddies are taking care of business and he wants you to settle your candied ass down and get some rack time while you can. He'll grumble at you when things are safe."*

In the distance, a woman screamed. A blood maiden?

Peabo walked farther down the passage beneath the tree. It ended in a loamy patch of soft ground. He sat down, leaned back against the surprisingly dry and comfortable soil, and closed his eyes.

It was hard to believe that less than a year ago his life had been relatively normal—and now he had his butt saved by something that he could only describe as an Ent. He wasn't much into fantasy stories—he'd grown up reading about cowboys and Indians—but he'd watched the *Lord of the Rings* movies, so he knew about Ents. He couldn't figure how he'd ended up in a world where Ents were *real*, but the movies had portrayed them accurately: as cool figures that took no crap from their enemies.

He wondered how J.R.R. Tolkien had nailed the description of these things, but quickly decided that was yet another mystery that he was never going to solve. So he allowed himself to relax, melting into what felt like the most comfortable mattress he'd slept in since coming to this world.

Peabo awoke to the sound of the pine groaning an all-clear at him. The tree had opened once more, and Peabo scrambled up into the darkness of the forest, fully expecting to find corpses of wolves and whatever else had tracked him to this place. There were no corpses, but he did find the area around the tree littered with some of the largest pinecones he'd ever seen. He picked one of them up, only to discover it was quite heavy.

He grinned at the tree that had hidden him. "I was wondering what was smashing into our visitors last night. This thing has to weigh at least ten pounds. I wouldn't want to get hit by one either." He dropped the pinecone and chuckled as he began jogging north.

It felt crazy talking to the forest, but he was living the literal version of *la vida loca*—the crazy life. He'd slowly become more accepting of the fact that almost anything was possible in this world. Here, crazy was often reality.

As the miles ticked past, the only sounds he heard, other than his own, were the chirps of crickets. Thanks to his unnaturally good night vision, he never had an issue seeing the terrain, which varied from thick carpets of moss to sandy and loose soil. But it was almost impossible for him to know how far he'd traveled, since he had no landmarks by which to judge distance. The entire time he was surrounded by nothing but trees, which all tended to look the same. If it weren't for his ability to sense Nicole's general direction, he could easily have gotten turned around and never realized it.

As he jogged across the forested hills and valleys, his stomach growled. Along the way, he'd managed to scare a few rabbits out of hiding, and he figured that one of those would make a decent meal, given his circumstances. He slowed his pace, looking for anything that he could use for a weapon. He stopped when he spotted an almost perfectly straight branch about half the thickness of his wrist and about five feet long. Using Max, he made quick work of stripping the leaves and smaller branches and giving the stick a respectably sharp point.

With his new spear in hand, he continued north once more, but slowly now, with his senses on high alert, listening for even the drop of a leaf.

It was almost immediately after his arrival in this world that Peabo first discovered he could hear people's thoughts, like transmissions coming from electrical signals up in the brain. For whatever reason, plainswalkers had the ability to receive those transmissions and understand them. The only thoughts he couldn't hear were those of higher-level individuals who'd learned to shield these transmissions. And most of the population was low-level.

The concept of levels had been a strange one for him to absorb, but now he thought of it almost like military rank. The vast majority of citizens didn't even rank at all. They were effectively a level one, which as a recruit to the military, started you off as a private. As levels progressed, ranks were harder to achieve. Level four was the threshold where people could block off their transmissions and he couldn't eavesdrop on their thoughts.

Animals were similar, but their thoughts were very different. He could hear what they were thinking, but it was hard to understand it. The way Peabo figured it, animals used a combination of thought, scent, and visual cues to communicate with each other, and he could only sometimes grasp pieces of it. It was enough for him to detect when an animal was nearby, but usually not much more than that.

As he walked across the loamy soil, he carefully picked where his feet landed. No breaking of sticks on the ground, no rustling of dried leaves if he could avoid it. He was a shadow in the forest, looking for—

He launched the spear even before he caught full sight of the rabbit streaking across the path not more than six feet from him. With a pitiable squeak the rabbit fell, the spear finding its mark, and Peabo claimed his breakfast. Or what *would* be his breakfast, if only he could cook it.

There was, of course, no way he was going to light a fire, even a small one, at night. That would be a shining beacon for anyone who might be looking for him, and he wouldn't take that risk despite his belief that he'd outdistanced any pursuers. That was another attribute of being a plainswalker that had come in handy over the time he'd been here: his stamina. He could jog at a brisk pace for far longer than he'd ever have imagined back home. At the moment he'd been jogging for at least a few hours straight, and he wasn't even winded.

For now, Peabo skewered the rabbit lengthwise, stuck it on the end of his spear, hefted the spear over his shoulder, and continued jogging northward. He was moving up the slope of a smooth hill, and after about ten minutes, the air grew cooler. The trees here weren't nearly as dense as they had been throughout most of his journey, and to his right he saw the brightening line of the horizon.

Dawn was approaching.

As he breathed in the clean, crisp air, he detected the scent of smoke. There was probably a town somewhere nearby.

Eventually he hit a downslope and the trees once more became plentiful. But despite the dense forest all around him, it wasn't long before the sun's rays were penetrating the forest canopy, some rays even hitting the forest floor. The scent of smoke was growing stronger, but with the way the winds were swirling about, he couldn't make out which direction it was coming from.

He slowed to a stop and cleared a space for his own fire. He figured if he couldn't detect where the smoke was coming from, others would have a tough time detecting the source of his own smoke, as long as he kept his fire banked.

He found some rocks and dried wood, and soon he had the first licks of flame coming up from a small campfire. He fed the fire for a bit, and just when he was about to start cooking the rabbit, the hairs on the back of his neck stood on end. Someone was nearby. He couldn't detect their thoughts, but he sensed their presence.

They were in pain.

Peabo stood and drew Max from his scabbard.

"What are you cookin', pea brain?"

Peabo turned his head, trying to determine the direction of the pain. He could sense it as easily as if he were picking up a broadcast signal. The sender couldn't be far, since the manner in which thoughts and emotions traveled was identical to that of sound, and would carry only as far as a voice did. He walked cautiously toward the source, and the feeling of pain grew stronger.

He looked upward and saw a rope hanging from a tree. Cautiously, he walked around a large collection of vines, and as he followed the rope down to the forest floor, he spotted the source of the signal.

A black cat had one foot caught in a metal trap. When it saw Peabo it let out a loud hiss, its blue eyes glaring as it tried yet again to pull its paw free. Peabo took an instinctive step back. The thing was only slightly larger than a house cat, but with those claws it could do a good job of shredding him.

"Hey, buddy, I'm not trying to hurt you," he said softly.

The cat yowled and bared long fang-like canines.

Peabo approached slowly and made a soothing noise. "It's okay. I'm just trying to help you get free. Can you understand?"

The cat's fur stood on end.

It didn't understand.

"This is stupid," Peabo grumbled at himself.

He examined the trap. It was much like a small bear trap, with a lever on each side of the metal jaws that clamped down on the cat's foot. To release the trap, he'd have to press down on both levers at once.

He grabbed a fallen branch and held it out in front of him. He continued to make reassuring noises at the cat, keeping his voice calm as he got closer. The cat sat Sphinx-like and growled, but it seemed to lack the conviction of its initial protests. Still, as Peabo reached out with the stick he did his best to keep out of range of the animal in case it decided to take a swipe at him after all.

Peabo managed to press the end of the stick on one of the

levers. "Good fuzzball, keep calm," he whispered. He inched closer to the trap, the cat watching his every movement, its tail swishing spasmodically. Peabo then reached forward, frightfully aware that his hand was now only inches away from the animal's trapped paw. He put just the tips of his fingers on the other metal lever, then pressed down on both levers at once.

The jaws released their tension and Peabo scrambled backward quickly, his heart racing. He'd expected the animal to bolt and race in the opposite direction.

It didn't.

The cat began licking its paw fervently. It seemed to not care a whit that Peabo was around.

Peabo chuckled nervously as he backed away from the scene. That had been a risky and stupid thing to do, but it had also felt like the right thing.

He returned to his fire, which luckily was still burning, and reached for the spear with the rabbit still skewered onto it. As he was about to start cooking the meat, the black cat, its ribs showing through its fur, wandered into his makeshift camp.

"Uh, hello there, Fuzzball." Peabo ripped one leg off the rabbit and tossed it to the cat. "You hungry?"

The cat looked at Peabo with icy blue eyes, sniffed at the hunk of meat, and began wolfing it down.

Peabo grinned as he began roasting the rest of the rabbit over his campfire. The sound of crunching bones competed for attention with the sizzling pop of the flesh on the spear. As he waited for the meat to cook, he re-focused on Nicole's position. He couldn't be sure, but it seemed like she might not be underground anymore. He hoped that was the case, because it would mean he'd have an easier time finding her.

He took a tentative nibble at a charred section of the rabbit's hindquarters, and though it still wasn't cooked enough, it tasted delicious. As hungry as he was, he was ready to eat almost anything.

The cat licked his paw and rubbed it on his face to clean up after his meal.

"Fuzzball, if you're still here when I'm done eating, I'll leave you the bones to chomp on. Just remember to stay away from those traps."

The cat looked at him, blinked, and again settled into a Sphinx-like position so he could stare at the cooking rabbit. It was as if he was waiting for the promised bones.

Peabo looked up at the sun. He figured he had about twelve hours left of daylight.

As he focused on his connection to Nicole, he wondered how far away she might be. For all he knew, it might be impossible for him to get to her without getting a boat or having to interact with people.

He lifted the rabbit carcass up from the glowing heat of the campfire, blew on the hindquarter for a bit, and took a large, satisfying bite.

There was only one way to find out where Nicole was, and to do that he needed to finish eating and get a move on.

CHAPTER FOURTEEN

In the several hours since Peabo smothered the campfire and resumed his jog, leaving the cat chomping heartily on the bones he'd promised it, he didn't once sense Nicole's direction vary in the slightest—further confirming that she was probably far away.

It was around midday when he heard the snap of a twig behind him. He immediately spun around, his heart beating rapidly and his skin tingling from head to toe with an adrenaline rush. But what he saw made him laugh.

The large cat he thought he'd left far behind leapt over a fallen log, sauntered over to him, and sat on its haunches as if to say, "Why'd you stop?"

Maybe it was a trick of the light, or Peabo's own faulty memory, but the cat seemed to have gotten longer and bulkier. It was no longer an oversized house cat; now it was a bit over two feet tall at the shoulder and probably weighed close to a hundred pounds.

With a shrug, he turned and resumed his run—but now, instead of a jog, he took off at a sprint. He didn't know if he'd somehow imprinted on the cat, or if the cat was just following a likely source of food, but either way, losing the cat in the forest was best for both of them.

Unfortunately, it wasn't that easy.

No matter how fast Peabo ran, he couldn't lose the damned thing. Sometimes it ran behind him, sometimes alongside him, and sometimes it even led him, as if it knew where he was going.

Peabo kept on running, right on through the day and into the evening. It was a cloudy night, and no moon or stars lent even the faintest glow to his surroundings, but his vision was sufficient to make his way, as was the cat's.

It was probably near midnight when Peabo at last felt his energy waning. He slowed and came to a stop.

He'd entered an area that was less wooded, more dominated by thick brush. He was on an elevated steppe, giving him a good view of the surrounding area, and he saw that he was literally in the middle of nowhere. No sign of civilization. No lights. No scents that hinted at people.

Off in the distance to the north—the direction in which he still sensed Nicole—he could just make out the dark outline of a mountain range. That was cause for concern. He could be running straight into an unclimbable mountain. For that matter, several people had hinted to him that the mainland had many unexplored places. Dangerous places. For all he knew, the area he was in right now was filled with indescribable monstrosities lurking in every shadow.

He was probably in a lot more danger than he even realized. He had utterly no intel on what was out here.

He walked a bit further and came upon a natural clearing. It was devoid of brush, and in its center was a giant rock that looked like a partially buried cube of stone. The sides were smooth, but the top looked rough, like it had stood taller in the past and the rest of it had broken off. Peabo ran his hand along the surface of the rock and gasped.

It wasn't a rock.

It was an amalgamation of pebbles and finer stone all congealed into a solid mass. *This is concrete.*

But concrete didn't exist in this world. Or at least, it didn't exist in the current time.

"Could this be an ancient ruin from the First Age?" Peabo wondered aloud.

The cat hopped up onto the rock, meowed, and settled into a comfortable position. Its black fur made it almost invisible against the dark backdrop. Only a small quarter-sized tuft of white fur on its chest truly stood out.

Peabo looked around once more. This seemed like as good a place to bunk for the night as any. The ground was dry, and there was no wind. He turned once more to the cat.

"Can I trust you to not do anything foolish while I try to get some sleep?"

He reached out to pet the cat, but when it hissed at him he quickly took two steps back.

"Sorry Fuzzball, I guess you're not the petting type. Got it."

He drew Max out of the scabbard, and the sword growled. *"Pea brain, are you lost again? Where the hell are we?"*

"I'm going to get some rack time. Do you think you can let me know if you see anything?"

"You are one dumb son of a gun, aren't you? Do you see any eyeballs on my blade? Do I look like a watchdog to you? I see what you see. Now, if you ask me if I feel anything creeping around like that bag of fur nearby, I can give you a zap and let you know something's about, but you'll have to ID it."

Peabo chuckled and sat on the ground with his back leaning against the rock. He couldn't see the cat that was still perched on the rock above. "Hey Fuzzball, I'm going to sleep for a bit. We'll catch something to eat when I wake up, okay?"

A cold breeze picked up from the west, and he shifted his position so the rock was blocking the wind. He felt fatigued from head to toe. The running didn't bother him while he was doing it, but whatever calories he'd consumed had long ago been used and his stomach grumbled. He sat cross-legged to conserve heat, rested his head against the stone, and with one hand on Max's hilt and the other hand inside his tunic, he tried to get some rest.

He heard the soft thump of the cat hopping off the stone, then felt it headbutt his left shoulder. As he turned toward it, he found himself face to face with the big cat. Now that he was sitting, he realized just how big this creature was. There was no doubt that it had grown since this morning. That was either a normal thing in these parts… or it was really really bad.

"What's up, Fuzzball? Are you going to get some sleep too?"

The cat rubbed the side of his face against Peabo's shoulder several times, walked in front of him, and then fell to its side. Half of the cat was lying in his lap.

"Okay. If you insist."

The cat pushed itself forward with its hind legs and managed to curl most of itself up onto Peabo's lap. The entire time, Peabo just stared in wonder at what this wild animal was doing. He'd had a cat as a kid—in fact it had looked like a miniature version of this one—but it wasn't the cuddly type, and had never sat in his lap. Next to him, sure, but never on him.

Either way, this was no house cat. By now it weighed a good hundred pounds. But it was giving off plenty of body heat, which meant the chance of Peabo turning into a popsicle during the night had diminished greatly.

He leaned his head back against the stone once more and closed his eyes. "Good night, Fuzzball."

The cat responded with a noise that sounded like a mix between a growl and purr.

Somehow, Peabo had gained an animal.

———

Peabo lurched up and onto his feet when he heard the sound of branches breaking. His hand was still gripping Max's hilt, and the sword yelled in his head.

"Aw, hell no. That pussy cat of yours just brought you back an MRE from hell."

The sun had just broken above the horizon, and as Peabo squinted he saw the back end of the cat moving toward him. Its tail was lifted up, and it occasionally wiggled as the cat growled and heaved at something Peabo couldn't see.

"Stop thinking so hard, you'll burn a hole through your skull," said Max. *"Go help the damned thing, you lazy son of a monkey's uncle."*

With drill sergeant Max in his ear, Peabo crept forward. "Need some help, Fuzzball?"

Suddenly, with one final yank, the brown body of what looked like an oversized elk broke through the underbrush and landed in the clearing.

"Holy crap," Peabo exclaimed. "That thing's huge!"

Peabo's first thought was that the elk had to weigh upwards of six hundred pounds. His second thought was that this cat was much more dangerous than he'd given it credit for.

Peabo set to work starting a small campfire, and when he had it blazing, he looked over at the cat, which was sitting next to its prize. With Max in his hand, he pointed at the dead animal.

"I'll go ahead and take off one of its haunches, and we can really feast on this thing. Okay?"

The cat stared at him for a few seconds and then began cleaning its face.

Using Max, Peabo made quick work of removing the back right leg of the beast. That chunk alone had to weigh over one hundred pounds. He removed the skin, then cut off large sections of the muscle. He tossed some to the cat, who immediately gobbled them down.

Peabo looked around for any sticks thick enough to act as a skewer, but eventually he gave up and just placed large chunks of the meat on the edge of the fire to roast. The cat stared quizzically at him as Peabo turned the roasting meat with a couple of skinny branches he'd yanked off a nearby plant. It let out a loud meow.

"Why burn the flesh?"

Peabo was about to answer the cat when his eyebrows shot up into his hairline. "You can *talk?*"

The cat hadn't actually *talked*. But it *had* made some vocalization that Peabo's mind had translated into words.

The cat just stared at him with its icy blue eyes.

"I suppose," Peabo said, "I burn it because I don't like to eat raw meat."

The cat yawned loudly and gave off an almost chirp-like sound. *"It tastes better raw."*

Peabo cut off a piece of the cooked meat, blew on it, and popped it into his mouth. It had the coppery taste of freshly butchered game meat that hadn't been salted or aged, but it was juicy and packed with nutrition. He sliced off another chunk and tossed it to the cat.

"Have you ever *tried* cooked meat? Maybe you'll like it better." He shook his head at the realization that he was having a conversation with a cat.

The cat sniffed at the roasted meat and gave him a baleful look as if to say, *Are you serious?* Then it made a horking sound as if it was about to puke up a hairball.

"Okay, fine," Peabo said. "Eat it your way." He motioned to the rest of the animal that was untouched.

The cat wandered over to the elk-like creature, dragged it closer to Peabo for some reason, and began gnawing at the animal's remains.

Peabo ate more than his fill. He'd probably consumed at least four or five pounds of meat before the idea of having another bite made *him* want to hurl up a hairball. But the cat was still going strong, and it had already eaten a shocking amount of meat.

He was contemplating how much of the animal to carry with them when he sensed something. The cat must have sensed it as well, because it stopped eating and began sniffing the air with a low growl.

"Peabo?" a voice whispered in his head.

Peabo jumped up from the campfire and looked to the north. His heart raced and his throat tightened as he reached out with his thoughts. *"Nicole? Is that you?"*

At that moment, Nicole's blonde head poked through the underbrush on the north side of the clearing. The cat let out a warning snarl and hiss, its hackles rising.

Peabo put his hand on the cat's head. "It's okay, I know her. She's a friend."

The cat sat back on its haunches.

Peabo ran to Nicole and caught her in a giant bear hug. He swung her around and buried his face in the crook of her neck. "I've missed you more than you can imagine."

Nicole returned his hug and wrapped her legs around his

waist. They stood in silence, breathing each other's air, for a full minute before Peabo set her back on the ground.

Nicole looked up at him with wide eyes. "By the Nameless One, you're glowing!"

"I am?" Peabo looked at himself and realized what she was talking about. "Oh, you mean my markings are glowing."

"Yes." Nicole stared at him for a few long seconds, then smiled and wiped tears from his cheeks. "We have so much to talk about." She nodded toward the giant cat. "For example: what is that?"

Peabo was surprised by the question. "You're asking me? I'm the one who's new to this world, remember?"

She shook her head in wonder. "I've never seen such a creature. It's not a displacer beast, because it doesn't have tentacles. Where did it come from?"

He led her back over to the animal. "I found him caught in a trapper's snare and helped release him. He's followed me ever since. Are you telling me you don't have cats or panthers in this world?"

She walked around the giant cat and shook her head. "I'm not aware of anything like this creature. Are you sure it's a he?"

Peabo grinned. "I guess I never thought to look." He stepped to the back end of the cat. "Fuzzball, can you stand up?"

The cat did, and continued its feasting.

"Okay." Peabo shrugged. "Looks like he's a she."

"And you call her Fuzzball?" Nicole raised an eyebrow,

giving him that familiar look of hers that meant he might want to reconsider a recent choice.

He turned back to the cat, who was face-deep in elk entrails. "Hey, do you have a name I should call you?"

That cat looked over her shoulder at him, blood and gore dripping from her whiskers. *"Fuzzball,"* it growled, then dove back into the animal's remains.

"Do you understand her?" Nicole asked.

Peabo made a so-so motion with his hands. "Sometimes she's pretty clear, other times I don't know. But it seems like Fuzzball is the name she wants to be called."

Nicole frowned. "That's not a very dignified name for such a beautiful creature."

The cat sneezed, spraying gore everywhere, then went right back to consuming her kill.

Nicole wrapped her arm around Peabo's and gave it a squeeze. "We clearly have a lot of catching up to do, and this isn't the place to do it. This is a very dangerous area. We need to get to safety. Let's grab what you have and get going."

Peabo nodded, then tried to send his thoughts to the cat. *"We have to go quickly. There might be danger. Are you ready?"*

Fuzzball's head popped up and she came sauntering over, her belly distended from the impossible amount of meat she'd consumed. She nudged the top of Peabo's leg with her shoulder and let out a low rumble. *"I'm ready. Is the woman ours?"*

Ours? He had no idea what the cat was getting at. He put his hand on Nicole's shoulder. "She's family."

"Okay." Fuzzball began purring and washing her face.

Nicole stared at the cat with amazement. "She's a tidy creature, isn't she?"

Peabo smiled. It was weird for him to have some experience that Nicole didn't have. He took it for granted that cats were fastidious about their grooming.

"So," he said. "Where are we going?"

Nicole motioned to the north. "We're going back to Myrkheim."

CHAPTER FIFTEEN

"How did you know to come find me?" Peabo asked as he ducked under the low-hanging branches of a species of tree he didn't recognize. He was barely keeping up with Nicole's rapid pace.

"Something changed a couple of days ago," she replied. "I sensed you in a much stronger way than I had since leaving you behind. I'm guessing there's something about the Sage's Tower or its surroundings that made our connection, I don't know how to describe it, but it made the connection dimmer. I could still sense you, but the connection was weak—very weak. And then all of a sudden it was like I could feel you on the other side of the room again. That's when I knew something significant had happened."

"I wonder if it had to do with whatever they have around the perimeter of that place that they tried to trap me with."

"Did they put a collar on you?" Nicole looked over her

shoulder and shuddered. "I should have known. I hated that thing."

Peabo chuckled. "Yup, not a fan either. I'd give it and the entire tower complex zero stars on its Yelp review if I could."

"Yelp review? Is that something I'm supposed to understand?"

He grinned. "No, it's just a bad joke from my world."

Nicole bumped her shoulder against his. "Your previous world. Need I remind you that this is now your world and you're stuck with it—and me."

Peabo wrapped his arm around Nicole's waist and gave it a light squeeze. He pointed north at the mountains, which were looming ever larger. "How long until we start heading underground?"

"If we continue through the night, we should get there before dawn—"

A sudden shriek from behind pierced the quiet of the late afternoon. Peabo and Nicole both spun around. Several hundred feet in the air—and aiming directly for them—was what looked like a dragon with a scorpion's tail. If he recalled the monster manual correctly, it was called a wyvern.

Nicole yanked at Peabo's arm. "We have to run! We need to get under the cover of the trees or we're dead!"

They ran together at top speed, but the trees were nearly a half mile away. The cat leapt ahead of them easily, but Nicole and Peabo had to plow through heavy undergrowth, Nicole slashing at it with a machete-like knife.

"Nicole," Peabo said, "there's no way we'll make the trees before it catches us."

He skidded to a stop, ignoring Nicole's yelled warnings. Instead he focused on the incoming wyvern, which was closing fast.

He stretched his arm out toward it and released the energy he'd been holding. Electricity arced at the tips of his fingers, forming a small ball of crackling energy that elongated and then streaked directly toward the incoming creature.

The wyvern let out a shriek as the light slammed into it. Its movements faltered, and it began tumbling toward the ground. The earth shuddered with the impact as it struck. One wing was bent at an odd angle and had smoke coming from it.

The thing could no longer fly, but it wasn't dead. It was rising to its feet. And it was no more a hundred yards behind them.

"We don't want this fight!" Nicole yelled. "Keep running!"

Peabo raced after Nicole, trying to recall all he could about the creature from his study of Brodie's monster manual. Wyverns were related to dragons, but they didn't have a breath weapon. Or at least, he didn't think they did. Its real weapons were its tail and its bite. The tail was deadly poisonous, and he wasn't sure if the bite was as well or not. The book had been fairly vague on that point, and his memory was spotty.

They made it to the trees and kept running. Peabo found himself ducking and running zigzag patterns to avoid smashing into a tree or getting garroted by a hanging vine. He heard a tremendous crash behind him and glanced over his shoulder to see the wyvern plowing into the forest after them, smashing the trees aside as if they were nothing, all in a mindless pursuit of its dinner.

Nicole skidded to a stop. "It's going to keep coming after us." She lifted her right hand, which was glowing white, and touched him on the shoulder. A warmth spread across his chest and through the rest of his body. "That's to make you harder to hit. Remember, don't let yourself get hit by the tail."

Before Peabo could respond, a shimmering, seemingly incorporeal war hammer appeared in front of her.

Peabo looked at the weapon and grumbled. "After this, you and I need to talk about you helping me use my powers."

"Use your sword," she snapped back at him.

A black blur raced past them. Fuzzball had joined the fight. As the big cat screamed a challenge, Peabo drew Max from his scabbard.

"It's about damn time, greenhorn. What have we—jumping Jehoshaphat, what the hell is that thing!"

Peabo felt adrenaline rushing through him. He and Nicole stepped forward. But Fuzzball struck first, sinking its teeth into the beast's three-foot-thick leathery tail and hanging on with a death grip. The wyvern spun, and Nicole seized the opportunity to throw her shimmering weapon. Her aim was true, and she struck it on the back of its head.

The ground shook as the wyvern roared and spun to face them once more, the cat still hanging on its tail.

The hammer reappeared in front of Nicole just in time. The creature opened its giant maw—large enough to bite a person in half—and with its elongated neck lunged at her. As she jumped to her left, narrowly sidestepping the attack, Peabo swung Max at the wyvern's face. His blow connected just below the left eye, and Peabo both felt and heard the crunch.

The head swung swiftly toward him and he just barely managed to fall to the ground as the head swept over him.

"Peabo!" Nicole yelled, and he'd only just managed to lift Max vertical before the wyvern slammed its head down on top of him.

Peabo felt the sword penetrate not one but two layers of bone. Still he was being crushed. The weight of an elephant was on top of him.

Nicole's hammer smashed into the wyvern's head again, distracting it just enough for Peabo to roll out from under the thing's jaw as it slammed to the ground, further impaling itself on Peabo's sword.

The wyvern lurched upward and let out a muffled roar through its skewered mouth.

Peabo got his feet under him and felt a surge of rage building within him. But his sword was still in the wyvern, and he didn't have another weapon, at least not one he dared to use. Pulling in power during daylight would certainly overwhelm him.

The wyvern swung its head down, aiming to smash Peabo like a hammer would a nail. Peabo leapt to the side—and then did what was probably the stupidest thing he could have done: he jumped onto the back of the wyvern's head and grabbed hold of its eye ridges.

The creature paused, as if unsure what was happening.

Peabo plunged his fist right into the wyvern's left eye.

He felt the sting of steaming fluid bursting forth. The wyvern convulsed and tried to throw him off, but Peabo he held on for dear life, tightening his grip with his legs.

He slammed his fist into the wyvern's other eye.

This time he didn't penetrate the outer membrane, but he still scratched furrows in the surface of the exposed eye.

The wyvern gave a massive heave, and Peabo found himself slipping off the wyvern's neck. He just managed to grab Max's hilt as he fell, and found himself hanging by one hand beneath the creature's lower jaw.

"Now what, pea brain? This is what happens when you let go of your weapon, numb nuts."

Another hammer slammed into the side of the wyvern. It spun around, lunging toward Nicole.

Nicole's voice sounded in Peabo's head. *"You blinded him. Now we just need to—"*

The wyvern managed to open its mouth for a full-throated roar, and Max at last slipped out of the lower jaw, sending Peabo falling ten feet to the ground. He rolled to his feet, finding himself near the back of the beast, and saw that Fuzzball had been doing more than just hanging on; the cat had gnawed almost halfway through the wyvern's tail.

Peabo raised Max and grinned.

The wyvern roared with frustration as it lunged at Nicole and got a mouthful of tree instead.

"I always knew you were into tail," Max said. *"You look the type, you grabasstic butt muncher. Fine, let's do this."*

Feeling a surge of desperate power, Peabo sent a mental warning to Fuzzball. The second the cat let go, Peabo swung his sword at the deep groove the cat had munched. He felt his entire arm vibrate as the weapon crunched through bone, severing tendons with audible snapping sounds and ripping through the remaining flesh, severing the wyvern's tail.

The creature roared so loudly that leaves shook right off of the nearest trees.

As it turned, another hammer slammed into the side of its head, and Fuzzball launched itself and bit down on the underside of the monster's throat. Blood poured down by the bucketful, but the cat held on, claws and fangs deeply embedded in the creature.

And within thirty seconds, the wyvern fell over, shuddered, and was no more.

Peabo wiped away some of the eyeball gore still on his hands and looked over at Nicole with a lopsided grin. "That was crazy."

"Are you okay?" she said, dismissing the shimmering war hammer.

"I'm fine."

A large shimmering blob of essence bubbled up from the body of the creature and drifted toward him. Absorbing the life essences of creatures he'd killed, or helped kill, allowed him to progress to a new level. Each level brought with it some kind of improvement in an existing skill, or sometimes even opened him up to a new skill. But since he'd just leveled, it would probably be quite a while until he leveled again. The higher the level the more effort it took to gain the next one. And sure enough, when the essence touched him, Peabo felt just the slightest tingle as his body absorbed the creature's life essence.

But when Nicole received her share of the wyvern's essence, she gasped.

"Did you level?" he asked.

She nodded, her eyes wide.

"Level eight?"

She nodded again and walked over to him, her hands already glowing. She started with his head, then slowly trailed her hands down until she hit his chest. He felt a warmth bloom inside him, and something snapped into place.

"Ouch! I guess I hadn't noticed that."

Fuzzball approached, looked up at him with her icy blue eyes, and let out a growl. *"There are worse dangers nearby."*

Peabo grimaced. He didn't want to think about what might be worse than that. "Fuzzball just said there's worse stuff nearby. We need to leave."

Nicole nodded, looked up into the sky to get her bearings, then pointed north. "We've got about five hours to go. We'll be there before morning."

The three of them set forth once more, setting a rapid pace. Fuzzball seemed to have gotten a nose for wherever it was that Nicole was taking them, because the cat took the lead as they jogged through forests and plains. Even in the dark, Peabo could see the mountains getting closer and closer.

At one point, Fuzzball veered sharply to the left and, with no vocalization whatsoever, projected a message into Peabo's head. *"Danger on the path. Going around it."*

Peabo silently repeated the message to Nicole, and she frowned as she responded.

"What kind of creature is this that we're involved with? How does she know there is danger?"

"Probably smell?" He knew dogs had good sniffers, and maybe cats did as well.

They continued west for a short period before turning north once more. About twenty minutes after the detour, an eerie wail sounded somewhere far behind them.

Peabo sent a thought to Nicole. *"What the hell was that?"*

Nicole shook her head. *"You don't want to know. That had the feel of an undead creature, and not a minor one."*

Fuzzball leaped over some fallen trees, which Peabo and Nicole had to go around. *"Like what kind of creature? Worse than a vampire?"*

"I can't be sure, but that sounded like something from another plane of existence. Maybe a ghost. Maybe worse. Neither of which do we want to mess with. And neither of which have a smell."

No smell? Peabo looked ahead at the cat, still leading them northward, and thought, *"Fuzzball, what are you?"*

"I've forgotten," she responded without hesitation.

"And how do you know where we need to go?"

"I got the image from her. She's ours, right? Family. Is it a wrong place to go?"

"It's okay. I'm sure it's right."

Peabo was surprised by the cat's blasé attitude toward being able to see images in other people's heads. Fuzzball was most certainly not just some random cat. But what was she?

At last they reached an open plain, with nothing between them and the sheer cliffs of a giant mountain range. As they continued onward, Peabo looked over at Nicole with concern. *"You look exhausted. Do you need us to slow down?"*

She shook her head. *"We're almost there. We can rest at the first shelter."*

Peabo spotted a dark blotch at the base of the cliff about half a mile ahead. The entrance to a tunnel. He pointed at it and thought to Nicole. *"Is that it?"*

She nodded.

When they reached the base of the cliff, the cat slowed and stopped. But it had led them to a spot about fifty feet to the right of the tunnel entrance. Peabo furrowed his brow in confusion, but Nicole merely raised a glowing hand and pressed it against the stone. The glow seemed to be absorbed by the rock, and an outline of a door appeared. The cat walked right up to—and right *through*—the stone door.

Nicole motioned for Peabo to do the same, and holding his breath, he followed the cat's lead. He found himself inside a tunnel within the cliff. Nicole hurried in after him, then sealed shut whatever it was that they'd walked through.

"Is that door an illusion?" he asked.

"No, it's real. But for the clerics of the Nameless One, we can enter some chosen places that others may not."

They walked down the tunnel only a short distance before it opened up into a chamber that reminded Peabo very much of the chamber Brodie had first brought him to. It was roughly twenty by thirty feet and was furnished with two straw mattresses and a chest. A glowing fire was burning some large wood-like slabs of dried mushroom.

Nicole pointed at the mattresses. "Let's get some rest. We're safe here. Tomorrow we head deeper into the caves."

As Peabo lay back on one of the mattresses, Nicole pulled a

blanket from the chest and tossed it at him. He stretched it over himself just before the cat hopped up onto his bed and lay across his legs. She sniffed the air a few times, then lay her head on his thigh and closed her eyes.

"Goodnight, Fuzzball."

Nicole collapsed on the other mattress. She began breathing heavily almost as soon as her eyes closed.

Peabo felt comforted by how familiar this shelter was. When he saw the banner hanging on the wall, he knew without having to be told that if he pushed on it, it would seem solid— but that by using whatever hocus-pocus the Nameless One had given Brodie and Nicole, it would lead to a passage out of here.

He closed his eyes and wondered what tomorrow would bring.

When he'd first traveled in the underground world they called Myrkheim, he was told how dangerous some parts of it could be. And given the kind of dangerous creatures just outside this shelter, he could only assume they weren't anywhere near the safer parts of Myrkheim, either.

Tomorrow, before leaving this safe haven, Peabo would need to have a talk with Nicole about what had happened at the towers.

He needed her help.

CHAPTER SIXTEEN

"No, I'm not joking," Peabo said. He and Nicole sat cross-legged on their beds frowning at each other, the cat resting her giant head on Peabo's lap. "That crazy woman nearly beat me to death trying to figure out how to get me to use this plains-walker power that I've got, and it ended up with me getting paired with someone who now probably wants me dead."

The furrow between Nicole's eyebrows deepened. "Hold on. Before we get to your plainswalker abilities, you're telling me that you literally ended up killing one of your instructors and then getting paired to another?"

Peabo winced at the memory of the pain he'd suffered at Leena's hands—or more specifically her feet. PTSD was definitely real. Several missions to Afghanistan and Iraq hadn't given it to him, but his experience in those towers had. "Leena was the one who beat the hell out of me and then tried to forcibly seduce me—"

"You mean rape?"

He grimaced. "I'd rather skip past that term and just say that it ended up with her trying to strangle me. Then something up here"—he tapped the side of his head—"snapped and I burnt a hole through that bitch. The other person, I thought she was a student, but I guess I was set up. She seemed to be having a hard time, seemed scared, and I got totally suckered because I'm the one who mentioned Scarlett's name to Ariandelle. She thought my choice was a wonderful idea, which should have set off a bunch of alarms in my head. I wasn't thinking."

Nicole shook her head. "They often have fake upper-level students embedded in the classes to monitor the other students. You can't trust anyone in that place."

"Anyway, in the end the pairing worked exactly the way it was supposed to, I guess. She was able to help control the use of my power, and it worked. The jig was up when she tried to push too far by digging into my head, and at the end something snapped yet again. I could see her connection to me and I was able to sever the pairing."

"You severed the pairing?" Nicole's eyebrows practically disappeared into her hairline. "I didn't think that was possible."

Peabo shrugged. "I guess I figured out a way. It was actually pretty easy. But when I did it, it knocked her out, and that's when I managed to escape the tower, which led me to being here with you now." He sighed. "I now have two blood maidens out there somewhere who almost certainly want me dead, so I kind of need your help in this."

Nicole grinned. "You probably have more than just those

two who want you dead, believe me. I was doing research with some of the scholars in Igneous City, and what little I could find about plainswalkers was scary. Ariandelle and the rest are probably scared to death of what you're capable of. They'll want to either kill you or control you."

Peabo pictured both versions of Scarlett—the young innocent girl and the older glowing woman who wanted to enslave him. "That girl who was posing as a student—she looked completely different than who she really was. Is that something blood maidens can do?"

Nicole shook her head. "No, that's a pretty rare ability. She must be a conductor of sorts, one who specializes in illusions."

"Could she make herself look like anything?"

"Not *anything*, I'd say. Though I'm not an expert. She can probably mimic most people, including their voices. It's like that skinwalker we encountered."

Peabo shuddered. Back on Dvorak Island they'd encountered a skinwalker that had imitated his own mother—right before he had to kill it. "I might be paranoid, but just in case, let's establish a secret word between the two of us that we can use to make sure it's really the other person. How about Twinkie?"

Nicole gave him a look that suggested he'd said something stupid again. "I probably don't even want to know what that word means. But since we're paired, there's no need to worry about someone using illusion. I can hear your heart from anywhere. I can close my eyes and see what direction I have to go to get to you. I've memorized your smell. There's no chance

I'd ever be fooled. And they don't know that, right? I mean they don't know we're paired."

Peabo shook his head.

"Good. And obviously, you wouldn't be fooled either."

Peabo winced at his own lapse in logic. At least he could count on Nicole for calling him out on the occasions when he flubbed something.

Shifting the cat off his lap, he moved over to Nicole, sat next to her, and looked her in the eye. "I need you to get inside my head and help me control this thing that I am."

Nicole looked serious. "Peabo... I don't think you understand what you're asking me to do." She was silent for a moment, staring down at her lap, then met his gaze. "This is a deeply intimate thing between two people. It forms a bond that is... deeper than just... well, it's just a very serious thing." She took a deep breath and nodded. "I'll do it, but before we do anything, you need to tell me what you know about how you use your power. Before I can help, I need to understand more about what it is I need to do."

It dawned on Peabo what she meant when she referred to this bond. She'd been paired before, and she had suffered greatly from her partner's death. A flash of guilt washed over him for having pushed this on her, but he didn't know of any other option.

He steeled himself against his rising apprehension and tried to keep his voice light and matter-of-fact. "It's all based on light. If I'm in a dark room with no lights other than, let's say, a lantern, I can breathe in the lantern's energy. The problem is, I don't have control over how much I take in. With a single lantern, it's not a big deal—there's only so much oil in it, only so much light it would ever produce, and thus only a limited amount of energy that transfers into me. When Scarlett was in my head, she was able to slow how quickly I breathed in the energy and even stop it completely. But when I'm outside, in the daylight, or even in the moonlight…"

"There's too much light available, and you can't stop your intake," Nicole said.

"Exactly." Peabo dug in his waistband for the pouch he'd hidden there. "I visited with Grundle—"

"Oh, he's still there?" Nicole smiled. "He's such a dear old man. One of the few treasures at the place. I don't know how he stands those women."

"Yes, he and I had a long chat near the end of my stay, and he helped me a lot. He even warned me about the women there, but he thought Ariandelle wasn't all bad, or least hadn't been in the past." Peabo opened the drawstring on the pouch, letting out a burst of white light. "Anyway, I was with him when I tried to use my power in the presence of daylight. He couldn't affect the rate at which I breathed in the energy; all he could do was close the shades after a second, cutting me off from the light."

Peabo held up the blindingly bright crystal. "This was the result. Had I remembered I had this, I could have used it against the wyvern. But I guess it's good that I saved it. If something terrible happens and it's dark, I can use this gem as a source for my power. It's good for emergency uses."

Nicole squinted and looked to the side. "Put that away." It really was too bright to look at.

Peabo returned the crystal to his pouch. "Do you know of any other crystal weavers like Grundle?"

"Not personally. But that's something we could ask Brodie or some others at Igneous City." She nodded at the pouch. "Just a quick second gave you that amount of energy?"

"Yes, and then I passed out. It was too much too quickly I suppose, even with Grundle limiting it to one second. Either I need to be much higher level to use daylight in any way, or I need someone slowing down how fast I'm taking in the light all around me." He reached over to Nicole's knee and gave it a squeeze. "And that's where you come in. I have no idea what I'm supposed to do in this world, or why plainswalkers even exist. But if I was brought here for a reason, it probably has to do with this ability of mine. Right now, the only thing I know is that I can do this—but only with you helping me."

Nicole took Peabo's hand and gave it a squeeze. "I'll try. That's all I can promise. Shall we practice with that?" She pointed at the fire in the middle of the chamber.

Peabo nodded. "That's a good idea. I'm ready whenever you think you are. Just tell me when."

"First let me try to see into your mind. If I can, I'll limit what you're pulling." Nicole squeezed Peabo's hand once more and let it go. "I'll say when."

Peabo felt a familiar pressure in his head and knew she was up there. After a few seconds the sensation changed, and a warm comforting caress raced through his entire body. It felt like a slow embrace from head to toe.

"I'm ready," Nicole said.

Peabo focused on the glowing planks of thick mushroom

and inhaled. The room dimmed, but instead of going instantly dark, the straw-like channel of energy narrowed to a mere trickle. He was still drawing from the fire—for the first time he could see the tiny streamers of raw colors coming from the glowing embers and flowing into him—but Nicole had slowed the transfer.

Even so, the planks of mushroom, which should have burned for days, had been nearly consumed in the blink of an eye.

Nicole whispered, "Try to stop yourself."

Peabo focused on halting that breath he'd started taking in. But he couldn't. It was as if the breath required a certain amount and it wouldn't be satisfied until it got its full allotment. He might be able to exhale, but he didn't know for certain that he wouldn't set something on fire in the process. And in an enclosed area, that wouldn't be good.

He was completely helpless. It felt like trying to wave an arm he didn't have.

The last of the mushroom planks collapsed into ashes, and just like that the flow of energy stopped, bathing the room in darkness. Peabo sensed Nicole moving, and a flicker of light bloomed from a lantern.

She smiled. "That was very quick. I thought I was ready, but I didn't anticipate just how fast that would happen. We'll need to practice that."

Peabo smiled back. "Isn't that exactly what we're doing?"

Nicole sat back down and ran her fingers across Peabo's arm. "Your markings are glowing again. The lightning patterns are apparently some sort of indicator of whether you're holding in some of this 'breathed-in' energy. I'd recently stumbled into a book talking about a plainswalker's markings in the archives of Igneous City, but that was when I detected something going on with you, so I raced out of there before I could read much about it."

Peabo chuckled. "I hope they don't take your library card away for leaving behind a mess. I seem to remember you covering an entire table with opened books last time we were in a library."

Nicole stood. "Don't joke. Those archive scholars are all approaching level twenty. They're all veterans of the lower levels and liable to beat you within an inch of your life if you mess up the way they organize their books. Especially there. That's the oldest archive there is outside of the Sage's Tower. But, speaking of leaving a mess..." She nodded at the ashes of the fire. "I need to replace those mushroom slabs. They should have lasted a full week. I'll be right back."

Before Peabo could say anything she'd fast-walked through the tapestry. A few minutes later she returned with several new slabs of mushroom. She swept the ashes into a bin and set up the new slabs for the next visitor to this little resting place.

With a glowing hand she motioned in the direction of the tapestry. "We have about a day's worth of travel before we get to the outskirts of Igneous City. It could be quicker, but we're going to have to avoid the main corridors. Ariandelle has eyes and ears everywhere, and with the way your markings are glowing, I doubt even the alchemist potion trick would disguise what you are. Eventually we'll have to come up with something else."

The two of them walked through the temporarily permeable tapestry, as did Fuzzball. They left the lantern behind, as it wasn't needed; the tunnels had their own glow, thanks to the spores of a mushroom that gave off a natural, dim light.

Peabo's stomach rumbled, and he wished they'd had a chance to find something to eat. Then again, he wasn't eager to find out what kind of food one could harvest from the wilds of Myrkheim.

Peabo followed Nicole through Myrkheim for what felt like half a day, and they spent most of that time in the same winding tunnel. The passageway was just barely tall enough for him to stand up straight, and it was so narrow that they had to walk single file. Occasionally they'd come across a hanging tapestry on the tunnel wall and would take a turn, but not often.

He sent his thoughts to Nicole. *"How is it that this tunnel even exists? It seems pretty uniform compared to the main traveling corridors we've been through before."*

"It was dug by the followers of the Nameless One many many centuries ago." She glanced over her shoulder at him. *"We're lucky it wasn't built more recently, because had the dwarves built it, we'd be walking hunched over the entire way. Thankfully, the first dwarves were said to be aboveworlders who came into Myrkheim to hide from the wars of the First Age. The archives say—"*

She stopped suddenly as the ground began quaking under

their feet. The sound of cracking stone echoed loudly from somewhere up ahead.

Fuzzball hissed. *"There are others nearby."*

"Um, Nicole, the cat just said there are others close by."

A belch of dust came rolling toward them, and they had to cover their faces with their tunics, but Nicole pushed forward.

"That sounded like a cave-in," Peabo whispered.

"Let's hope not."

Nicole led the way through the thick cloud of dust. Slowly it began to settle, and soon their fears were confirmed. There *had* been a cave-in—and the tunnel was completely blocked just ahead.

Nicole surveyed the damage. *"This happens on rare occasions. We'll have to turn back and take a different route."*

They retraced their steps for what Peabo estimated was a quarter mile before Nicole stopped them beside a tapestry. She pointed at a red square at the top right of the weaving. *"That signifies an unprotected area. I'm not sure where we'll end up, but our goal is to go out, race to the nearest hidden entrance, go back into it, and hope that it gets us past the cave-in."* She looked at both Peabo and the cat, and spoke aloud for Fuzzball's benefit. "You two ready?"

The cat's tail swished spasmodically as she nodded, apparently understanding, and Peabo said, "Ready."

With a wave of Nicole's hand, the tapestry took on a different sheen, indicating that for the next few seconds it could be passed through. They stepped through to the other side—and were greeted with the sounds of war.

CHAPTER SEVENTEEN

The coppery scent of blood hung in the as a gout of flame burst from the depths of some multi-headed, long-necked creature. Peabo froze at the unexpected scene of carnage and everything seemed to progress at a snail's pace.

They were standing in a giant cavern, its ceiling at least fifty feet high. Hundreds of goblins to their left were yelling high-pitched battle cries, and hundreds of pig-snouted orcs to their right bellowed their own blood-curdling yells. And directly between the two sides loomed a twenty-foot-tall hydra, its many long-necked heads snapping and tearing at its enemies on both sides. Two of the hydra's heads lay limp, dragging on the ground, but even as Peabo watched, four new heads sprouted from the creature's main body, their eyes glowing.

"Go back!" Nicole shouted in his head,

At that moment two of the hydra's heads noticed Peabo and

his companions. The heads opened their mouths and sent two billowing gouts of flame directly at the newcomers.

Without thinking, Peabo breathed in.

Streams of energy flew at him from all directions. The hydra's flaming spittle exploded into clouds of ash, their energy absorbed by Peabo, who was beginning to glow like a beacon in the dim world of Myrkheim. Flaming debris on both sides of the battle were likewise snuffed out in the blink of an eye, their torrents of energy being sucked in as well. Even the glow from the cavern's mushroom spores was snuffed out, and a million gossamer threads of energy rushed into Peabo.

Peabo's body quivered with the energy he'd absorbed. It was more than he'd ever absorbed before.

But there was no time to dwell on the sensation. Two of the hydra heads lunged at him, and arrows were launched at him from either side.

He exhaled.

A fountain of sizzling energy and blinding light burst forth from his body.

The incoming arrows were incinerated in the blast of power. The attacking heads of the hydra were struck by Peabo's light-based assault, and the entire beast convulsed, its heads whipping about spasmodically, white-hot light shooting from their maws and eyes. The entire cavern was swept through with the crackling heat and cleansing light of a plainswalker's true power.

There was no more yelling. The only sounds in the cavern were the popping of heated gristle and the thud of falling bodies.

Then, out of the darkness, three brilliant jets of deadly flame shot toward Peabo, launched from three dark figures at the far end of the cavern. Another flare of light came streaking toward him from another direction, looking very much like a lightning bolt.

Still operating on instinct, Peabo breathed in. The flames and the lightning were extinguished, and Peabo mentally pushed back at where he sensed the attacks had come from.

This time, the shimmering lights that emerged from him, four in total, had a rainbow-like coloration, the individual wavelengths coruscating in threads that had previously looked white to him, but now Peabo plainly saw the variety of colors within. What was more, each color now had a unique sound, and together they formed a symphony.

The beams of light swerved, each moving of its own volition, tracking their targets. They struck the four conductors—wizards, in Peabo's mind—and though two of these conductors had some type of shielding, the light penetrated these shields and shot right into Peabo's attackers. A shock wave was both felt and heard throughout the cavern as the four bodies exploded, simultaneously, from the burst of energy.

Peabo's knees buckled, and he would have fallen had Nicole not caught him. Exhaustion didn't even begin to describe what he was feeling. He'd been drained of something that he wasn't sure he'd ever get back. Nicole was shouting something, but he couldn't make out the words. His mind was numb. The smell of charred flesh was everywhere. His tongue and throat were coated with ashes, and he felt nauseated.

Was this what being a plainswalker was about? Mass killing?

Nicole summoned a light orb, which hovered over her head. It was barely strong enough to illuminate a fifty-foot radius, but that was enough for him to see the extent of the carnage. He shuddered at the sight.

Then, suddenly, something clicked, and he had his wits about him once more. He could hear Nicole's heavy breathing, along with the sound of receding footsteps.

"Peabo? Are you there?" She was shaking him, practically yelling.

He nodded. "Did I lose consciousness?"

"You didn't... I guess maybe. You were there, but unresponsive. I think we're out of danger."

"What about those footsteps I'm hearing?"

Nicole shook her head. "Whoever didn't get killed is running away. I don't blame them."

Peabo looked into the darkness, then gasped as it lit up suddenly with many hundreds of shimmering balls of essence.

The essences of those he'd killed.

"By the Nameless One, I've never seen such a thing!" Nicole said, her eyes wide.

"You see the essences?" Peabo asked, perplexed.

"Yes! They're everywhere."

"I thought they could only be seen by the person who was receiving the essence. The person who killed the creature."

Nicole shrugged. "Yes... that's interesting. I was inside your head as it happened, watching you carefully to better understand your power. I didn't do anything, but I guess my keeping tabs up in your head resulted in my receiving undue credit."

The essences streamed toward the two of them. Peabo had never killed so many things at once, and the essences hit him in a rapid-fire barrage. The countless tingles of received essences built into a crescendo that sent him over a precipice. He leveled, and as he glanced at Nicole, he saw the look on her face and could tell that she'd leveled as well.

She smiled weakly. "I never thought I'd see the day when I hit level nine."

And still the essences continued coming. And as Peabo absorbed the last of them, he felt another surge.

He'd leveled *again*.

Time seemed to stop. New sounds and feelings coursed through his body. The gossamer-thin connection between him and Nicole was brighter than he'd ever seen it. Fuzzball, who was swishing her tail nervously and growling into the darkness, glowed with a preternatural light that he'd never seen before. And when he looked at Nicole, he could hear her thoughts as easily as if he'd crawled inside her head.

He was level eight. Something that had seemed unimaginable just a few months ago.

Despite the darkness of the cavern, he could see all the way across its expanse now. An ability that, at this moment, he wished he didn't have. As he took in the full view of what he'd done, he bent over and heaved stomach acid onto the pebble-strewn ground.

Nicole ran her hand over his back as he continued dry-heaving for nearly a minute. He felt her silent compassion.

"Peabo, I know this is a lot to absorb, but we have to go. This isn't a safe place."

Peabo wiped his mouth and nodded.

Nicole led them quickly through the bodies strewn across the cavern. And despite the vomiting, the trauma of what had happened, and the absolute exhaustion he'd felt just moments earlier, Peabo felt stronger and faster than he could have imagined possible.

There was so much about this world, about his journey, about who he was, that he wanted to savor. To explore slowly. But it seemed like there was never time to do anything but run.

As Peabo gazed at the burning mushroom slabs that heated the shelter, he noticed something he'd never noticed before. "Is there something different about these mushrooms?" he asked Nicole. "I'm seeing different colors than I'm used to."

Nicole shook her head. "Not that I know of." She looked at the fire. "I don't see anything unusual. What are you seeing?"

"I guess I'm seeing a rainbow-like hue around the light. It's not very noticeable, but it's there. Could I be seeing it because of leveling?"

"It's possible. I've never heard of anyone ever gaining two levels in a week, much less in a moment, especially after advancing to above level five. You might be experiencing a side effect of that. To be honest, I can't believe I'm level nine. I'll need to study and practice, but I should be able to do some of the things that we saw Brodie do in that battle with Lord Dvorak."

"Like calling down flames and stuff?"

Nicole nodded.

"One thing about that," Peabo said, "and we should probably have discussed it earlier. Anything that you do with light, you don't want it active when I'm using my skill. At the tower, a lady who was also a healer ended up almost passing out because—well, I guess I sucked all of the energy out of her through the light she projected."

Nicole's eyes widened. "That's an amazingly powerful ability. You're probably a weaver's worst nightmare. You've proven you can breathe in and attack very quickly." She looked up at the ceiling. "It's no wonder why the plainswalker is mentioned so prominently in the histories. Especially if you can master the use of daylight. Entire armies could fall beneath your scythe of burning light."

Peabo lay back on the mattress. This shelter was furnished almost identically to the previous one. "How much further until we get to civilization?"

"A few hours, no more. I can hear your stomach growling. We'll find something to eat then."

Peabo turned to the cat, which was laying across his legs. "I assume you could use a bit as well, eh, Fuzzball?"

The cat opened her mouth wide in a dramatic yawn, her four-inch canines shining brightly in the reflected firelight. *I will eat when there is food.*

Peabo glanced over at the pile of additional slab mushrooms on the far side of the shelter. "When we leave, is it okay if I breathe in whatever's left of the campfire's energy? I'm feeling almost naked not having something loaded inside me."

"That's fine, but your glowing markings will remain a problem when you're holding energy. We'll need to consult with Brodie about solving that problem. I have no idea what Ariandelle has in mind for you, but that woman is more dangerous than anyone you've ever met."

"Well, if she's a conductor I'd think she'd be—"

"Don't get ahead of yourself, Peabo. Not every attack involves a source of light. What if she manages to charm you? What about sending a noxious cloud of poison to suffocate you? Or even pulls down a cliff on top of you? Never underestimate your opponent or think you've got the upper hand."

Peabo nodded. He remembered the strange feeling of compulsion that had emanated from that woman, and that was when Ariandelle probably wasn't even trying to do anything. He didn't want to imagine how powerful she could be when she tried.

Nicole gave him a comforting look. "Try not to worry about it. Get some rest. We've got a long day ahead of us."

Peabo closed his eyes, but instead of trying to rest, he practiced using his new, leveled-up senses. Even though they were sealed away in a hidden chamber deep underground, he could sense the tiny scratching sounds of claws skittering across rock. Something was out there somewhere, crawling around. The vibrations told him it was something very bulky—likely not something he'd want to mess with.

True, he'd just wiped out a small army. But they had been foolish enough to use fire and light against him. But with a normal brute—like an ogre, or some other day-in-the-life monstrosity that lived underground—he wouldn't have that same advantage.

Fuzzball placed a fist-sized paw on his chest. *"The one who is ours is correct. Sleep."*

The cat was much more intelligent than Peabo had initially assumed. Which made him wonder: had his encounter with Fuzzball truly been random?

But it had to be, didn't it? The cat couldn't have set up the whole trap scene on purpose. There was no way. Still, there was something very odd about the animal. It was like a furry guardian angel by his side.

But what if…

He shook his head. He was being paranoid.

CHAPTER EIGHTEEN

As Peabo stepped through the shimmering tapestry, his ears popped due to a sudden change in air pressure. The scent of damp stone and the echoes of distant voices greeted him as Nicole led their party down a short passage to one of Myrkheim's main travel routes.

"We're here," she said. "Do you remember passing through this city?"

Peabo faced a breathtakingly large tunnel that must have begun, long ago, as a magma tube. Now it was a major underground thoroughfare, easily two hundred feet wide with the ceiling at least fifty feet above. A short way down the underground boulevard, two blazing bonfires burned on either side, with a dozen dwarven soldiers stationed next to each. And about four hundred feet beyond that was the enormous entrance to Igneous City, where two forty-foot-tall statues stood like granite sentinels. They depicted proud, stoutly built dwarves, each wielding a tremendous hammer. Beneath their gaze, dozens of dwarves passed through into a massive city carved out of the bedrock.

Peabo shook his head. "I must have been really out of it. I don't remember this place at all."

Nicole draped an arm over his shoulder. "You were in and out of consciousness for most of the trip. I wasn't sure you'd even make it as far as the Sage's Tower."

A squad of dwarven soldiers approached and stopped in front of the three of them. These guys—and one gal, Peabo noted—looked like they meant business. Their leader had a brace of glittering daggers strapped across his chest and a pair of glowing maces holstered near his waist. His gaze skipped right over Nicole and stopped on Peabo and the giant cat, whose tail was swishing nervously.

Peabo silently sent a thought at the cat. *"Don't attack anything unless Nicole or I do."*

Fuzzball opened her mouth wide, exposing her teeth, and let out a loud yawn. *"These are not a threat."*

To the dwarven leader's credit, his only reaction to the yawn was a slight widening of his eyes. He gave Peabo a quick look from head to toe, then clicked his armored feet together, stood at attention, and slammed his fist to his chest. "Plainswalker, I'm pleased to see you've arrived in one piece. I'm with the Igneous City Security. I've been instructed by the prelate of the Nameless One to escort you to the church's security perimeter."

The leader looked to one of the dwarves to his left, and the other dwarf's hands began to glow.

"Wait a minute," Peabo said, the hair on the back of his neck standing on end. "What's he doing?"

Nicole put a hand on Peabo's shoulder. "It's okay."

"It's to obscure other's people's view—just for a moment," said the dwarf with the glowing hands. His voice was surprisingly nasal and high-pitched.

A series of coruscating golden threads projected from the dwarf's hands and began racing around the gathering, weaving what looked like a glowing spider web. And as the web was being woven, Peabo heard a chittering noise, almost as if there really were some invisible spider building the ephemeral wall around them.

He sent a thought to Nicole. *"What are those threads doing?"*

"Threads?" She gave him a questioning look. *"What threads?"*

What threads? Was he the only one seeing this?

The weaving and noise stopped, and the threads puffed out into a giant wall of gray fog that completely encircled them. Peabo heard the grousing of several passersby who'd been caught in the instant cloud bank that had fallen in the underground passage.

"By the Nameless One, warn a fellow when you do such things..."

"Oy there! I'm walking here!"

Both he and Nicole were handed cloth bundles. "Please put those on," the leader said. "They will help keep your identities hidden from curious eyes until we get to safety within the church's walls."

Inside Peabo's bundle was a long robe made of a gossamer-thin cloth. It had a shimmering, mirror-like quality to it, and when he put it on and looked down at himself, he gasped. Instead of seeing his body, he saw a slightly warped image of what was on the other side of him. It was almost, but not quite, like he was invisible.

Nicole leaned closer to the squad leader and asked quietly, "What's going on? Is there already a security threat?"

The leader also spoke in a low tone. "We have two newly arrived blood maidens under watch. They arrived only hours ahead of you. Unfortunately, due to the treaty we have with the Sage's Tower, we cannot hamper their travels without cause."

Nicole put her robe on, and one of the soldiers pointed at the cat. "What about that creature? Should I try to cloak it?"

The leader looked to Peabo. "It would be better if none of your party is seen. Henry can cast a temporary cloak of invisibility on your... animal. Is there any danger in doing so?"

Peabo looked questioningly at Fuzzball, who let out a low growl. *"I have no objection."*

Peabo nodded to Henry. "She's okay with it."

"That was an agreement?" Henry said skeptically, but he proceeded with the procedure. Golden threads jetted from his hands, wrapping Fuzzball in a glowing, gauzy cocoon that evidently only Peabo could see. Then the web unraveled, fell to the floor, and vanished with a fizzle.

Fuzzball wasn't even the slightest bit invisible.

The dwarven conjurer looked dumbfounded. "I don't understand. It somehow... resisted the spell."

Fuzzball hissed, and her fur stood on end. *"Danger is approaching."*

The dwarves all took a step back at the angry-sounding hiss, but Peabo explained. "She's warning us there's danger nearby."

The squad leader made a knife-hand gesture at Henry. "Get them out of here, *now*."

A woman's voice called from beyond the fog. *"Peabo! I know you're here somewhere."*

"We must be touching each other," Henry said, grabbing Nicole's and Peabo's hands. Then the dwarf's entire body began to glow, and Peabo felt a tingling sensation.

"You can't hide from me in this fog, you fool!"

The woman's voice sent a chill up Peabo's spine.

The fog vanished with a pop, and the ground began to shake violently. Dwarves were thrown to the ground, and screams sounded from all up and down the tunnel.

The world flashed white.

With a disorienting rush of colors and sounds, Peabo, Nicole, and Henry popped into existence in a dark stone passage barely tall enough for Peabo to stand.

"Follow me," Henry yelled, and he raced down the dim tunnel.

Peabo looked around for Fuzzball, but the cat was nowhere to be found. He hoped she could take care of herself, because there was nothing he could do for her now.

"Hurry!" Nicole screamed in his head. She yanked on his arm, and they chased after the surprisingly fast dwarf.

A clanging bell sounded in the distance. It was not unlike a bell he'd have expected to hear at a fire station. *"What's that mean?"* he thought at Nicole.

"It's a security alarm. Normally it indicates an attack on the city by some creature, but this time..."

She didn't need to finish. This time it was no creature, but a blood maiden. Somehow, despite the cloaking, that woman had known Peabo was there.

The dwarf halted at the end of the tunnel and began glowing. "Keep hold of my arms, duck down, and do *not* let go as we go across the plaza ahead. I'm going to create an anti-magic shield around me, but you have to stay very close for it to protect you as well."

Protect us from what? Peabo wondered, but he dutifully grabbed the dwarf's arm.

The air around them sizzled with power and grew blurry, and with a loud crack, a see-through bubble appeared around the tiny group. It was very close quarters; if Peabo so much as straightened up, his head would poke through.

They began fast-walking across a circular plaza that was about a quarter mile across. It was ringed by ornate buildings, many of them larger than anything Peabo had seen on Dvorak Island, where he'd started his unlikely adventure. People were walking everywhere, almost all of them dwarves, but no one paid the trio any attention, thanks to the invisibility robes. Still, Peabo sometimes felt a glance in their direction just after they passed someone.

What would you expect someone to do after they saw a weird blur pass by? The dwarves probably figured they needed to check their eyesight.

They approached the far end of the plaza, where several dwarves appeared at the gated entrance to a sprawling compound. The buildings in the compound were huge, and looked like they had been precisely carved from the bedrock itself, and the entire area was enclosed by a wall that gave off a near-blinding white aura.

Standing just inside the gate was a dwarf who had the same preternatural glow as Ariandelle.

The moment they crossed the threshold of the compound, Henry dropped his protective shield. The short man sighed with relief, their quick escape looked to have taken something out of him. Peabo gratefully stood at his full height, towering over everyone but Nicole.

A familiar face rushed up to them, and they clasped arms.

"Brodie!" said Peabo. "It's good to see you again."

The dwarf grinned and clapped him on the shoulder. "You've grown in many ways, Peabo. You're looking like the plainswalker that destiny would have you become."

"Not yet, Brodie. Our plainswalker has a long path before him." It was the dwarf with the shimmering aura who had spoken. He looked young, much younger than Brodie, whose dark beard and hair were shot with streaks of gray. "Given time, however, we can hope that what was done can be undone."

Brodie cleared his throat and faced the glowing dwarf. "Prelate of the Nameless One, I'm privileged to introduce you to a man you've spoken to before, but from afar. This is Peabo, a true plainswalker, as the stories foretold." He turned to Peabo. "Peabo, this is the prelate of the Nameless One, head of our church and the first in our order to rediscover the means by which to commune with the Nameless One himself."

Peabo recalled the time when Brodie set up what almost seemed like a Ouija board drawn in some sand to commune with the Nameless One. It had seemed crazy back then—to speak to a higher power and actually get responses—but with all that Peabo had seen since, it seemed almost normal.

The prelate looked at Peabo from head to toe, and Peabo realized he was still wearing the robe. He quickly took it off.

The dwarf chuckled. "You need not have done that for my benefit. I can see you as you truly are."

"The Robe of Cloaking affects only the common eye," Brodie explained. "We had hoped to avoid rumors of your arrival."

The prelate smiled. "I think that ox has already escaped the corral."

Someone screamed outside the gate, and Peabo turned to look, expecting the worst. Something dark was approaching across the plaza.

"Close the gates!" Brodie shouted.

"No!" Peabo said, stepping closer to the gate. "I know this creature. She's a friend."

The dark shape loped toward him, and Peabo couldn't help but smile as Fuzzball raced across the plaza.

"What in all the hells *is* that thing?" Brodie muttered.

Fuzzball approached the open gate but didn't come

through. She sat on her haunches on the other side of the barrier. Her maw was covered with fresh blood, and her icy-blue eyes looked directly at the prelate.

Several of the dwarves took a step back, but the prelate looked curious. "In all my years, I've never witnessed such a thing," he said in a whisper. He turned to Brodie. "The creature just spoke in my mind and asked permission to enter."

Peabo sent his thoughts to the cat. *"Where did that blood come from?"* He had nightmare visions of dead dwarves on the street along whatever path she'd taken to get here.

"There was a danger. One is gone. The other is eliminated."

Peabo turned to the prelate. "I think the cat might have killed one of the blood maidens. She's sort of a guardian of mine."

"A guardian?" Brodie and the prelate asked in unison.

Nicole nodded in agreement. "The creature joined Peabo before I intercepted him in the Aboveground. She's traveled with us the entire way since, and she does seem protective toward the plainswalker."

Everyone looked to the prelate, who seemed to be in a staring contest with the cat. The dwarf blinked first.

He motioned the cat forward. "As guardian to the plain-swalker, you are given temporary asylum within the Nameless One's domain."

Fuzzball rose and stalked through the gate. Peabo heard a sizzle, like arcing electricity, as the cat penetrated the glowing barrier. But he saw no golden threads.

The prelate gestured toward a building that looked to Peabo

like a chapel, complete with a tall stone spire despite being deep underground. "Please join me inside. Before we do anything more, I'd like to understand what truly happened today. If these are rogue maidens, that is one thing, but if the tower is seeking a battle, we may be on the cusp of a war."

CHAPTER NINETEEN

Peabo stared wide-eyed at the glowing communication ring on the desk in one of the church's inner chambers. The room was bare other than a desk that Brodie was sitting behind, while he and Nicole were sitting on the chairs on the opposite side of the table. Fuzzball lay sprawled at Peabo's feet.

"The body is being brought here?" Peabo asked. "Is there anything else you can tell us about what happened?"

The communication ring gave off a bluish-white glow, a sign that it had an active connection to a mated pair. He'd only seen such a ring once before in this world, but he understood it served the same purpose as a point-to-point intercom system. This one evidently connected to someone at the front gate.

A gravelly voice projected from the ring. *"Plainswalker, that is correct. The squad leader who engaged with the maidens is bringing the corpse to your location. I am but a gate guard, so I do not know anything more."*

"That is all, Tarek," Brodie said with practiced finality. "We'll wait for the gurney's arrival. Let me know if there's any word about the second blood maiden."

"Yes, sir."

Using two fingers, Brodie squeezed the sides of the ring. The bluish-white glow vanished, severing the connection.

He looked over at Peabo. "Reports say that three people died at the entrance today, not including the blood maiden. It will be very interesting to see if you recognize the maiden who died."

Peabo replayed in his mind the voice from earlier today. *"Peabo! I know you're here somewhere. You can't hide from me in this fog, you fool!"*

"One of the maidens is someone I knew from the tower," he said. "I recognized her voice when she called out to me in the fog. She called herself Scarlett—though I have no idea if that's really her name, since everything else about her was a lie." Peabo's jaw clenched. "At the very end she tried to take over my mind. Prior to that she pretended to be a student. She looked young. And she had bruises from getting beaten, which made me... sympathetic. I was an idiot."

Nicole looked over at Brodie. "An illusionist?"

Brodie nodded. "And a high-level one to cast a permanent illusion." He turned back to Peabo. "Did you share a room with her?"

Peabo nodded.

"And when she slept, did she look any different?"

"No. She looked exactly the same, and we were inches

apart. I never knew a thing until the end, when the illusion dropped."

Brodie's lips pressed into a thin line. "Necromancy is a forbidden art, and it's nipped in the bud as soon as it's discovered, but an illusionist... they're real trouble. They're supposed to be outlawed, but the rules are difficult to enforce. And I've heard rumors that the king employs illusionists as special assassins, though there's no solid proof. When someone can make themselves appear like anyone, affect perceived reality, cause mass suggestion, create veils of nature... it's powerful stuff."

"Hold on, Brodie. You're speaking in cursive. I don't know what you're talking about... create veils of nature?"

Nicole chimed in. "It's not just that she can change her own appearance, Peabo. She could make you see a flat road continuing onward where there's really a cliff ahead of you. And she can pass through all but the most advanced security without even trying hard. An illusionist can be a thing of nightmares."

Peabo remembered the feeling of her trying to take over his mind. How had that related to illusion? But he decided to ask about something else.

"What does it mean when someone glows?"

"Glows?" Brodie raised an eyebrow. "What do you mean?"

"Well, Ariandelle and Scarlett—after her illusion fell—both gave off a glow. The prelate does too. I'm just wondering what that's all about."

The looks on Nicole and Brodie's faces made it clear that they'd never seen such a thing.

"Interesting," Brodie said, raking his fingers through his

beard. "I've never heard of someone glowing—or of a plain-swalker being able to see such a thing. Perhaps that's a plain-swalker ability that's simply not documented. As for why these particular people share this trait? The only thing I can think of is that both Ariandelle and the prelate are very high level."

"How high?"

"The prelate is level twenty-three."

Peabo widened his eyes.

"I do not know Ariandelle's level," Brodie continued, "but I believe it is at least nineteen or twenty. As to your illusion-ist… to be able to create a seemingly permanent illusion—one that would suffice in fooling you up close—would require at least a level twelve. Beyond that, I have no idea."

A knock sounded on the door, and the squad leader Peabo had met earlier poked his head into the room. He looked like he'd been through quite a battle. The right side of the squad leader's face was almost completely without hair, and what little hair was left had curled up into a kinky wiry mess. He'd probably been burnt to a crisp, and this was what he looked like after being treated by a healer.

"High Priest, may I enter with my burden?"

"Come in." Brodie stood, as did Peabo and Nicole.

The squad leader rolled a cart into the room. A blood-stained sheet covered its cargo. As the dwarf grabbed the sheet to pull it back, Brodie forestalled him.

"Hold on that. First tell me what happened at the city entrance."

The squad leader stood at ease and spoke simply. "Immedi-ately after Henry teleported away with our charges, we were attacked by a tremendous fireball and a barrage of poison darts. One of the darts penetrated our protections and got Jenkins. It was laced with extract of acidwort."

Nicole explained silently to Peabo. *"Extract of acidwort destroys flesh. It also makes it so the victim cannot be resurrected."*

The squad leader motioned to Fuzzball. "The fight was joined by the plainswalker's companion as well as the gate guards. One of the maidens vanished into thin air, and even with true seeing, we couldn't spot her. The other..." He nodded to the gurney. "It was a quick and vicious encounter. It was lucky we were there, because those women fought like demons." He glanced at Peabo. "Even with the famed powers of a plainswalker, I don't know how you would have fared if they'd caught you unaware."

"And what of Jenkins?" Brodie asked.

The squad leader sighed. "She did not survive the resurrection."

Brodie clapped his hand on the soldier's shoulder. "May the Nameless One keep her and hold her tight for eternity." He pointed at the gurney. "Now let's see what we have."

The soldier unceremoniously removed the sheet. The figure beneath had lifeless blue eyes and blood-streaked blonde hair. A look of surprise was etched on her face, and it was obvious why. Her throat had been torn out.

Fuzzball began to purr. *"It was a danger to us."*

Nicole moved her fingertips across Peabo's back. "Do you recognize her?"

"Yes. It's Leena."

"The one who tortured you?"

Peabo nodded. "It's funny. I would have figured that I'd be dancing a jig to see her dead… again. But I feel nothing."

"That's a good thing, Peabo. Holding hate within you only gives others power over you," said Brodie. "Now please step back. Let's see what she has to say for herself."

"What?" Peabo choked out the word as he imagined the woman without a throat being resurrected yet again. "You're not bringing her back to life, are you?"

Brodie chuckled and shook his head. "Don't worry, plains-walker. She is far too dangerous to allow her to live."

"He's going to speak to her spirit," Nicole thought at him. *"The spirit can be compelled to answer a few questions truth-fully, for a short period of time after the body dies."*

Peabo shook his head. Any time he dared to think he was getting a handle on what was and wasn't possible in this world, he was proven wrong yet again.

Brodie held his hands over Leena's corpse, and they began to glow. The air crackled with energy, like static, and it grew from loud to near-deafening in only a few seconds. Then, suddenly, the room fell silent.

A shimmering white ball bubbled up from the corpse, looking much like the life essence that arose after kills. But this one was gauzy and almost transparent.

Brodie's voice sounded distant yet powerful. "Did you come to Igneous City for a specific purpose?"

"Yes." The voice was Leena's, but it too sounded distant, as if Brodie was talking to Leena's spirit on some other plane of existence.

"Who was your target?"

"The plainswalker."

"Were you to do harm to the plainswalker?"

"Yes."

"Were you sent by someone?"

"Yes."

"By someone in the Sage's Tower?"

"No."

Everyone's eyes widened at the ghostly response.

"Who sent you to harm the plainswalker?"

The shimmering ball of Leena's spirit turned jet black, and with a resounding crack the room was cloaked in suffocating darkness. Peabo felt disembodied fingers clutching at his throat, and maniacal laughter echoed all around him.

Peabo tried to move, to escape, only to realize that he had no body. And yet he was choking. He had no sense of himself, anyone else, or time. He floated in the never-ending laughter of a maniac.

Had he suddenly gone crazy?

Was he dead?

If he didn't have a body, why did it feel like he was gasping for air?

He strained against the darkness, his thoughts growing more jumbled and confused.

His mother's face flashed in his mind's eye... but he couldn't remember the details. Her face was a smudge. A forgotten thought.

He tried to remember the others in the room, but their

memories were burnt away. His mind was being drained of all that it had, all of who he was.

Would anyone find him in the darkness?

It was so cold.

This was what death was really like… nothingness.

He was nothing.

Suddenly a pinpoint of light appeared in the distance. It was so far away, but it was something…

As he strained to reach it, words broke through the laughter.

"By the power of the Nameless One, begone."

The light grew just a bit larger. But he couldn't reach it.

"By the power of the Nameless One, begone."

Again the light grew larger, now the size of his fist. He reached for it and heard the words a third time.

"By the power of the Nameless One, begone!"

Peabo lurched forward and fell to the floor, gasping for air.

The darkness was gone.

The others were all in the same condition, except for the cat who seemed unfazed.

The prelate stood in the doorway, glowing with a holy aura that rivaled anything Peabo had seen since coming to this world.

The head of the church waved one hand and brought down a pillar of searing flame onto Leena's body. Everyone scattered at the blast of heat, and in moments all that was left of the corpse was ashes and a few tattered fragments of cloth.

The prelate turned to Brodie. "What just occurred in this room?"

The high priest got back to his feet, looking pale and shaken. He quickly explained what he'd done.

"Was it a demon that possessed her?" Nicole asked. "Even into death?"

The prelate shook his head. "That was no demon. No demon could bypass the wards set on this site. I don't know what it was." He turned to Peabo. "Plainswalker, there is much at risk with you here. Both to us and to you. We need to get some answers. Answers that I'm afraid may only be available in Myrkheim City."

"The oracle?" Brodie asked.

The prelate nodded. "It will take me a few days to summon the appropriate party. In the meantime, don't do anything like that again. Are we understood?"

Brodie's hands were shaking as he nodded his understanding. It was the first time Peabo had ever seen the man rattled.

Whatever had just happened was way above Peabo's pay grade.

The prelate left the room, and the squad leader departed with him. Brodie took a deep breath and looked back and forth between Peabo and Nicole.

"We still have a maiden out there, and we have to presume these two were on the same mission. When heading to Myrkheim City, you can't afford to have a known enemy of the illusionist's caliber at your back. Before you depart—"

"You're not coming?" Peabo cut in.

Brodie shook his head. "I know this might come as a shock to you, but I'm not a high enough level to be useful on this trip." Peabo felt his eyes widen. "Nicole will accompany you only because you two are paired," Brodie continued, "and she'll complement your weaknesses with her strengths. Now, as I was saying, before you depart, we need to know how these women were able to track you here. Do you have any ideas how they managed that?"

"I think I do," Nicole responded.

Brodie made a rolling motion with his hand for her to continue.

"Peabo was paired with the illusionist."

Brodie's eyes widened. "Oh crap."

CHAPTER TWENTY

"I can assure you that I've never heard of a pairing being severed without one of the parties having died," Brodie said. He, Peabo, and Nicole were sitting cross-legged on the floor of one of the church's so-called 'safety rooms.' "Now tell me again how you did it."

Peabo frowned and began to explain what he was able to see. He touched his sternum. "Starting here, I see a golden see-through haze." It seemed weird to him that nobody else could see it—not even Nicole. "It shoots out to the same spot on Nicole's chest." He passed his hand back and forth through the ephemeral connection. "I can't touch it or interact with it. When I was paired with Scarlett, I saw a similar thread connecting us. Normally when I direct my energy, I focus it onto a tangible target, and this time I focused on the connection. When my attack connected with the thread, it exploded in a rainbow of colored sparks. Scarlett screamed and fainted."

Brodie's eyes widened. "I wonder if you're seeing things in different planes of existence."

"That would explain a lot," Nicole said. "We know that images can sometimes bleed through from other planes. A ghost, for example, is on both the physical and ethereal planes. And if Peabo can see things on a different plane, it stands to reason that he can attack things on a different plane, too."

"Wait a minute." Peabo made a time-out motion with his hands. "I thought the ethereal plane wasn't actually a real place. You gave us a potion that changed how our cells vibrated so that... oh!" Suddenly it clicked. "I get what you're saying. Because something is vibrating at a different frequency, it looks invisible, but it's really there. When we drank that potion to sneak into Lord Dvorak's castle, that was an example of that. So if the energy involved in the pairing was operating at a different frequency, you wouldn't be able to see it. Except that I can. I couldn't before though..."

"You know that as one advances in levels, your abilities advance," Brodie said. "And those changes in ability can be different for each person. My recent advancement to level ten has brought with it some mysteries that I'm still trying to work out, and I'm sure Nicole will have similar struggles with her recent advancements. You, my dear plainswalker, are experiencing the same changes, except that your changes are radically different than most people's."

He paused. "But none of this explains why this Scarlett can still sense where you are even after the pairing has been severed." He stroked his beard. "Peabo, can you see your connection to Nicole better in the dark?"

Peabo shrugged. "I guess I never paid attention."

In the blink of an eye, Brodie extinguished the light that had been hovering above them, cloaking the room in darkness. "Can you still see the connection?"

"Yes." With no other light sources, Peabo was easily able to see the shimmering golden thread. "It's interesting, because although the thread itself glows brightly, it doesn't shine any of that light on anything around it. It should be bright enough to at least show parts of Nicole, but all I see is an inky blackness where she is."

"Interesting." Brodie's voice echoed in the dark chamber. "That lends credence to the theory that the connection itself is not on the material plane."

Peabo shifted the angle of his head. "Hold on. I see another thread! It's so thin that even in the dark it's almost impossible to see, but it's there. It's about two hand spans higher than the first thread. I think it's—yes, of course—it's connecting our minds."

Nicole's voice had an excited tone. "You said you severed only one thread with Scarlett. Can you see the other? Is it still there?"

Peabo stared into the darkness and turned slowly, tilting his head. "I see it!"

"Can you sense her?" Brodie asked. "If she can sense you, there's no reason you couldn't turn those tables."

"Shouldn't he just cut the remaining tie?" Nicole said, an edge to her voice.

"No, at least not yet. Peabo? Can you detect her?"

Even though it was dark, Peabo closed his eyes as he would

when meditating. "I'm trying, but… it's hard with Nicole right here. It's like trying to see a piece of grass on fire with a bonfire as a backdrop. Hold on…"

With Nicole, he'd always sensed two things through the connection: her heartbeat and her location. The heartbeat was the stronger and "louder" of the two. But with Scarlett, he'd severed that heartbeat connection, leaving only the quieter of the two, and it was now being drowned out by Nicole's heartbeat. He took a deep breath and focused once more.

"Got it!" Peabo felt the pulse of Scarlett's presence along that gossamer-thin line. It was like playing phone with two cans and a string. "It's weak, but it's there. I can sense her signal through the connection."

The light came back on above Brodie. "Now that you know what you're looking for," Brodie said, "can you see the connection in the light?"

Peabo saw a single strand of the translucent golden web shooting off into space. He pointed at the door. "She's in that direction. But it feels like she's very far away."

There was a knock at the door, and three armored dwarves entered. The one in front had a puckered scar running across his right cheek and into his thick red beard, and when he spoke, his voice sounded like rough sandpaper. "High Priest, we are here."

To Peabo, the man glowed just like Ariandelle and the prelate.

Brodie hopped to his feet. "Menkins, you shouldn't be here on assignment. By the Nameless One, you're in your time of mourning for your sister."

The soldier took a step forward and glowered. "Jenkins was not just my sister, she was my twin. I'm owed an opportunity to avenge her." He spit on the ground. "Dying of poison—a coward's weapon. I will see this done."

Nicole thought to Peabo, *"Menkins is a paladin for the Nameless One. He's somewhat famous... a legend of sorts in certain crowds."*

"Paladin?" Peabo wondered if that meant the same thing here as it did in the stories back home—some kind of holy knight. Though the short man didn't look the part.

"Think of him as a holy fighter."

Suspicion confirmed.

"Not only can he heal, he's said to be a man possessed in a fight. A few years back he was attacked by a tribe of orcs and killed over one hundred of them before they fled. The only damage he took was a splinter from one of his maces when its handle broke during combat."

Brodie made a clicking sound with his tongue and shook his head. "Fair enough." He motioned to Peabo. "This is Peabo, a real plainswalker come to life, as if he stepped right out of the stories we've heard since we were children."

"It's good to finally meet you, lad," Menkins said. He stepped forward, grinning toothily through his red beard, and they clasped forearms. "This is quite the adventure you're on, isn't it?"

Peabo couldn't help but return the gruff soldier's smile. "There seems to be a new surprise at every turn."

Menkins roared with laughter and slapped him on the back. "Isn't that always the way?"

Brodie motioned to Nicole. "Our plainswalker is paired to Nicole. She will be accompanying him wherever he goes."

Menkins bent on one knee, gently grasped Nicole's fingertips, and gave them a light kiss. "It is a pleasure to meet one so lovely and so deadly. A true blood maiden is a joy to behold and a fear to encounter."

To Peabo's shock and amusement, Nicole actually blushed.

Menkins stood, stretching on his tiptoes to just over four feet. He grinned. "The hair and eyes are a dead giveaway." Then he turned to Peabo and winked. "Lad, you most certainly have a handful to deal with, with that one."

The soldier then took notice of the cat. He crouched down beside her. "You are not what you seem to be, are you?"

Fuzzball leaned forward and rubbed her head against the soldier's cheek.

"You recognize this creature?" Brodie asked.

Menkins stood and shook his head. "No. But I sense something very familiar about it. It is as if I know this creature—but somehow I have forgotten why or how I know it. It is not in its natural state, of that I am certain. But I don't know what that natural state might be."

Brodie looked to Peabo. "Where exactly did you find her?"

"It was somewhere in the woods, but..." Peabo felt a moment of confusion. "Somehow I can't remember precisely where or how I found her."

Brodie raked his fingers through his beard, then shrugged and faced Menkins once more. "Our plainswalker has the ability to detect the general direction of the illusionist blood maiden. Though at the moment she's keeping her distance."

Menkins slapped his hands together with a metallic clap. "Well, that settles it. First stop, let's get something to eat. Next, we track down my sister's killer."

Peabo, Menkins, and Nicole sat at a table in a bustling café in the middle of Igneous City, while Menkins's two fellow soldiers stood guard at the eatery's entrance. The prelate had given Peabo permission to go out into the city without the Robe of Cloaking. He liked not having to hide his identity, but with that exposure came the stares.

Tall people were common enough not to draw excessive attention, but the glowing marks all over his exposed skin were unmistakable, especially in the dim lighting of the restaurant. The funny thing was, Menkins drew nearly as much attention as he did. Nicole must not have been exaggerating when she said the dwarf was a legend in this area.

A tiny waitress walked up to the table and gave them all a big smile. "What will you have?"

Nicole glanced again at the menu. "Country-fried purple worm with pickled fire radish."

The waitress jotted that down on a notepad. "And to drink?"

"An ale."

"We have bitter, sweet, and pumpkin-spiced."

"Pumpkin-spiced sounds lovely. I'll take that," Nicole said with a surprising amount of enthusiasm.

Peabo wondered what was with women and pumpkin-spiced things. His mother had been a huge fan as well.

The waitress turned to Menkins and her eyes widened as her mouth hung open for a few long seconds. She stammered and asked, "And you, s-sir?"

Menkins scratched his chin. "I'll have what the blood maiden is having, but none of that pumpkin nonsense. A bitter ale for me, thank you."

"What?" said Nicole. "You think you'll turn into a girl if you drink it and decide you like it?"

The dwarf gave her a lopsided grin. "Call me a traditionalist. Pumpkin-spiced...? Blech!" He looked at the waitress. "I have two friends standing watch. Can you arrange for something for them too? Whatever you have that they can eat while keeping one hand on their weapon."

The waitress nodded. "Two roasted giant frog legs should tide them over." As she turned to Peabo, her cheeks flushed red. "And you, my dear? What can *I* do for you?"

Peabo nodded at the menu. "I don't see it on here, but do you have any spiced fungus stew?"

"Of course. How *spicy* do you like it?" She leaned closer and smiled.

Peabo grinned. "Medium spice, I suppose. And I'll take a bitter ale as well."

The waitress leaned even closer, her bosom threatening to explode out from the top of her blouse. "You know... I've got some really excellent sweet ale at my home if you have some time later tonight."

Fuzzball, who was lying under the table, let out a small growl. *"She's in heat. Be aware."*

Peabo nearly choked as he tried not to laugh at the unexpected commentary from the cat. But that did remind him that Fuzzball needed to eat.

"Do you have anything raw that my companion can eat?" Peabo asked, pointing under the table.

The waitress clearly hadn't noticed Fuzzball before now, for when she looked under the table she squeaked and backed up three steps. "What is… um, y-yes, I can bring something out. Is a whole raw ham okay?"

"That will do," Fuzzball purred.

Peabo nodded. "Thank you."

"That will be two gold and four silver royals for your drinks and meals, plus another gold for the ham and giant frog legs."

Nicole slid four gold across the table. "Keep the change."

As the waitress pocketed the money and left, Menkins opened his mouth to speak, but Nicole quickly said, "The high priest gave me funds to cover our food costs."

The dwarven warrior nodded, then turned to Peabo. "Is she still far away?"

Peabo nodded. "I've kept my focus on Scarlett's whereabouts since leaving the church's compound. The moment I stepped out into the plaza I could sense her more easily."

"I had the same experience with you while you were at the tower," Nicole said. "You were a dim signal I could barely feel, and then when you left the tower complex the signal was suddenly so strong I thought you were right next to me. But remember, if you can feel her presence easily, she can feel yours just as well."

"I'm very well aware," Peabo said.

"So where is she right now?" Menkins asked.

Peabo pointed across the restaurant. "That way, and down a bit. Probably at a lower level."

Menkins nodded. "We'll find out soon enough, that I can tell you."

The waitress returned with their drinks and food, and another waiter carried a platter holding a twenty-pound ham. He looked below the table with some trepidation, then set the tray on the floor and used his foot to slide it toward the cat, who'd begun to purr loudly.

Peabo sniffed at his stew. Its warm, savory smell made his mouth water. But before he could even try it, Nicole pulled the bowl away from him, dipped her spoon in, and tasted it first.

That was something blood maidens were trained to do. Taste for poison.

"You're positive you're immune to poison?" Peabo said with a grin.

She grabbed his beer, took a long sip, swirled it in her mouth, and swallowed. Only then did she push his food and drink back over to him. "There's no poison," she said. "And it's pretty good."

Under the table Peabo patted Nicole's leg, and she bumped shoulders with him. It was the closest they ever got to public displays of affection.

"Enough talk," said Menkins. "Everyone eat before the food gets cold. We have a traitorous witch to hunt down and kill."

CHAPTER TWENTY-ONE

As the small team of soldiers moved down a slope leading to a lower level of Myrkheim, Peabo felt Nicole's touch in his head.

"I'm here for you if you need me. I'll only hold back your abilities if you ask—or if it seems you're overwhelmed."

"Thanks," he thought back to her.

Thanks to the personal connection they had, Nicole being in his head felt very natural. A stark difference compared to what he'd experienced at the tower.

Their current surroundings were nothing like the civilized environment of Igneous City. They were in large passages that were lit only by some of the naturally glowing fungus that was everywhere in this subterranean world. The air was musty—it didn't circulate much down here—and the walls dripped with condensation that left dank puddles along the ground.

Upon approaching an intersection of passageways,

Menkins halted the group. "Plainswalker, where is she, and is she on the same level as us?"

Even with his eyes closed Peabo could point in the direction of the illusionist, but he kept them open so he could look for that almost invisible thread. He had a plan, and that plan involved being able to sense that intangible connection precisely.

Since he'd discovered the existence of the umbilical between his mind and Scarlett's, it had become more and more apparent to him. Now he could sense it pulsing with a rhythmic energy, almost like a heartbeat. Peabo thought of it more like an EEG, a device that reads signals from the brain as pulses of electricity. He wondered if it was possible to reach across that connection and hear her thoughts. He hoped it wasn't, because if he could do it, so could she.

Peabo pointed to his left, where the thread vanished into solid stone. "She's that way. Closer than before. And I think we're on the same level."

Menkins's hand glowed, and he touched each member of the party on the shoulder, skipping over the cat. Peabo felt a warmth bloom from the point where the dwarf had touched him. The sensation flowed into his chest and through the rest of his body.

"He's placing a blessing on us," Nicole explained. *"It makes us more difficult to hit and less likely to fall prey to the magicks an illusionist may employ."*

The soldier turned to Nicole. "Blood maiden, you have the ability to cast true seeing?"

She nodded. "But I'm not confident as to how long it might

last." She saw Peabo's confused look and explained aloud. "True seeing is the ability to see through all forms of illusion. I can't do it all the time, though. I have to summon the ability, much like healing."

Fuzzball growled deep in her chest. *"I can sense when there is something unnatural."*

Peabo crouched in front of the cat. "Are you a weaver in cat form? Can you see illusions?"

The cat head-butted Peabo in the chest. *"I am not affected by illusions or any such spells. But I can sense them."*

Peabo saw that the team was watching him curiously as he conversed with the cat. He smiled. "She says she can sense when illusions are being used."

"Excellent." Menkins turned back to Nicole. "When the creature informs the plainswalker we have illusions about, employ your true sight. We'll need you to guide us on what's real and what isn't." He pointed at the two other dwarven soldiers, who looked like twins. "Jasper and Gypsum, you listen for the warning. When you hear it, I want one of you to cast dispel magic and the other to stretch time on us all."

"Those two must be conductors of sorts," Nicole thought to Peabo. *"Dispelling magic is essentially canceling something a conductor has done—in this case illusions. Stretching time makes time seem to progress slower, which improves our reaction times and speed of attacks. Both spells are limited in area."*

The light hovering over Menkins grew brighter, chasing the shadows from every nook and cranny if the surrounding passageways. "Okay, weapons out. I lead. Plainswalker, you stay just behind me to help guide us toward our objective. If we're careful and smart about this, it shouldn't take long."

Peabo winced. Anytime anyone ever said those words, reality usually ended up proving quite the opposite.

He drew Max from his scabbard.

"It's about damn time, pea brain. Just remember, the rules of engagement are that there aren't any rules. That bitch deserves whatever she gets. Don't hesitate to stick me in her. I'll mess her stuff up."

Nicole drew a shimmering short sword that she'd checked out from the church's armory. It sizzled as she cut the air with a few practice strokes.

They moved along a meandering passage for about ten minutes before they hit another intersection. Menkins looked to Peabo for guidance, and Peabo pointed to the left. The crew headed down that passage.

The brilliant light dipped and bobbed just below the ceiling, always hovering over Menkins. Some of the passages were only a few inches taller than Peabo, so for a good portion of the journey he needed to avert his gaze or it would be like staring directly into the sun.

But mostly he focused on the illusionist. She was getting unmistakably closer. When the strength of her signal approached the strength of Nicole's, Peabo tapped Menkins's shoulder and whispered, "We're close."

Menkins made a hand signal to the twins, indicating for them to get ready. The two dwarves shimmered with what looked like a scintillating second skin. A shield of sorts?

They soon came upon another intersection. The sound of

dripping water, which had been ever-present for a while now, was louder here, amplified. There were two tunnels ahead of them, both deep in shadows despite Menkins's light, but the rightmost one was unusually dark.

Fuzzball hissed, and she raised her hackles. *"I sense something ahead."*

Peabo whispered a warning.

"Blood maiden," Menkins whispered. "What do you see?"

Nicole's eyes glowed white, then shimmered, giving them a cat-like appearance. "The one on the right is spelled with darkness. I can't see much beyond its entrance, other than that it veers to the right."

"Let's get some!" Max cried out with glee.

Wielding two glowing maces, Menkins motioned the twins toward the darkened tunnel.

Peabo wasn't sure which of the two dwarves was Jasper and which was Gypsum, but one of them aimed a glowing hand at the tunnel while the other faced the group and held out two glowing arms as if to embrace them all. At almost the same moment, a *pop* sounded somewhere in the tunnel and Peabo felt a strange tingling sensation. The air seemed thicker somehow. Was this time being stretched?

As Menkins led the way toward the tunnel, a chorus of ear-splitting shrieks burst forth from the darkness. Even the grizzled dwarven warrior winced as the sound drilled into everyone's skulls.

And then absolute silence. Peabo wondered if the sound had been so strong that he'd been rendered deaf.

Menkins raced into the tunnel and began attacking something, and Peabo was rocked with the all-too-familiar sensation of someone grabbing at his mind and squeezing.

Scarlett.

But this wasn't like it had been back in the tower. Back then, Scarlett hadn't actually been angry, just frustrated. But now he felt the woman's raw anger bearing down on him. His arms went numb and he dropped his sword and fell to his knees, trying desperately to wrest control from the woman whose hatred he could sense even through their whisper-thin connection.

Suddenly the chamber filled with an impenetrable fog. He felt Nicole at the edges of his mind, trying to help, trying to loosen the madwoman's grip, but Scarlett was far too strong.

He felt something fly past his left ear. A dart?

Scarlett's fingers dug deeper into his mind.

Suddenly the fog vanished and Peabo was flooded with a cacophony of sounds.

The two spell-casting dwarves gasped for air and held panicked looks on their faces as they tore at the collars of their tunics with glowing hands.

"I hate shriekers almost as much as I hate illusionists!" Menkins shouted. "Show yourself, you evil sow!" And then he gasped. "No!" he cried out, a look of terror in his eyes. He looked back at the rest of the team. "Run for your lives! I'll hold him!"

The heavily muscled warrior squared off against what looked like empty air. "Brangromuth the Unholy, I know you! Demon, you cannot have escaped your confinement!"

One of the twins stood statue-like, as if paralyzed, while the other sat on the ground crying, his arms wrapped around his knees. Peabo was sprawled on the floor, having lost control of his limbs. It was all he could do to keep conscious against the iron grip the other blood maiden had on him. Images from his past flashed before him as Scarlett dug into his mind.

"Menkins!" Nicole shouted. "There is no demon!"

"Run!" Menkins shouted back. "Don't make my sacrifice be in vain!"

Fuzzball roared.

Peabo tasted blood. It was dripping from his nose and splashing on the floor.

He was dying.

He could barely think anymore, but he knew it was almost over.

Someone was touching him. Holding him. He felt warmth and a tingling sensation. Nicole. She had wrapped her arms around him, pressed her head against his. She was healing him. Trying to help in the war that was being waged in his head.

Peabo closed his eyes and sensed the two women. Nicole glowed white and warm. But the illusionist... she was utter darkness. Darker than the black of night. If there was such a thing as infinite black, that was what was on the other side of that golden spider's thread.

He embraced the white. For an instant he sensed *all* of Nicole—all her thoughts, her memories, her love that was lost, and a love that was rekindled with him.

The pressure on Peabo's mind faltered, and he lashed out with all that he had left within him.

The cord attached to the darkness exploded in a cloud of

rainbow-colored sparks, and his vision immediately snapped back to normal. Scarlett's scream of fury echoed off the walls of the tunnels.

Peabo staggered to his feet. Ahead of him, a rainbow-hued sphere of energy emerged from a craggy shadow of stone. It expanded, then exploded with a deadly spray of color. The sphere had separated into different-colored laser-like spears—one aimed at every member of the team.

Peabo breathed in deeply, pulling energy from every source of light. The launched rays dimmed and vanished, and the chamber was cloaked in absolute darkness.

And still he pulled. Without Nicole stopping him, he continued to draw energy from within the darkness.

Two sources.

He heard the sound of an armored body collapsing, then the thud of a body hitting the floor.

Now crackling with energy, Peabo sent Nicole a thought. *"Light."*

A dim light appeared in the chamber, revealing a robed woman slowly getting up on all fours.

Peabo breathed out.

All of the energy he'd drawn in—from the campfire, from the prismatic spray, and from Scarlett and Menkins—formed a searing column of white light that blasted into Scarlett's body and exploded from all of her orifices. In mere moments the heat of the attack set her clothes ablaze, melted her skin, and then cremated what remained. The heat was so intense that when Peabo was finally drained, the stone behind her glowed red with heat.

Menkins sat up and groaned. Peabo had inadvertently drained him of all his energy, but he was all right. He looked at the glowing rock and the ashes settling to the ground, and he shook his head.

Scarlett's life essence appeared above the ashes and drifted toward Peabo, and he absorbed it.

Fuzzball emerged from the dark tunnel ahead. She had a backpack in her mouth, and she dropped it in front of Peabo. Inside was a black silk robe. When he pulled it out, Nicole gasped.

"That's got the king's insignia on it," she said.

"What does that mean?" Peabo asked. "She worked for the king?"

Nicole shook her head. "Worse. If that's really hers, it means she's a royal. Part of the king's extended family."

Peabo knew nothing about the king or what any of this meant. "I guess that's bad?"

"It's not good. Killing a royal brings a death sentence not only upon the person who does it, but also on their entire family. That's why it rarely ever happens."

Peabo dug into the backpack and pulled out a black ring and some onyx bracelets, all engraved with the same insignia. Nicole shook her head.

"From the quality of these items, I'd say she was much more closely related than Jakub ever had been."

Jakub was the man Nicole had previously been paired with. She'd told Peabo little about him, but Peabo knew Jakub was the fourth son of a rich merchant who was in some way related to the king.

"I don't give a rat's ass what family that bitch belonged to," said one of the twins. "The king holds little sway in Myrkheim."

Peabo returned the items to the backpack, then noticed Menkins crouched down, looking at the spot where Scarlett had burned away. Peabo followed the dwarf's gaze to a necklace lying on the ground. It was black as black could be. So much so that it seemed to suck the light from its surroundings.

Menkins growled. "I've never seen a thing give off darkness."

Fuzzball hissed. *"It's not of this world."*

Peabo repeated what the cat had said, and Menkins nodded in agreement.

"It feels evil," Nicole whispered. "We can't just leave it behind. What if someone finds it? We have no idea what it does or what it would do to someone."

Menkins pulled a dagger from his belt and used the tip of the blade to lift up the necklace. "Let's put this thing in the bag, seal it up, and take it to the prelate. He will know what to do with it."

Peabo held open the backpack and Menkins carefully deposited the necklace within. Though it was only a thin metal chain, the backpack suddenly felt much heavier.

Then Menkins turned, lowered the front of his trousers, and peed on Scarlett's ashes. "You had too easy of a death, and may urine stain your grave for eternity. Jenkins, I'm sorry it came to this, little sister." He spat on the wet ash heap. "I hate illusionists, and so does every decent citizen of this world."

Nicole looked around. "Does anyone need any healing before we go? Menkins?"

The dwarf waved her away. "Nay, girl. I just need some rest. I don't know how that bitch did it, but somehow I feel like everything inside me has been drained." Then he grinned at Peabo. "That was some light show, plainswalker."

CHAPTER TWENTY-TWO

Peabo stood in the church courtyard, where the prelate had used a glowing rod to inscribe a circle that was at least one hundred feet in diameter. Many people had gathered to watch the summoning—though *what* the prelate was summoning, Peabo had no idea.

Working with the prelate was a very short figure, and that was saying something since the prelate himself was only four feet tall. The prelate's assistant was a good foot shorter, with a lithe build and dark brown skin. He glowed just as fiercely as the prelate did, which indicated that he had achieved a very advanced level and was not someone to underestimate.

Peabo was about to whisper a question to Nicole when she put her fingers to her lips. *"Thoughts only. This is a very dangerous procedure. The prelate and Spam need to focus."*

"Spam?" Peabo's first thought was how unfortunate of a name that was. Then again, this world wouldn't have heard of

the luncheon meat. He swallowed the immature thought with a grin.

"Yes. He's a gnome. They're sort of a cousin species to the dwarves. You've probably never seen one since they reside mostly in the deeper levels of Myrkheim. Spam is a very powerful conductor. He's placing wards around the summoning circle, just in case."

"Just in case of what?" Peabo asked. *"What or who's being summoned?"*

Nicole shrugged. *"I'm not sure. You saw the prelate's reaction to the necklace—he nearly had a fit. But I guess we'll both find out soon enough."*

The gnome raised his hands in the air and sent a glowing arc of sizzling energy over the inscribed circle. The arc duplicated itself, rotated slightly, then duplicated itself again. It did this quickly, hundreds of times, until it had created a dome-like structure of glowing energy over the circle. It sizzled and popped, and Peabo felt its vibration in his chest. The reverberations seemed to be getting stronger by the second. But nobody else seemed to be having any reaction to this immense pyrotechnic sight, so it was probably another of those things that only Peabo was able to see.

Suddenly, with a particularly loud *pop*, the dome vanished, leaving just a slight iridescent blur between the onlookers and whatever was inside of the shielded circle.

All this because of a necklace?

The prelate pulled out a golden sphere, and Nicole nudged Peabo in the ribs. *"He's about to do it. I've only seen a summoning once before, and it was a very minor demon. It was amazing to behold."*

Peabo's eyes widened. A demon? He'd read about them in the monster manual, but didn't imagine he'd ever see one. *"Are the circle and shield there to keep the creature from attacking?"*

Nicole nodded. *"With a summoning, there's always a risk. The act opens a gate between our world and wherever it is the prelate is attempting to summon from. Sometimes you call for one thing, but another responds first. Precautions are a must."*

The prelate held up the fist-sized golden orb, and it began glowing. The glow brightened, and a crackling sound erupted from within the circle. A bright vertical line had appeared right in the middle of the shielded circle, and was growing slowly in both size and brilliance.

The prelate's voice boomed across the courtyard. "Baham! It is I calling you. Baham!"

"Baham?" Peabo thought to Nicole. *"Is that a name or a thing?"*

She waved his question away, transfixed by what was going on.

"Baham! I am calling upon you to service a debt. Your wisdom is needed. Come forth."

The courtyard was deathly silent as everyone watched the thirty-foot tall portal created within the shielded circle.

Five seconds passed.

Ten seconds.

Fifteen seconds passed, and a gigantic scaled foot pierced the portal and thudded onto the stone courtyard. The foot alone was the size of the prelate, with scales like polished silver, and its claws were the length of a short sword.

Another foot followed, then a giant spiked head, a long neck, a tremendous body, and a serpentine tail.

Peabo was stunned. This was a *dragon*. It was at least seventy feet long, with glowing, lantern-like eyes, and smoke curling up from its nostrils.

Nicole grabbed Peabo's arm and practically squealed with delight. "It's *the* Baham! I wasn't sure if it could be possible, but it is!"

A murmur rose up in the courtyard as the creature calmly unfurled its wings and gazed upon everyone from within the domed barrier.

"And Baham is...?" Peabo asked.

"He's the first of his kind. Ancient beyond measure, and hasn't been seen in this world in millennia."

Millennia? Note to self: dragons live a long, *long* time.

The dragon looked down at the prelate and spoke with a booming voice that sent vibrations through the air. "Richard, we meet again."

Richard? The prelate's name was Richard?

The prelate spoke in a normal tone, but his volume had been amplified by some means. "Baham, I have an issue that I think you might be able to help with."

He held up a wooden box and opened it. Even from where he was standing, Peabo could see the darkness emanating from the necklace contained within the box.

Baham pulled back and hissed. "What is this thing? How did you come by such an artifact?"

The prelate pointed at Peabo, and the dragon's head swung toward the plainswalker, coming within inches of the barrier. Peabo held his ground, gazing up at the massive creature. The dragon was a majestic beauty, a work of art. No movie could ever capture the mirror-like shine of the scales, or their iridescent sheen that glowed with a tremendous internal life force. The entire dragon was humming with power. To face such a creature in combat would be utter folly.

"Plainswalker."

The dragon's voice was a mere whisper, but the vibrations rattled Peabo's chest.

"It has been a very long time since I've seen one of your kind."

Peabo's mind was blown by that statement, since from what he understood of this world's history, there hadn't been a plainswalker in this world for at least a hundred millennia. Could a creature really live *that* long?

Baham's lizard-like eyes darted down to Fuzzball, which had been sitting between Peabo and Nicole. When Fuzzball hissed, the dragon reared its head back and blew out a gout of snow that coated the inner side of the barrier. Peabo realized, to his astonishment, that the dragon was laughing.

"So, the Forgotten One has returned, and it no longer remembers itself. That is funny beyond belief."

Peabo looked from the cat to the dragon. "I don't understand."

The dragon lowered its head once again and gave him a toothy and terrifying grin. "You will not understand until it is time. And even then you will forget. That is the nature of such things."

Baham continued. "Plainswalker, you are a danger to this world. It is time you undo what has been done." The creature looked back at the box in the prelate's hands. "That *thing* is a sign that this world is certainly doomed. The Darkness is coming. It cannot be avoided. You were created to be a light within the Darkness, but it is past the time for you alone to fix things. You will need help. Only together can you hope to bring light when the Darkness arrives. What the other has done must be undone."

To Peabo, the dragon was speaking in riddles. "I'm sorry," he said. "I don't understand."

The dragon nodded. "You will. It is time for the plainswalker to emerge from his cocoon. Become what you were meant to be. When you go back, it will be time for the Prismatist to emerge."

The giant creature lowered its head almost to eye level with Peabo, and spoke directly to his mind. *"Remember what I say, or we will all die in nothingness. Do not trust your allies of the past. Those who know you, they mean you harm. They intend to lead you astray. In the end, it will be only you who stands against the Darkness. Be man enough to embrace the suck, because you have not yet experienced what true suckage is like."*

The dragon swung its head away from Peabo and faced the prelate once more. "You will not be able to destroy this thing—though believe me, I wish you to. Hide it instead. Keep it from others who might use it. For it is a tool of the Darkness."

244

Peabo's mind reeled. Everything about the dragon was mind-blowing, but the thing that struck him the deepest was that the dragon had used Earth-based terms when addressing him. "Embrace the suck" was a frequent saying in the American military. It meant to consciously accept circumstances that were extremely unpleasant—and push through. Only someone in the military would even know that phrase.

Maybe the creature had somehow plucked that out of Peabo's mind. That had to be it. Because the alternative was impossible. Wasn't it?

The prelate spoke. "Baham, could you keep this in your fortress, away from prying eyes who might use it?"

"I could. But..." The dragon extended a claw and scratched at the shield, which caused sizzling sparks to fly in every direction. "You will have to lower the shield and cross the circle."

The church members who had come to witness the summoning gasped and shook their heads. But the prelate merely looked down at the gnome and nodded permission. The gnome waved a glowing hand and the dome vanished with a *pop*.

The prelate stepped across the inscribed line, and the entire circle vanished in a puff of smoke.

The dragon stood in the courtyard with absolutely nothing between him and everyone else.

The prelate closed the box and held it up for the dragon to take.

Baham chuckled, a loud booming noise that caused most of the crowd to back away. With two claws, the dragon plucked the wooden box from the prelate's hands. "Richard," it said, lowering its head to face the prelate. "You were always too trusting. Never allow a summoned creature its freedom. You know better than that."

The dragon began glowing from snout to tail as if it was building up for some kind of massive attack. Peabo was over-come with fear, and when he glanced over at Nicole, he saw that same desperate fear reflected in her eyes.

Then the dragon grinned widely, exposing its spear-like fangs and blinked out of existence.

It was a few hours after the summoning, and the entirety of the church was still talking about what they'd seen. But Peabo and Nicole had returned to their room to rest, and now they lay in bed together for the first time since being reunited.

Peabo vividly remembered what he had seen in Nicole's mind in that moment during Scarlett's attack when their consciousnesses had merged. He knew how she felt about him, and the feeling was mutual. Yet here they lay chastely in bed like brother and sister. He wondered if that would ever change.

He could barely see her shadow next to him. The room was dark, and he'd breathed out all the energy that caused his mark-ings to glow. But he sensed her there—as he sensed the pres-ence of Fuzzball, sprawled across the foot of the bed.

"I really thought the dragon was going to eat the prelate in one gulp," Peabo whispered.

"I feared the same," Nicole replied. "It was a gutsy move. The prelate was willing to risk his life to get the necklace in a safe place, so we can only imagine how dangerous that necklace is."

"The dragon referred to 'the darkness' a lot. Is that supposed to mean something?"

"I don't know. I've read that phrase in some passages, but I always assumed it was a mere euphemism for evil. The way Baham spoke of it, though, it seemed like he was referring to a tangible thing."

"What about what he said to Fuzzball?" Peabo chose to think these words at Nicole so the cat wouldn't overhear. *"It was like he recognized her."*

"Yes, that was particularly odd. What did he say again?"

Peabo was about to repeat the words, but recalling them was like trying to catch smoke. The memory just disappeared. *"Wow, I... I can't remember. Why can't I remember what Baham said just a few hours ago?"*

"I don't know." Nicole patted him on the shoulder and turned to her side, her bare back facing him. "Get some sleep. Tomorrow will be a long and possibly dangerous trek."

The dragon's warning sounded in Peabo's head. *"Do not trust your allies of the past. Those who know you, they mean you harm. They intend to lead you astray. In the end, it will be only you who stands against the Darkness. Be man enough to embrace the suck, because you have not yet experienced what true suckage is like."*

Allies of the past... Did that mean Nicole? Or maybe the people in the tower? But those people had never really been allies of his. Whoever these allies of the past were, evidently they were going to be trouble for him.

The dragon had also said, *"It is time for the plainswalker to emerge from his cocoon. Become what you were meant to be. When you go back, it will be time for the Prismatist to emerge."*

Emerge from his cocoon? Peabo supposed that made *some* sense, given that he was evolving as he leveled. He was getting stronger, and he was seeing things he couldn't see before. But what about *When you go back*—what could that mean? Back to where? Earth? Unlikely. The tower? God, hopefully not.

And this Prismatist… he had no clue what that meant, and neither did anyone else. He'd even asked the prelate, and the dwarf had never heard the term. A prism split light into its constituent colors, so maybe it had something to do with that? And he'd been seeing lots of color variations in the lights that he hadn't before, it might all be related.

But he was just guessing.

Nicole turned to face him. "I can sense your mind is racing. It's keeping me awake. What's wrong?"

Without thinking, Peabo blurted out what he hadn't intended to talk about. "I love you, and I think you love me. Why do we not—"

"Peabo…" Nicole's voice was soft but firm. "I will never love anyone more than you, but because I love you, and because you're so important to the welfare of this world, I can't get in the way of you finding a true love. One who can return it in the way love should be returned. One who can give you children."

A surge of frustration heated Peabo's cheeks as he faced the shadowy outline of his partner. "We have no idea what my destiny is or how important I am or am not to the world—that's all speculation. In the meantime, why can't we be together in a more… in a way that's more like a husband and wife?"

"Because I can never give you children."

Peabo was about to interrupt when Nicole put her hand over his mouth.

"Shush and let me talk. It is because we don't know much about you and what will happen that I cannot be your wife. For all we know it might not be you but your son or daughter who somehow rescues this world from a threat we don't yet understand. All we know is that the threat *is* coming. Our being together cannot produce a child, and I know you well enough that unless I make the decision for us both, you won't. So we cannot be."

Peabo's throat tightened, and he took a few deep breaths. "How is it that your inability to have children can't be cured? Surely the prelate—"

"The prelate has tried before. What is done in the tower is irreversible. Some things are burnt out of a maiden's system as a sacrifice to our advancement. It is in part why we are called maidens. We can never have children. Just accept this. I have."

Peabo moved closer to her, and she pushed back on his chest.

"No, Peabo. If this is a problem for you, I'll go to another room." Her voice cracked, but she quickly recovered. "This is hard for us both, but respect my wishes as much as I respect the duty I have to us and to the world we live in. Do I need to leave?"

Peabo shook his head. "No. I'm sorry."

She reached out and stroked his cheek. "Not as sorry as I am. Now get some sleep. Tomorrow we'll meet the excursion team."

Peabo laid his head back, and a wave of exhaustion washed over him. Between the fight with Scarlett, and the bizarre experience with the dragon, and now being emotionally drained... it took mere seconds once he'd closed his eyes for his mind to finally get some rest.

CHAPTER TWENTY-THREE

Standing in an empty stone chamber underneath the main chapel, Peabo stared in amazement at the clean-shaven gnome who was looking right back up at him from crotch level with a bemused expression.

"How in all the planes of existence can you breathe the air way up there?" Spam asked. "You must be constantly light-headed. Was your mother a cloud giant or something?"

"I don't know," Peabo replied. "I was actually wondering how you manage to climb the stairs in any multi-story building. Do you always carry climbing gear in your pack or do you ask a human toddler for help?"

Spam snorted and nodded approvingly.

"Okay, enough with you two clowns." Menkins walked into the chamber followed by the prelate and another dwarf who looked like he'd just sucked on a lemon.

Spam walked over to the sour-faced dwarf, and they fist-bumped. "Looking cheerful as always, Hosten. Your wife pour bleach in your gruel again this morning?"

Hosten raked his fingers through his beard. "No, but I'm surprised after all these years you *still* haven't hit puberty."

Peabo guffawed, and Nicole patted him on the shoulder. *"Gnomes are known for insulting those they like. It's sort of a contest with them. The worse they talk about each other, the closer they are."*

Peabo thought back at her, *"I noticed Spam didn't approach you at all."*

"You noticed correctly. It's a long story, but let's just say I misunderstood the way of gnomes and got very angry when he insulted my previous partner. Spam hasn't forgotten it."

"What? You tried to kill him?"

Nicole shrugged. *"Maybe."*

The prelate snapped his fingers to get everyone's attention. "Menkins, Hosten, and Spam are going to be the guides into Myrkheim City." He motioned to Peabo and Nicole. "Menkins is already acquainted with everyone, but Spam and Hosten, the large fellow is Peabo. He's the plainswalker we talked about. The woman to his right is Nicole, his blood maiden."

"Oh?" Spam muttered, giving Nicole a look.

Nicole shot back the same glare. "Some things change over the years, unlike Spam's soiled tunic and likely his underwear."

Spam smirked. "Hopefully this time around you don't try your foolishness again, or maybe I'll show you how soiled my underwear are."

Peabo's eyes widened, but Nicole retorted with a snide

tone. "You couldn't reach that high even if you had a ladder, pipsqueak."

Spam gave her a wink.

"Are you friends now?" Peabo thought at Nicole.

Nicole maintained eye contact with the gnome and grinned. *"I probably won't try to kill him today."*

"Very well," the prelate continued without missing a beat, "Menkins leads, Hosten is the group healer, Spam will zap anything that gets in the way. I've secured a passageway that should bypass most of the intervening levels and get you to Myrkheim City in less than an hour. I've already gone over the route with Menkins. Does anyone have any questions before I bid you farewell?"

"I do," Peabo said. "The dragon mentioned the Darkness, and I was wondering if you had any information about what that actually is."

"Good question," the prelate said. "Much of what Baham said is shrouded in mystery; it's the way of dragonkind. But I did some research last night, and I found a passage in the *Chronicles of Eve* that talked about the Prophecy of the Forgotten One. It states the following:

'Woe to you Aboveworlders and Myrkheimers, for The Darkness sends his minions with wrath, for he knows the time grows short.

'Let the one whose destiny it is reckon the solution, for it is a solution that can only come from the one bearing the markings of the Prismatist.'"

"There's that Prismatist again," Peabo said. "Baham said I'm supposed to emerge from my cocoon. Become who I'm supposed to be. And something about going back… and when I do, it will be time for the Prismatist to appear. It all sounds dire and ominous, yet I don't understand a word of it."

The prelate grinned. "Aye, and that's why you travel to Myrkheim City. Consult with the oracle, if she will see you. Only she might have the answers we're all looking for."

The prelate walked over to a section of the wall that was bare of any glowing fungus and pressed a glowing hand on it. There was a grinding sound and the head of the church stepped back as a stone door yawned open, revealing a swirling vortex of colors. Peabo sensed a strong field of energy that swirled slowly counterclockwise, crackling and popping.

"Okay folks, follow me," said Menkins. "We're going to bypass a day's worth of travel going this way. Hold hands and don't let go until we arrive on the other side."

Without warning, Fuzzball came up behind Peabo, reared up, and put her paws on his shoulders, nearly knocking him off balance.

"Okay, Fuzzball, I figured it might come to something like this," Peabo said as the cat draped her front legs over his shoulders. She then planted her back paws firmly on his hips, and Peabo had a passenger.

Peabo held Nicole's hand with his right, and with his left he clasped Spam's tiny hand. With everyone linked together in a chain, Menkins led them into the swirling vortex.

The moment Peabo stepped over the threshold, the world began to swirl past at unimaginable speed, flowing past in blurs of stone and darkness, punctuated by sporadic flashes of light. He felt himself stretching unnaturally, and his ears were full of the constant crackling sound of electricity—and occasionally other sounds.

Inhuman screams.

Deep and bellowing roars.

The sounds of combat.

As they raced along what felt like this world's equivalent of a slip-and-slide, Peabo wondered how it was possible to create a passage between two places like this. He had the sensation of movement, but had no sense of how fast they traveled. Everything was such a blur, there were no points of reference. And it was all he could do to keep his balance, especially with a giant cat on his back.

He sent a thought to Nicole, unsure if it would even work. *"What is this thing we're traveling through?"*

"It's called a gate," she thought back. *"A gate connects two points in our world, or even connects our world to another plane of existence. I've never seen anyone create one, but I know the prelate is capable of establishing them, as are a few others."*

Peabo was collecting a long list of mysterious things he couldn't even begin to explain. Several questions came to mind: how is a gate established, what's the mechanism of transport, how is it even possible to send people through such a thing, et cetera. There were quirks in real science, such as quantum entanglement and even quantum teleportation, that made it possible for something to happen in one place and instantly affect another place, and he'd heard that teleporting had been proven possible at the atomic level... but this? This was beyond anything he would ever have considered possible.

And it bugged him that he didn't understand how it worked.

Peabo's ears popped, and he found himself stepping through the other end of the portal and staggering into another stone chamber. He felt a moment of dizziness, and was grateful when Fuzzball hopped off of him and swished her tail. The others also seemed to be a bit unsteady on their feet. Nicole gripped Peabo's shoulder with one hand and bent over looking like she was about to throw up.

"Damn I hate those things," Menkins groused. "They scramble my giblets something awful."

Peabo looked back at the portal, but there was nothing there to see but a rocky wall. Nobody would know that this was a path to Igneous City. Or maybe it wasn't? Perhaps it was one-way only, and there wasn't a path back at all.

When they'd all recovered, Menkins faced the team. He shrugged his shoulders and leaned his head side to side, cracking his neck. "The gate dropped us about an hour's march from the main entrance to Myrkheim City. The city is spelled against anything gating in closer than that. We'll be skirting past the city and heading directly toward the oracle's alcove. Be wary: that path is not normally patrolled, and we may encounter something along the way. I'm taking the point position." He pointed to the gnome. "Tiny, you take the rear. The rest of you, don't get dead. You got me?"

To Peabo, Menkins sounded a lot like some of the sergeants he'd served with in the service, which he found oddly comforting.

Peabo drew his sword, and the glow was obvious in the dim

room. *"I felt you drop me, pea brain. Do that again and I'll start thinking about ways to PT your ass until you drop and see how you like it."*

Peabo sent his wordless apologies, which seemed to mollify Max. Who knew that an inanimate object could get its feelings hurt?

Menkins motioned to the only exit from the chamber, and the team moved forward.

———

As Peabo followed along through the passages of this confusing realm, he wondered how Menkins managed to keep track of all the turns and detours, around fallen rocks and past gaping chasms. At the lower levels they were currently wandering about, Myrkheim felt different. It was warmer, for one thing. And instead of glowing mushrooms to light their way, the rock itself gave off its own glow. Peabo hoped that wasn't an indication that the rocks were giving off some type of radiation.

Was a cancer a thing down here?

Peabo felt a tingle at the base of his neck. He was just about to say something when an invisible presence slammed into him, and he recognized the feeling of something trying to invade his mind. The image of Scarlett loomed large in his mind's eye.

He focused his thoughts and spotted the threads of energy spooling forward from a barely visible figure on the other side of the cavern they had just entered. Peabo's anger rose at the indignity of what the figure was trying to do to him and mentally pushed back against the intruder.

Peabo gripped his sword and stepped forward, but he felt something completely alien trying to hinder his progress.

The air was thicker here; it was like wading through honey. He realized then that everyone else was unmoving, as though time had stopped.

But his fury fueled him. He pushed harder, and Peabo strained mentally as he battled whatever it was on the end of the cavern. Gritting his teeth, he shoved against the alien thing attacking him and felt something give way.

Peabo slowly strode forward.

He was now close enough to see the figure clearly. It was cloaked in robes that melded perfectly with the coloration of the rocks behind it, but its face was visible—unfortunately. It looked like someone had stuck squid tentacles on a ghastly pale face.

Peabo had read about this kind of creature in the monster manual.

A mind flayer.

He pushed harder, and the mind flayer took a step back. It was no match for Peabo's assault. He thrust his anger ahead of him, a spear targeting the creature's mind. And after a long struggle, the flayer's defense collapsed completely.

Peabo now had a firm mental grip on the creature's mind. He sensed its entire life—or to be more accurate, lives. Inside it were all the many lives it had claimed each time it had consumed the brain of a victim. Peabo was repulsed by the thing's sheer disregard for others. It cared nothing for those in Myrkheim, or anywhere else.

Peabo mentally squeezed down on the soft tissues of the creature's brain until it fell to its knees. Then with a swipe of his sword, Peabo separated the squid head from the humanoid body.

He heard sounds within the chamber once again.

"How the hell did you get up there so quickly?" Menkins yelled from far behind him.

A life essence bubbled up from the convulsing body, and as it touched Peabo, he felt a thrill race through him. Everything around him seemed just a bit brighter than it had before.

As the team raced to join him, Nicole looked curiously at him and smiled. "You leveled just now, didn't you?"

Peabo raised an eyebrow. "How'd you know?"

"I felt it." She tapped her chest. "In here."

Menkins slapped Peabo on the back and chuckled. "I've never seen such a thing. You were by my side as that damned flayer attacked, and in the next blink you're here killing it. Did I fall asleep in between?"

"I saw the same thing," Spam said. "How does someone so big and fat move so fast, I wonder?"

Peabo pointed at the tiny wizard's belly. "You have no room to talk, butterball. If you were any rounder, you'd be rolling instead of walking."

Menkins chuckled again, then gestured forward. "Enough jibber-jabber. We're almost to the guardians of the oracle."

As they continued their march, Nicole sent her thoughts to Peabo. *"What just happened? It did look like you blinked from one place to the next and instantly killed the mind flayer. How'd you do that?"*

"Honestly, I'm not sure. The attack was a lot like what Scarlett tried to do to me, just much weaker. I got angry. Really angry. I know something happened because the air seemed thicker and time slowed for me. It slowed a lot. You guys looked like you were statues. But to be honest, I was so focused on the mind flayer and its attack, I lost track of everything else. The next thing I knew I'd subdued it, realized the kind of thing it really was, and killed it."

Nicole rubbed her fingertips across his back. *"It's extremely unusual to gain levels this quickly. There's probably a lot more that you can do that you don't even know."* She bumped her shoulder into his and gave him a warm smile. *"Do you realize we're the same level now? Who'd have thought?"*

Peabo had just opened his mouth to reply when, with an explosion of rock, a five-foot-tall boulder rolled from the wall. Only it wasn't just a boulder. It had arms and legs—three of each. And on its top surface were two bulbous eyes and a huge, jagged-toothed maw.

With blinding speed, Menkins whirled his maces at the creature. The rock thing began to sink into the stone floor, but before it could escape, Spam sent a crackling bolt at it. The boulder burst open like a ripe cantaloupe.

"Xorns are idiots," the gnome grunted.

Peabo had just witnessed a fight with one of the strangest creatures he had ever laid eyes on, and it was all over in under ten seconds. It was a true testament to how powerful his team-mates were.

As Menkins walked past the xorn's corpse, which was halfway buried in the floor, the dwarf bashed in a few of the thing's teeth. "You didn't have to kill him that quickly, Tiny," he said over his shoulder. "I was just starting to have fun with it."

The gnome put his hands on his hips. "When a creature as stupid as a xorn tries to phase through stone right in front of me, you think I'm not going to take advantage? You've got the wrong gnome if you think that."

Menkins waved for the group to continue. "If I recall correctly, we're right on top of the oracle's alcove."

They walked up a long slope, and as they cleared the underground rise, they entered a large cavern. In the distance, there was a temple with tall white columns. It was nearly identical to some Greek temples Peabo had seen photos of, and for a moment he wondered if this was the place Greek society had modeled their architecture on... or vice versa.

He heard the sound of scales rubbing against stone, and from the shadows on either side of the path appeared two enormous snakes. Each one was twenty feet long, with gold scales, green markings... and women's faces. The faces would have been beautiful were it not for their unblinking, snake-like eyes that shined with a golden hue.

The air around both creatures crackled with a sound that Peabo felt more than heard, indicating that there was a lot more to these snakes than just their size.

The snake on the left hissed, displaying her fangs as her red, forked tongue flicked in and out. "Are you ready to die?"

Peabo gripped the handle of his sword, and Max grumbled

in his head, *"I don't care how drunk you ever get, not with those two, you hear me, soldier?"*

"Not something you have to worry about," Peabo thought back.

But no one else so much as moved, and Menkins sheathed his weapons and laughed heartily. "Rita," he said, "you're not half as scary as you think you are."

The snake woman's expression turned from ferocious to disappointed.

Menkins looked back at Peabo. "These two ladies are the guardian nagas, Rita and Chloe. They keep the riff-raff from disturbing the oracle." He grinned at Rita. "And this big fellow is a plainswalker. He's here to see the oracle."

The two snake women slithered over to Peabo and leaned their heads down, examining him. "Oh, you're adorable," said Rita. "The oracle said you'd be arriving."

"She did?"

"Plainswalker, follow us. The rest of you wait here."

The two snake-ladies turned and slithered up the path toward the temple.

Peabo looked to Menkins, then to Nicole. "Do I follow? Is it okay to go alone?" He realized at that moment that the cat was nowhere in sight. "And where's Fuzzball?"

Nicole nudged him. "Yes, go on. This is why we came here. I'll look for the cat."

Peabo jogged after the two snake women. He wondered what he'd gotten himself into.

CHAPTER TWENTY-FOUR

Though Peabo had never been to Greece and had only seen its buildings in pictures, the underground temple was quintessential Greek architecture, with the post and lintel style of having horizontal blocks of stone held up by vertical pillars. The pillars were detailed with intricate carvings of dragons, nagas, and many other creatures he'd never seen. Even a xorn was represented.

The snake-women paused at the steps leading up into the temple. They smiled, and despite their fangs and unblinking eyes, they seemed pretty nice—especially considering they could probably squeeze his bones into jelly. The information on nagas in the monster manual had been pretty sparse, but it suggested they could not only crush their victims, they could also cast spells and kill them with poison. That was enough to make any sane person wary.

One of the snake-women motioned with her head toward the dark entrance. "The oracle will see you."

"Thanks, Rita."

The woman's expression turned sour. "I'm Chloe. One of the scales under Rita's chin is red, unlike mine, which isn't marred with that abnormality."

Peabo smiled. "Of course, I should have known. You're both so beautiful, I was blinded to the difference."

As he started up the steps, Rita and Chloe chatted behind him.

"He's quite nice, don't you think?"

"Yes, but now I think he's put off by my red scale."

"Nonsense. Nobody can notice it."

"They certainly notice it if you insist on pointing it out."

Peabo chuckled at the banter as he walked out of earshot.

The moment he crossed the temple's threshold, two half-height pillars began glowing a bluish-white, illuminating the interior. The central chamber was square, about one hundred feet on each side, but empty.

Then Peabo noticed a glowing mark on the right-hand wall —a purple handprint. It looked like something fluorescing under a black light.

"Here goes nothing…"

Peabo placed his hand against the glowing handprint. His hand was exactly the same size.

But nothing happened.

Fuzzball appeared out of the shadows. *"It isn't for you to use on this day."*

He looked down at her. "How did—"

"I've been waiting for you. It's time."

Peabo sensed movement to his left, and turned to see that an opening to another room had appeared on the temple's rear wall. He could have sworn that doorway wasn't there before.

He stepped through the opening into a throne room, its ornately carved white marble throne occupied by a surprising character.

An ordinary little girl.

She looked to be about ten or eleven, with dark hair, a plain white dress... and completely white eyes.

Okay, maybe this wasn't exactly an *ordinary* girl.

"Are you the oracle?" Peabo asked.

The child smiled and said nothing. He felt no hint of magic.

Fuzzball approached the child, and she looked the cat in the eye. "You are me."

The cat meowed, and an otherworldly voice sounded in the chamber. "I am you."

Fuzzball turned into a cloud of black mist, and the child *breathed* the cloud into herself.

Peabo backed up a step as the child morphed into a gray cloud. The cloud grew until it was twenty feet tall, with flashes of lightning shooting about within it.

A deep voice reverberated from within the cloud. *"You are mine. I created you. But there was a mistake in your original design. Hold out your left hand."*

Peabo did as he was told even though his mind was reeling. What was this thing? What was it talking about? This thing *created* him?

A thread of mist erupted from within the cloud and formed

a semi-opaque miniature image of Fuzzball. The cat leaped toward Peabo's outstretched hand and condensed into a thin black rope that swirled around his ring finger. Peabo felt a burning sensation as the rope cinched itself around the base of his finger and buried itself in his skin, leaving behind a blackened and raised welt. It looked much like one of his many lightning-shaped markings.

"You are now complete—and you must undo what has been done. Your purpose lies behind you and ahead of you."

"What does that mean?" Peabo said to the cloud.

The cloud rose up to the rafters of the temple, then dropped a sheet of rolled-up paper that landed at Peabo's feet. He picked it up, unrolled it, and read it.

It wasn't written in the runic symbols of this world, but in English. And it wasn't handwritten. In fact it looked like it had been printed on a laser printer.

Sage's Tower: Basement
  Crate: A03
  Carrington's Last Wish

The booming voice from within the cloud spoke in his mind. *"Your next steps lie in the Sage's Tower. Be prepared. If you fail, everything and everyone you know will be consumed in darkness for eternity."*

With a loud clap of thunder, the cloud vanished.

His hands shaking, Peabo looked at the document once

more. *The Sage's Tower.* It was the last place in the world he wanted to go.

As he turned back to the entrance of the temple, he felt nauseated.

The tower... those women... Ariandelle.

Peabo looked once more at the paper and shook his head. Did he even have another choice?

His stomach gurgled.

He not only had to return to the tower, he had to somehow talk his way into the basement so he could rummage around in Ariandelle's precious relics. And there was no way she'd give permission for that. Which meant only one thing.

This sucked.

"Be man enough to embrace the suck."

The dragon's words were probably going to haunt him for the rest of his life—however short that might be given his current mission.

He took a deep breath and let it out slowly.

The dragon was right. It was time to embrace the suck.

———

Standing in the enclosed courtyard that was said to be the prelate's private retreat, Peabo stared in amazement at four swirling vortexes of white crackling power. The vortexes hovered in midair, and every thirty seconds or so one of the vortexes would spit out another arrival from God-knows-where. Soon nearly one hundred people of all shapes and sizes had arrived. And almost all of them had an aura of white. Some were armed with swords, maces, flails, or bows. Others had no weapons at all but wore thick cloth robes much like Spam's, the only wizard Peabo had met thus far.

It had been only two hours since Peabo and the rest of his group had gated back to Igneous City and been debriefed by the prelate. In that short period of time, the man had assembled this small army of what looked like very dangerous people.

Now the prelate waved his hand with a flourish, and the threads of energy that sustained the vortexes unraveled, flying back into the prelate and the other priests who had created them.

From what Peabo could deduce from these threads, the gates required a constant stream of energy flowing into them. But that was mere speculation. The whole thing was still beyond his comprehension.

The prelate walked to the center of the courtyard, and when he spoke, it sounded as his voice was being amplified by a megaphone.

"You've all been summoned here from the far reaches of the mainland for a mission that's been foretold for centuries uncounted." The prelate motioned toward Peabo. "We have all read the tales left behind by our ancestors, tales that speak of a plainswalker and what had happened at the end of the First Age. The war that ensued. The collapse of all that the first world knew.

"We rebuilt. We survived. We thrived. But a warning was given to us many years ago: a warning of an approaching Darkness. That threat still looms, and it is now directly in our path.

Even the legendary Baham, the first of dragonkind, acknowledges the danger.

"The Nameless One has set us as guardians for this world. It is our job to keep it safe from the Darkness that threatens all life. Yet the Darkness has already begun to infiltrate some among us.

"It is foreseen that the plainswalker is the key to combating the Darkness. He is to be the light for all of us in the dark times to come. It is our duty to assist the plainswalker in whatever way we can.

"The plainswalker now needs to return to the Sage's Tower to retrieve something from within its domain. Even though the women of the Sage's Tower have always been allies, they have now become suspect. Thus I have gathered you all together to provide an escort and to ensure the plainswalker's goal is not threatened.

"Are there any questions?"

A gnome who was even shorter than Spam pushed his way to the front. "What are the rules of engagement with these maidens? Do you expect trouble?"

Peabo had his own suspicions about how the women would react to his return, but he looked to the prelate, curious how the man would answer.

The prelate looked grim. "I hope for cooperation from Ariandelle and her people, but our priority is the safety of the plainswalker and his mission. If there's a threat to him, I expect you to act by whatever means necessary."

The gnome grinned, as tiny sparks arced between his fingertips. Of the new arrivals, his internal glow was the brightest, second only to the prelate's. It was clear that in this world, power wasn't defined by gender or size. Peabo wouldn't be surprised if the little guy could wipe out a huge swath of enemies just by blinking at them.

"We will meet back here in one hour," the prelate said. "Eat, drink, and do whatever you need to prepare. The bell on the steeple will ring five minutes before we are to leave, so be listening for it."

The prelate dismissed the group with a wave, then motioned for Peabo to follow him.

As they walked alone down a dim corridor, the prelate spoke in a whisper. "I've arranged a place for you to recharge your skills, so to speak. Your blood maiden will have prepared the room by now, and she'll assist."

Peabo looked down at the glowing beacon of a man who represented the head of an entire church. "Do you know Ariandelle?"

"Aye, lad. I knew her when she was but a child. But I'm afraid that she's no longer the person I knew. She was a delightful child, but as a woman, or at least at this stage, she's... murky." He patted Peabo on the arm. "We'll keep you safe, that I can assure you. No maiden will harm you. But you cannot allow yourself any complacency within that tower. It's full of ancient things, secrets, ghosts. Always keep looking over your shoulder. That's not just a lesson for now, it's a lesson for life."

Peabo chuckled. One of the first lessons he'd learned in the army had been to watch his six.

The two of them turned through an open doorway and

stepped into a blindingly bright room. Hundreds of lanterns were scattered about the small space, nearly all of them lit. Nicole was waiting for them, lighting the remaining lanterns, while using one hand to shield her eyes.

"I think I've taken every lantern in the church," she said with a grin.

The prelate nodded with approval and closed the door behind him. He too was shielding his eyes from the glare. "Peabo," he said, "I think it's wise that before you leave, you have your own form of attack ready. Against a blood maiden, especially some of those at the tower, your sword will probably not do you much good." The man grinned. "And besides, I've never had the chance to see a plainswalker use his abilities."

Peabo nodded with relief. Walking around "unloaded" felt weird at this stage.

Nicole laid a hand on his shoulder, and he felt her presence in his mind. "In case this is too much, I'll help you stop if you need me to."

"Thanks." Peabo turned to the prelate. "You may already know this, but while I'm absorbing the lanterns' energy, don't do anything that produces light—which includes using your own abilities. I'll inadvertently suck your energy away as well. I can't help it."

"I appreciate the warning." The prelate winked. "The blood maiden already gave me a report on that."

Peabo looked back and forth between the two. "You guys ready?"

They both nodded.

Peabo breathed in. The world went completely silent, and

everything seemed to slow and then stop. The flames flickering in the lanterns paused as if frozen. He was between heartbeats, yet hundreds of threads of energy flew from the lanterns into him.

The markings all over his body began to glow. Peabo felt the energy coiling up inside him, almost as if charging a battery. And before his heart even took its next beat, the energy flow stopped and the room fell into darkness.

Time resumed, and Peabo heard the prelate pull in a breath of air. "Amazing. Is it safe to turn on a light now?"

"Yes," Peabo said. "I'm done."

A white glow appeared above the prelate's head, bathing the room in light. "Now then," he said. "Are you ready for a trip?"

Peabo shrugged, trying to rid himself of the tension that had been building up in his shoulders. "I'm as ready as I can be, I suppose."

The prelate nodded. "Good. It's time to play out the next step in your destiny. Let's go."

CHAPTER TWENTY-FIVE

Peabo staggered out of the gate. The others ahead of him were wincing from discomfort, but he felt none of the disorienting nausea the others seemed to be going through. All he felt was a kind of mild unsteadiness, as if he'd stepped back on land after having been on a boat for a few hours.

They were at the edge of a forest.

He scanned his surroundings and saw the towers, only about a quarter mile away. A shiver raced up and down his spine, and he took a few calming breaths. He had no idea how this was going to work out, but the prelate had said he'd be the one doing the talking, so as the crew assembled, Peabo walked to the prelate's side. Nicole joined him.

The prelate had a mischievous expression. "She's meeting us at the entrance to the central tower to talk."

"Who, Ariandelle?" Peabo asked. "When did you get a chance to speak to her?"

The prelate held up his hand and wiggled his pinkie. It had a communication ring on it. "We have a matched pair, the headmistress and I. I don't use it often, but it is a convenient artifact of the past."

Peabo raised his eyebrows. "That's an invention of... the First Age?"

"Aye, it is."

The prelate motioned for the others to gather around, then spoke only loud enough to be heard by the group. "We are meeting with the headmistress directly. The plainswalker and I will advance; the rest of you hang back at the edge of the tower complex. I expect that the headmistress has already sensed our presence and called her people to the fore. Just in case things go sideways, you should prepare defensive and offensive measures as appropriate. You all know what to do."

He turned to Nicole and nodded curtly. "I'd like you to stay back with the others. I know there's a thing with blood maidens and those who—"

"I understand," Nicole said.

Peabo looked confused, and Nicole sent her thoughts to him. *"The prelate's right. I'm still considered a failed blood maiden. I'm a pariah to those in the tower, an example of what not to do. I'm not supposed to return to the tower area. It's okay. Just reach out to me through our link if you have any trouble in there. I'll let the others know."*

"Peabo," the prelate said, "bend down so I can reach your face."

Peabo did as instructed, and the dwarf held up three glowing fingers on each hand.

"Close your eyes for a second."

Peabo again did as he was told, and the prelate placed his hands on the sides of Peabo's head. Peabo felt a warmth building up around his forehead, cheeks, and eyes.

"What I'm doing will temporarily stimulate parts of your mind," the prelate explained. "It will enhance your sight as you travel within the tower. This will help you see past illusions, spot traps, and give your senses a boost. I hope you don't need it, but just in case, it's there. Now go ahead and open your eyes."

Peabo opened his eyes. He didn't see anything different from before.

"Okay, folks," said the prelate, "let's move."

As the group walked through the outskirts of the woods and into the cleared area leading to the tower, Nicole pressed a glowing hand on Peabo's shoulder, sending a tingle through him. She whispered, "This'll make you a bit harder to hit and improve your chance of hitting your target, if it comes to that."

Peabo gave Nicole's hand a quick squeeze, then moved forward with the prelate as they approached the perimeter of the tower complex.

Ariandelle was waiting for them up ahead, standing directly in front of the center tower's entrance, her glowing form flanked by at least twenty other blood maidens. They were a formidable force, but Peabo's side had the numbers, and likely the level advantage. Still, the last thing anyone needed was a battle. Besides which, Peabo himself was at a way lower level than most of these people. If it came to a battle between these powerful forces, he'd probably get squished like a bug.

"Stop daydreaming, plainswalker," the prelate said under his breath as they crossed the outer barrier of the tower complex. "Keep your focus."

Ariandelle walked toward them and stopped about ten feet away. She was a different woman than the one Peabo had seen last. She looked older than he remembered. He noticed slight bags beneath her eyes, and her hair wasn't nearly as full or luxurious.

He pulled in a breath and pressed his lips together to avoid smiling. His guess was that Ariandelle always looked like this, but that she used some sort of illusionary makeup to look better and younger—to project an image of her former self. But now the prelate's vision trick had improved Peabo's ability to see past the illusion.

Vanity—even the headmistress of the famous Sage's Tower suffered from it.

"Ariandelle." The prelate bowed his head. "It's been a while. I hope you're doing well."

The headmistress panned her eyes across the array of people behind Peabo and the prelate. "Richard, Peabo. It's good to see you both again. I see you've brought friends. That wasn't necessary." She sighed as if disappointed, then focused on the prelate. "You said this was urgent and it concerned something grave? What is it that you need?"

The prelate smiled warmly. "I've communed with the Nameless One. Many of the prophecies are coming to pass in our age. And because of that, the plainswalker must refer to an item that happens to be in the main tower's basement. All we ask is for free passage to seek what is needed, and then we will be gone."

"This is the *dire* situation you referred to?" Ariandelle looked incredulous. "Some random prophecy? Richard, you of all people know how inaccurate and misleading those prophecies can be."

"Some of our guidance comes from the oracle herself."

Peabo was watching Ariandelle's face closely, and he saw her left eye twitch. Maybe some nervous condition?

The headmistress frowned. "I cannot allow your people down in the archives. Many of those items are irreplaceable and have yet to even be catalogued."

The prelate patted Peabo's arm. "My people will stay outside. Just the plainswalker will go."

"Just the plainswalker?" Ariandelle shifted her attention back to Peabo and narrowed her gaze. Finally she gave a nod. She removed a set of white linen gloves from her waistband and handed them to him. "You may not touch anything with your hands. The oils from your fingers can damage the ancient manuscripts. And you are not allowed to remove *anything* from the archives. Do you understand?"

Feeling paranoid, Peabo studied the gloves, but he spotted nothing unusual about them. And when he slipped them on, nothing happened.

"I understand," he said.

"Who else is in the tower right now?" the prelate asked.

"I've asked the girls to remain in their rooms," Ariandelle said. "They won't be in the way. All other staff is out here with us."

"Can I have the key to the basement door?" Peabo asked.

Ariandelle gave him a half-smile as she removed a long golden chain from around her neck, with a key strung from it. "I seem to recall you not needing a key, but here it is." She stood aside and with a sweeping motion, pointed at the entrance. "It's all yours."

As Peabo walked to the main tower's entrance, he faintly heard Nicole's voice in his head. *"Remember, there are no friends in that tower, only enemies. Be careful down there."*

"I will."

Peabo winced as he inserted the key into the lock on the basement's door, but there was no electric jolt. He turned the key, heard metal slide against metal, and opened the door.

With a sigh of relief, he lit the lantern on the hook at the top of the stairs. He closed the door behind him, and then, spotting a broom leaning against the wall, decided to place it loosely against the door. If someone opened the door, the falling broom would at least make a noise to warn him. Peabo wasn't normally the paranoid type, but inside this tower, he wasn't about to take anything for granted.

A musty scent of age wafted up from below as he walked down the steps. The scent was comforting, but as he reached the lower level of the tower, he couldn't shake a nervous feeling. With one hand on the pommel of his sword and the other on the lantern, Peabo strode into the underground chamber.

He quickened his pace, knowing that the marked crates

were at the far end of the basement. Finding some, he rushed forward, and followed the path that swung to the left. The nearest crate was CB01. The crate at the head of the next row was CA01. He was going in the right direction. That meant that A03 had to be at the far end of this wing of the basement. He continued jogging.

He had gotten only as far as AB01 when he heard the sound of metal brushing against metal. He spun around to find three soldiers in full plate mail about twenty feet behind him, blocking his exit. Then three more soldiers appeared to his right, three more to his left, and three more ahead of him. Twelve soldiers in all. All of them had weapons drawn, and those weapons had a reddish aura. Clearly there was something enchanted about the swords.

Even in the dimness of the basement, Peabo could see the crest on their breastplates. It was the same symbol that was on all the gold, silver, and copper royals that served as this land's currency.

These were the king's men.

One of the soldiers blocking his exit spoke. "Plainswalker, you are being detained in the name of the king."

"Nicole, there are king's guards down here. Any advice?"

From each direction, one of the soldiers lit a bull's-eye lantern and cast a bright beam of light directly onto Peabo's face, making it hard for him to see.

"Nicole?" He yelled his thought to her, but got no response. She probably couldn't hear him from inside the basement.

He drew his blade, and Max yelled in his head. *"Good job,*

pea brain, we're surrounded. At least that makes things simpler."

The twelve soldiers advanced simultaneously. There was no way Peabo could fight them all at once.

This was a trap. A setup. Somehow, Ariandelle had known he was coming for something in the basement, and had placed them here.

Anger washed over Peabo at the thought, and with it, a sixth sense awakened within him. Suddenly he could feel each soldier's presence in his core. He didn't even have to look at them. They weren't soldiers anymore. They were blobs of energy heading for him.

With a quick inhalation, he sucked the light from all of the lanterns and blasted the twelve figures he saw in his mind's eye. Twelve laser-like threads of light shot out of him.

There were no screams. There was no time for that. There was only the sound of sizzling—a wave of searing heat washed over him from all four directions as the energy poured out of him.

The breastplates of each soldier glowed red with heat, each of the armored figures convulsed as the heat intensified.

The armor glowed white-hot just before the metal failed, and white light exploded from their helms as Peabo felt his reservoir run dry.

He heard crashing metal as the soldiers collapsed to the ground.

The scent of burnt flesh and scorched wood permeated the air.

His hands shaking from the adrenaline, Peabo listened in

the darkness for any other enemies. But all he heard was his own heart beating at a surprisingly moderate pace.

The twelve tiny balls of life essence bubbled up from the soldiers' bodies. They drifted toward Peabo, and he absorbed them.

It was dark, but not completely so. One of the lanterns was still lit. Peabo walked over to it and looked at the nearest corpse. A fist-sized hole had been burned directly through the man's breastplate. The smells of burnt flesh and copper-scented blood permeated the air.

"Well, that's one way to take care of business," said Max. *"I guess you weren't up for having a little chit-chat with your friends, eh?"*

Peabo sheathed his sword and grabbed a dagger from the dead soldier's waistband. The weapon's leather-wrapped grip was almost too hot to handle. It, too, had the king's insignia on the pommel. He would show it to the prelate when he got out of here.

Grabbing the lantern, which had somehow remained lit, he continued moving toward his destination, but now he was jogging. He didn't know how much time he had. He reached row A, and quickly located Crate A03. He had to lift off the top in order to get to it, and set them aside. Then he pulled A03 into the aisle, jammed the soldier's dagger in the seam just underneath the lid, and pressed down.

The dry wood splintered and gave way, and the lid shifted slightly upward. Using the same technique, Peabo moved the dagger along the edge of the lid and kept slowly prying it open until the lid finally popped off altogether.

Beaming the light into the wooden box he saw the gleam of some gilded books and carefully lifted one out of the box. It was an unfamiliar title, so he set it aside, and continued until the crate was nearly empty.

With a rising level of concern that he maybe had wrong information, he pulled out the second to the last book in the crate, which was wrapped in an oilskin covering that had long ago dried out and was brittle.

Peabo carefully removed the protective covering. The book within was covered in a metal leaf that gave off a slight glow. And when Peabo saw the front cover, he smiled.

The titles on all the other books looked to have been either block-set printed, like on an old-style printing press, or written by a calligrapher who clearly had too much time on their hands. But this one was different. It was handwritten—nothing fancy, just ordinary handwriting—with what looked like a Sharpie marker.

The title was "Carrington's Last Wish."

This was the book he'd been sent to find.

CHAPTER TWENTY-SIX

Peabo opened the book and read the opening paragraphs.

My name isn't important. Just know that I am the chief assistant to THE Dr. Carrington, and I have been for over twenty years. From now on, I will refer to him simply as Carrington, because that was his preference. For those who may be reading this long after I have passed, know that Carrington was a genius. He was the most intelligent and revolutionary scientist of our era. It was my privilege and honor to work for him and to call him my friend. He saw the dangers that were coming long before anyone else did.

But as always, the politicians of both sides refused to listen to reason. "This will be better for us all in the long run," they would say. It wasn't.

It was Carrington's last wish before the bombing started

that I preserve his thoughts and do what is necessary for the time to come. When this hell is over and we are back in a time of peace, maybe these things that I describe, these things that Carrington invented... maybe they'll be of use.

Peabo skimmed the pages, looking for something important. He couldn't help but wonder why he had been directed to find this particular book. It was a contemporary firsthand record from the end of the First Age, which Peabo found fascinating, but he didn't have time for fascinating. He needed answers. He was ever conscious of the dead bodies lying not far away and the people waiting on him in the courtyard.

There were various mentions of the Nameless One and the Twins. Both seemed to be nation-states of some kind, ruled, respectively, by someone without a name and a set of twins. But these rulers were different than everyone else. They were treated like gods. Supremely intelligent, and powerful. They were spoken of in the way a worshiper describes a deity. Only these deities were corporeal. People had literally visited with them. Saw them in the flesh.

Yet despite this society's religious backdrop, they had been very advanced. The book spoke of satellites—and then of these satellites being shot out of the sky by a great "light-bearer." Peabo wondered if that was just another name for what he was capable of. There was no mention of a plainswalker or a Prismatist, but this account could have preceded the adoption of those terms.

The society also had bombs powerful enough to wipe out

entire cities. And evidently there were cities everywhere. Cities holding millions of people.

Peabo continued skimming. It was a short journal, and it didn't take him long to get to the end. He slowed as he read the final passages:

Near the end, just before the Twins vanished, Carrington said that they'd handed him the knowledge to undo what was to be done.

We worked in secret for over a year. Myself, Carrington, and twenty other scientists. The data was all beyond my comprehension, but the design was clear. It was like putting together a puzzle. I just had no idea what it was that I was building.

Only after half of the scientists had succumbed to the nano-virus plaguing the world did Carrington finally divulge to me what he knew of the purpose of the device we'd spent countless hours assembling. It was, he said, a means to travel beyond space and time.

And then Carrington himself succumbed to the plague. By then various parts of the AI were sealed off from all who might access it—other than the one it was meant for.

I never expected to be the last survivor. But here I am. And it is with my last ounce of energy that I write this log for those who might come.

I have sealed the site for another time, another generation. Another world. This will all be used, so Carrington assured me, but it isn't meant for us. It isn't meant for now.

Maybe it's punishment for a deed that was done unbe-knownst to us, or maybe a deed that hasn't been done. I'll never know. All I can tell you is that whatever this is, this invention, it's meant to reverse the damage we have done to each other.

There's a great evil afoot. I can feel it in my bones. I've seen it televised on the video broadcasts any time a politician speaks. They've doomed us all. I just pray that there will be someone to read this someday and make our sacrifice not be for naught.

I've prayed to the Twins, to the Nameless One, and to any other higher being who might listen. Asking for another way to fix the wrongs that have been done. But I've never gotten a response.

The broadcasts have been silent for months. The airwaves are still. For all I know, I'm the last person living on this planet and our species is truly doomed. I hope that's not the case.

This is my last testament. To the one who will read this account, I leave this warning:

I have no idea what will occur if you do this thing.

I've set the seeker's AI to transport you to this place, hidden from all living things. I pray the world is cured by your actions.

May the Twins guide your hand.

A deep sorrow filled Peabo as he imagined what it must have been like for this nameless survivor.

Suddenly he heard the shuffling of feet. Focusing his

senses, he detected several people out there, in the darkness of the basement. Once again, there were twelve of them. Beacons of shimmering power that shone to him like torches in the night.

He was sensing them on a completely different level than that of light and dark. Could he truly see the echoes of people and things on different planes of existence? Was that how he was detecting whoever was out there?

A woman's voice called out. "We know you've expended your powers," she said. "Give up now or face the consequences."

Fury washed over him as the many people he'd met within the tower flashed in his mind's eye. The executors, the so-called teachers, even the students. They were all suspect. They could all be the enemy.

And then he remembered some faces that were different. Binary. The middle-aged man who curated for the museum of First Age equipment in the northwest tower. And Grundle, the old crystal weaver in the southeast tower.

The crystal!

Peabo dug into his waistband, pulled out the leather pouch, and plunged his hand inside. The moment he touched the crystal he felt an indescribable surge of energy.

"This is your last warning, plainswalker. You have five seconds to comply."

He had no idea who the woman was, or who the other eleven people arrayed against him were, but as Nicole had rightfully said: they were enemies.

He breathed in, and using his connection to the charged

crystal, he sent torrents of blinding light in twelve directions. Some of the beams had to blast through crates and walls to reach their target. A rainbow-like effect bloomed throughout the darkened basement, and everything was bathed in preternatural light. Screams were locked frozen in the women's throats as Peabo's light attack blasted through them and shot from their mouths and eyes.

In that other plane, which seemed to be laid over everything else in front of him, Peabo saw the women's life forces blink out of existence, one by one.

He clenched his gut to stop, and by some miracle, his attack ceased. The gem was still glowing brightly.

Peabo allowed himself a smile of triumph. He'd stopped himself. And there was nobody in his head helping.

The essences bubbled up from the bodies, and as he absorbed them, Peabo felt himself gain yet another level.

Level ten.

And this level was different.

Previously he'd seen flashes of some rainbow effects. Strange auras with various colorations. But nothing that was consistent. Now the world shimmered with an abundance of color. Colors that went far beyond the rainbow he knew. It was as if he'd been colorblind all his life and had just now been introduced to color for the first time.

He knew that humans could see only a small part of the light spectrum. Now he was seeing beyond that. He was seeing colors for which there were no words.

The last words from "Carrington's Last Wish" replayed in his mind.

I've set the seeker's AI to transport you to this place, hidden from all living things. I pray the world is cured by your actions.

May the Twins guide your hand.

He knew where he had to go next.

As he began jogging back to the stairs, he almost tripped over a body. The woman was blonde, and wearing a dark robe. He crouched down and ripped the robe open, revealing a necklace that seemed to absorb light, just like the one Scarlett had worn. And the woman's tunic had the king's insignia on it.

Peabo spit on the corpse, then raced forward through the wreckage. Several crates had been blown apart; golden pages of books scattered in every direction. He hadn't realized just how much damage he'd done with his last attack. Ariandelle was going to be pissed.

Peabo smiled at that thought. He had half a mind to lay waste to everything down here just to spite her. But that wasn't what needed to happen.

He took the steps two at a time and burst through the door, practically knocking it off of its hinges. As he fast-walked down the hall, he encountered one of the older students, and without thinking he sent a stream of high-powered light straight into her mind. She stopped, frozen in shock, as he rummaged through her thoughts.

The girl's name was Candace. She was seventeen. She was afraid of failing. She was deathly afraid of him. But she was innocent of any crime.

He walked past her and said, "Go back into your room. It's not safe."

Peabo encountered no one else on his way out of the tower, but the moment he exited, he found Ariandelle waiting, a look of surprise on her face.

She clearly hadn't expected him to return.

He sent the same high-powered invisible light into her mind. He was only able to stay inside Ariandelle's mind for a split second before she managed to expel him, but in that moment he sensed a dark pit of evil. It sat at her core, controlling her.

Peabo breathed in and attacked at the same time, sending a glowing pillar of light slamming into Ariandelle. Peabo pulled in more energy than he'd ever done before, launching exploratory threads at all of the other blood maidens at once, searching their minds to determine who was friend and who was foe. In the blink of an eye he was sending three more pillars of light into three other corrupted blood maidens. It was all Peabo could do to not be torn apart by the stresses of the powers flowing through him.

And then he felt Nicole's soothing presence. The power ebbed, and he let it go. He collapsed to his knees, the world spinning around him.

For a brief moment he might have passed out. Then he felt himself being lifted up. He looked at Ariandelle and the three other blood maidens he'd attacked. They were now nothing but ashes floating away in the wind.

Peabo shrugged off the help and managed to get back onto his feet. With nearly a hundred high-level soldiers and wizards directly behind him, he walked to the several dozen blood maidens arrayed in the main tower's courtyard. Though he'd brushed their minds for only an instant, he knew them. He felt their bewilderment and confusion.

"Your headmistress and some of your peers were possessed by something beyond description," he shouted. "Evil doesn't begin to describe it. A great darkness is coming over the land. You all need to be on the lookout. Steel yourself against the evil that's coming. War is approaching. Prepare yourself. You are either an ally or a foe. Each of you... get ready. The Darkness comes."

Peabo turned from the group, walked up to the prelate, and showed him the dagger he'd gotten from the soldier in the basement. He quickly filled him in on everything that had happened.

The prelate grew pale as Peabo spoke. "And did you find what you came for?"

Peabo nodded. "I think I know where I need to go next."

The prelate turned to the blood maidens and spoke loud enough for the entire courtyard to hear. "Who is your new headmistress?"

All heads turned toward one woman, who bowed her head and took a step forward. "It is I, prelate. My name is Eileen."

Peabo felt a surge of relief as he approached her. She was one of the good ones. "Eileen—or should I now say, Headmistress Eileen. I'm sorry things had to happen this way. But you must have noticed that something changed in Ariandelle somewhere along the way, and that's why you're in this position now."

She nodded. "You're right. I did notice a change. About a year ago. But who could I have said anything to?" Her cheeks flushed, and she looked Peabo in the eye. "I apologize for everything I put you through, plainswalker."

"It's fine. You were doing your job."

The prelate clasped forearms with the new headmistress. "It is a pleasure to meet you, headmistress. I'm sorry to tell you that your term begins with more trouble than you're already aware of. In your basement are the dead bodies of a dozen king's maidens and a dozen king's guards. I would suggest hiding the bodies, but that is up to you. None of us are ready for a war with the king, but we all might need to be if what is happening isn't an isolated incident. You should prepare."

Eileen nodded. "And are the tower and the church of the Nameless One still allied?"

The prelate smiled. "Always."

It wasn't until they were all well away from the Sage's Tower that the prelate asked the question that had surely been on his mind the entire time.

"What is it that you have to do next, plainswalker?"

"I have an appointment with the Seeker."

"The Seeker?" the prelate said, sounding confused. "Oh!" His eyes suddenly widened. "The Seeker from Dvorak Island?"

Peabo nodded. "I'm headed back to where I started. Back to the Desolate Plains."

"Those plains are treacherous," the prelate said with a grimace. "The sands swallow entire armies whole. It's impossible to navigate. And the Seekers that travel over those plains are monsters unto themselves. Are you sure that's your next stop? Are you going to battle one of those? Because if you are, it has been tried before—and it was a disaster."

"No," Peabo said. "I believe the intention is for me to somehow *ride* the Seeker. At least that's what Carrington's assistant had written."

"Ride the Seeker..." The prelate repeated the words as if Peabo had uttered a string of gibberish. "Very well then." He motioned for the others to gather around. "First stop will be Igneous City. Nicole, you will collect Brodie, since he is normally stationed there, and the three of you will be off to Dvorak Island to find the Seekers. But first you may want to check the church's library, as well as the Igneous City Library archives, for any information you can find on these Seekers. It would be unfortunate if our plainswalker were to become a snack for an ancient creature with a bottomless appetite."

CHAPTER TWENTY-SEVEN

After gating in from Igneous City, Peabo stood with Brodie on the edge of Raiheim, a small farming town on the island of Dvorak. It was the first town he'd encountered in this world, after arriving here nearly a year ago knowing nothing about where he was or even who he was. He now knew a lot more, but it was never enough. Even now he was still encountering things that he felt like he should have known but didn't.

He gazed out at the vast expanse of gray, hard-packed soil known as the Desolate Plains. "I can't believe we're back where we started," he said to Brodie. "Had I just stayed exactly where I was when first arriving, I'd be in exactly the situation I'm about to put myself into, but nearly a year earlier."

Brodie patted Peabo on the arm. "Aye, that might be true, then again it might not. I'd assert you're now much better equipped, both in experience and your ability to deal with dangers, than you were when you first arrived."

Nicole gave his hand a squeeze. "And if you had never left the Desolate Plains, you would never have saved me from the fate the auctioneer had for me. I believe some things are destined to be, but not always in the order that might make sense to us at the time."

Peabo nodded. "I'm not saying any of this was a mistake, I just find it ironic."

Brodie turned to Nicole. "You realize that even if the Seeker accepts Peabo as an appropriate rider, it may consider you a threat and attack you. I still say you should allow the plainswalker to fulfill his destiny on his own."

"Brodie might be right," Peabo said. "I'm fine doing this myself. If you insist on coming, I won't try to stop you... but it is a risk."

Nicole's tone brooked no argument. "I won't be separated from you again. We're a team. This is how it is."

Brodie harrumphed. "Fine. Nicole, you have the communication ring on you, so if there's any trouble, you let me know."

Peabo and Nicole clasped forearms with the tough old dwarf, then took their first steps onto the sandy soil of the Desolate Plains.

Holding Nicole's hand, Peabo walked south, further into the Desolate Plains, knowing that at some point something was going to happen.

Nicole tightened her grip on Peabo's hand. "How can you be so calm? My heart is racing."

Peabo grinned, feeling her rapid heartbeat through their connection. "I just figure that whatever this Seeker really is, it's probably programmed to take me somewhere in one piece. Otherwise what's the point of all this?"

"Programmed?" Nicole frowned. "I don't know that word."

"Programmed is a term from my world—and perhaps from your world in the First Age, too, when you had machines that no longer exist today. The Carrington journal I read in the tower referred to something called 'AI,' or artificial intelligence—something we use in advanced machines. The exact phrase from the book was, 'I've set the seeker's AI to transport you to this place.'"

"Are you saying the Seeker isn't really a creature?" Nicole said.

"I'm saying I suspect the Seeker is some type of artificial creature. Not natural, but man-made. And to 'program' it means to give the creature—or machine—instructions that it's supposed to follow. Not unlike training an animal."

"You think the Seeker has all this time been looking for a plainswalker to transport?"

Peabo shrugged. "That's what that book said. I guess we're going to—"

An ear-splitting squawk sounded from high above, and a large shadow temporarily blocked out the sun.

"It's here!" Nicole cried. "What do we do?"

"I need to identify myself," Peabo said.

He quickly scanned the terrain, spotted a boulder, and used a tight burst of energy to send a beam of light at it. He did his best to control his power, making the light as harmless as possible. Sure enough, when it struck the stone, there was no obvious damage.

"Hopefully that's enough to let the Seeker know who and what I am."

Nicole looked at him in surprise. "Your skin markings are still glowing. You stopped your power by yourself?"

The shadow swooped past again, and this time Peabo spotted the tremendous figure high above, skimming just beneath the clouds.

"Since I hit level ten, I've had more control," Peabo said. But even as he said it, he felt the scar on his ring finger throb. Perhaps it was whatever that oracle and Fuzzball had done to him that had helped him gain control. There was no way of knowing.

Nicole pointed. "It's coming around again."

The Seeker came in on a slow decline, like a jet on approach. And though it looked bird-like, it didn't perfectly mimic a bird's flight. There was too much flapping and not enough gliding. Also, it seemed to be decelerating without making the adjustments to its wings that a bird would normally make.

But the biggest thing that differentiated it from a bird was its size.

It was gigantic.

It not only came in like a plane, it had the wingspan of a C-17 transport.

As it came closer, Peabo got a better look. In many ways it reminded him of an impossibly oversized pterodactyl, but it had feathers. Its long-toothed beak opened and let out a shriek.

If that was a warning, Peabo thought, it certainly sounded very convincing. It was no wonder the people of this world were terrified of this thing.

It slowed even further, to a pace that would make any flying machine or non-flapping animal drop out of the sky. Yet it didn't. Peabo heard a sound that couldn't be made by an animal, or even by a jet engine—it was more like a hum, like the sound of a high-voltage transformer.

The Seeker glided in slowly and settled on two clawed feet about a hundred yards away. It opened its mouth wide, and Peabo's eyes went wide.

The jagged toothed ridges in the beak weren't teeth. They were *stairs*.

"I guess we better get on board," Peabo said. He started forward, and Nicole was practically glued to his side, matching his steps.

"Are you sure about this?" she thought to him.

They were close enough now that Peabo could see inside the Seeker. Deep in its gullet was a large wingback chair, very reminiscent of the chair Kirk sat in on *Star Trek*.

"I am," he thought back.

They reached the stairs. The scent of age emanated from deep within the creature. Except from here, it was clearly no creature. It was an aircraft. It has just been made to resemble an animal—from a distance, anyway.

Together they climbed the steps. As they reached the top, the lower jaw raised up behind them. Just before it closed, lights flicked on, illuminating the interior.

Unfortunately, there was only the one chair.

Peabo shrugged. "I guess you can sit on my lap."

They did exactly that. As soon as they were both seated, seatbelts automatically threaded over them both, cinched up the slack, and pulled them in tightly, but not uncomfortably. Then Peabo felt them lifting up from the ground.

"Is this thing some kind of gate?" Nicole asked.

Peabo smiled. How to explain an airplane to someone who'd never even seen a car?

"It has the same purpose," he said. "I guess we'll find out soon enough where we are going."

Nicole leaned her head against his chest and sighed. "At least we're not dead."

"Not yet anyway." He chuckled.

Suddenly the vehicle put on a burst of acceleration, and they were both pressed hard against the back of the seat. Peabo felt his cheeks pushing backward, and Nicole's weight was nearly crushing him. He'd been in his fair share of fast-movers before, and he knew a jet's acceleration rarely exceeded one g. This thing had to be accelerating at three or four times that rate.

"I'm crushing you, aren't I?" Nicole thought.

"I'm okay," he lied. Peabo tightened his core and focused on trying to pull in a breath and let it out slowly.

The acceleration seemed to continue forever, but in reality it probably lasted only a minute or two before the pressure let up—and was replaced by a feeling of weightlessness.

Peabo's eyes widened. Were they in space? He tried to calculate the distance they would have traveled if they'd been accelerating at a rate of four g's over two minutes. He wasn't sure if his math was right, but if they were nearly two hundred miles above the surface, and moving quickly enough, they really could be experiencing the same zero-g effects that satellites experienced.

"What's going on?" Nicole asked.

"I don't know how to explain it. Let's just say I think we might be very, *very* high up in the sky right now."

The zero-g effect wore off, and the entire aircraft began to vibrate.

Now it made more sense. The vehicle had taken a parabolic path to shoot past the atmosphere to avoid friction. It was like throwing a baseball forward and up into the air. At the peak of the arc, the baseball would also seem weightless. That was what they'd just experienced.

And now they were going back down again.

Thankfully, the way down was less intense than the way up. No extreme g-forces, no burning up in the atmosphere, just the occasional bounce and tremor as the Seeker raced to its destination.

For the next fifteen minutes Peabo and Nicole silently experienced the ride together, neither one knowing where they were going or what might happen next. At last Peabo felt the aircraft settle smoothly onto something solid. The mouth of the giant bird yawned open, and the restraints automatically unlocked and recessed back into the flight chair.

Nicole and Peabo stood, and Peabo stomped his legs to get his blood circulating properly again. Then they walked down the stairs onto what looked like a desert island. A palm-tree-lined beachfront was about a quarter mile away.

Strangely, it appeared to be late in the evening. It had been morning in Raiheim, and they'd only traveled for maybe half an hour. That raised a lot of questions for which Peabo had no answers. How big was this planet? How fast had they gone?

Nicole pointed straight ahead. Looming in front of them, not that far off, were two giant stone figures carved in a cliff face on the side of a mountain. The statues were at least a hundred feet tall, with determined expressions, and they wore what looked to Peabo like togas with open-toed sandals.

"I wonder who they are," he said.

"They're the twins," Nicole said with certainty. "We're in a very ancient place."

Between the two statues, at the base of the cliff, was a large door. That, it would seem, was their destination, so they walked toward it.

As they drew close, another light blinked on above the door. A modern-style electric floodlight, the first Peabo had seen since arriving in this world. And the door looked modern, too. In fact, it looked like the kind of door that a bomb shelter might use. It was made of metal, and large enough for a bus to pass through. There was no obvious way to open the door, but next to the entrance was a square panel.

Emblazoned on the door was the image of the twins.

"I've never seen such a thing in my life," Nicole said.

Peabo walked up to the panel and flipped open its cover. Inside was a glowing purple handprint, just like the one he'd seen in the oracle's temple.

"What point would an empty box serve?" Nicole asked.

He looked over at her, and then back at the panel. "You don't see anything?"

"Just the box." She shrugged. "Why? What do you see?"

Peabo took a breath and placed his right hand on the glowing image.

The door began to yawn open. It was a good three feet thick, strengthening Peabo's feeling that it was meant to be bomb-proof.

"What did you do?" Nicole asked.

"I wish I could tell you," said Peabo.

Beyond the door was an empty hallway, lit by light panels all along the ceiling. At the end of the hall was a swirling vortex of white.

Nicole pointed at the vortex. "At least that I understand." She looked at Peabo. "Shall we?"

They stepped into the empty hallway, and the door closed behind them. Holding hands, they walked forward to the vortex, and Peabo reached out and touched it.

Instantly, everything froze.

"Your purpose lies behind you and ahead of you..."

The voice sounded in Peabo's head. It was the same voice he'd heard in the oracle's temple.

"What's happening?" he said.

He felt himself drifting forward, but Nicole remained behind, frozen in time.

"Nicole!"

"The maiden shall remain in stasis. It is not permitted for one of this universe to travel into the past for the purpose that we seek."

"I don't understand. Who are you? What do you want from me?"

Peabo felt himself spinning head over heels, images rapidly flashing by, but he had no sense of inertia or dizziness, just a feeling he was being stretched and pulled in every direction. And moving—quickly.

"I am one who cannot be remembered. The others are banished. You have been brought from another place to help undo what has been done. You have been engineered to combat that which wants to end existence for all."

At this point Peabo felt like he was swirling around a drain, faster and faster, with absolutely no idea which way was up or down. "How am I supposed to do that?" he asked. "I don't even know what you're talking about or what's been done that needs to be undone."

Peabo saw images of a world devastated by war. Cities ruined, people starving, vast populations dying. Chaos and near extinction.

"I cannot tell you what to do, because even if I did, you would not remember."

In his head flashed images of war, explosions, cities being flattened, people dying under collapsing ruins, praying for help that would never come.

"You will not remember me. It is my nature. It is why I am still here. Unknown, yet present."

Peabo saw bustling cities, skyscrapers, hovering vehicles taking people back and forth across continents and vast oceans.

"You will be given an opportunity to affect what has been done, because at this moment that you are now in, it has not yet occurred. You are the light in the darkness. You are that which shall come, shall undo, shall restore... or we are nothing.

"You are the Prismatist."

Peabo lurched forward and fell to his knees.

Gone were the swirling lights, the stretching sensation, the images. The air smelled heavily of sulfur.

Staggering to his feet, Peabo realized he recognized where he was. The bluish-white glow coming off of the two half-height pillars were the giveaway.

He was in the oracle's temple.

He went to the entrance, looking for the twin snake guardians. They weren't there. There was no sign of anyone.

He ran up the path toward what should have been the entrance to the oracle's alcove—but was met instead with a solid stone wall.

He heard the sounds of several jackhammers smashing against the rock. Then, suddenly, the wall cracked.

Peabo stepped back.

A man-sized hole was hammered through the bedrock, and someone yelled, "Hold it!"

The power equipment stopped, and a dark-skinned man wearing a breathing apparatus peered through the hole. When he saw Peabo standing there, he stared in shock.

"How did you get in…? Are you alive?"

Peabo was startled by the question. "Shouldn't I be?"

The man seemed flummoxed. "The air at this level of Myrkheim hasn't been cleared for habitability yet. Are you insane?"

Though the air was stale and unpleasant, it didn't seem unbreathable. Peabo stepped through the newly dug entrance to find nearly a dozen people there, all with mining equipment, what looked like rebreathers of some sort, and hardhats. All of them were staring at him like he was an alien. One of the men looked to his neighbor and said, "What's with the sword and strange clothes?"

Not one of them was a dwarf. Something was very wrong.

The first man handed him what looked like a spare breathing apparatus. "Put this on before you die. There's poison gases down here."

Peabo waved the thing away. He didn't need a breathing apparatus, he needed to understand what was going on. The last thing he remembered was being on an island with Nicole, and now he was just outside the oracle's temple. What had happened? He had to get answers.

"I need to go to Myrkheim City," he said, "to visit the temple of the Nameless One."

"A temple, down here? You've got to be kidding me," the man said. "There ain't no city nor any temple down in the mines. You want a city, go up top to Brevard, that's the closest outpost to the mining operation." He dug a plastic card from his pocket. "But you'll need a pass-key to work the elevators."

"What?" Peabo clenched his hands into fists so the others wouldn't see them shaking. "What about Igneous City? I know there's a temple there."

An older miner approached. He took the breathing apparatus from the first man and began unraveling the straps. "Son," he said gently, "I think the gas has poisoned your mind. There's no place I've ever heard called that."

"It has two huge dwarven statues lining the entrance. The city is full of thousands of dwarves."

Peabo was beginning to feel like he was going crazy. He allowed the man to place the mask over his face. At least it removed the bad smells from the air.

The miners began talking, and the first man, who seemed to be the leader, pulled out what looked like a walkie-talkie. "Charles," he said, holding the device to his head, "we've found someone down here, and he's a bit confused. We need a medevac."

"You found someone? On level nine? Alive?" said a voice through the device's speaker.

"I know, it sounds crazy. I'm just telling you what happened. The gas has clearly gotten to him. He's talking about dwarves and underground cities and temples."

"Dwarves? Like actual *dwarves?"*

"I told you he was confused. Who knows how long he's been without breathing protection down here. Just get us a stretcher down to my team. I've turned on my beacon."

Peabo's mouth dropped, and it all hit him.

Carrington's journal had said: *All I can tell you is that whatever this is, this invention, it's meant to reverse the damage we have done to each other.*

Reverse the damage.

Peabo had been at the island, and now he was here.

No underground cities—*yet.*

And the dwarves, who'd lived underground for countless generations, didn't exist—*yet.*

Peabo was in the past. And judging by the man's modern communication device, he was some time in the First Age.

With a humming sound, a floating stretcher with a flashing

light zoomed toward them and stopped only about ten feet away. It floated with no obvious means of support.

The older man helped Peabo onto it. "It'll be okay, son. You just need some fresh air. The docs will look after you. Everything will be just fine."

The other miners were giving him looks of genuine concern, so Peabo nodded his thanks and lay down.

The moment he rested his head against the stretcher, straps automatically looped across his legs and chest.

The stretcher began moving. It went horizontally for a short distance, then started up a vertical shaft. All the while, Peabo struggled to remember what had happened. How had he gotten from the island to the temple? From the present to the past?

He couldn't remember. His memory between those times was completely blank.

Then Peabo realized something that sent a chill up his spine. He couldn't sense Nicole. The two threads attaching them were still there, stretching outward, but there was no one on the other end.

He supposed that made sense. If he really was in the distant past, Nicole hadn't even been born.

Everything he knew about this world had just been flipped upside down.

He was in the First Age.

A modern world.

A world on the brink of total disaster.

PREVIEW OF THE PRISMATIST

Peabo held his arms out to the sides as the doctor pressed a stethoscope against the left side of his chest.

"Breathe in deeply," the doctor instructed. "Then breathe out."

Peabo did as he was asked, all the while staring at the posters on the doctor's wall. They advertised new drug treatments for ailments Peabo had never even heard of.

When the doctor repeated the process, switching sides to listen to the right side of Peabo's chest, the posters on the wall suddenly flipped over and displayed a new set of advertisements and medical trivia. Peabo would never have guessed it just by looking at it, but the wall seemed to be some kind of video display. But it looked just like the real thing, complete with 3D effects that simulated the posters having tiny fold marks and curled corners.

The doctor took a step back. "Mr. Smith, you have

somehow managed to avoid any physical side effects from the gases in the mines. On that point, you're a lucky man. As to your amnesia, that's a bit of a concern." With gloved hands, the doctor tilted Peabo's head upward so that he was facing the ceiling. "These marks are all over you. Were you born with them, or are they some kind of tattoo?"

"I don't remember," Peabo lied.

The doctor, who looked very much like a brown-skinned version of Max Decker, Peabo's boot camp drill sergeant, frowned and shifted his attention to his tablet. He swiped upward, his eyes darting back and forth across the screen.

Peabo had been in this new world for less than an hour—not nearly enough time to come up with a good explanation for how he'd gotten into Myrkheim, which he'd learned was some kind of secret government project. Instead of trying to come up with a series of half-truths, he'd fallen back on the easiest thing he could come up with: amnesia. At least that gave him some time to figure out what to do in this place where he didn't know the rules, didn't know what he needed to do, and didn't want to talk his way into a corner.

The doctor swiped one last time on his tablet. "Mr. Smith—"

"Please, call me Peabo."

"Peabo…" The doctor turned the tablet so Peabo could see it. "What does that tell you?"

Peabo looked at the screen and breathed a sigh of relief when he saw that the rune-like symbols were familiar to him. "It says that patient Peabo Smith has no identification." He looked up at the doctor and shrugged. "I guess that means there's probably some kind of glitch in the system?"

A red light began blinking on the wall. The doctor swiped his index finger across the flashing light, and it vanished. "It's not possible for someone to not be in the system. You can't enter any building without a retinal scan. There's no backup embedded ID anywhere on you. Even your clothes have no micro-tags indicating where the fibers were manufactured. And that sword... and the glowing gem..." There was a knock on the door. "I'm sorry, but outpost security had to call the regional authorities. I'm releasing you to them for follow-up."

The door opened and a beefy man in a dark paramilitary uniform with a nightstick hanging from his utility belt walked in. He gave the physician a nod before turning to Peabo and motioning for him to get up.

Peabo hopped off the exam table and gestured to his medical gown. Like the ones from back on Earth, it tied in the back and left a bit of a breeze where there shouldn't be a breeze. "Can I change back into my clothes first?"

"Your clothes and other items are being examined in a secure lab," the officer said. "We're taking a tube transport to the RBI headquarters. They'll figure out the situation with your belongings when we get there."

"One second," said the doctor. He opened a cabinet, rifled through a pile of folded blue scrubs, and handed Peabo a pair of pants and a shirt. "These should fit you."

The officer nodded in approval, and Peabo changed into the scrubs.

So far, everyone here had been very polite and had treated

him well. But it was clear that his being here posed some kind of security breach, and they were trying to figure out who in the world he was and what was going on. Peabo wanted an answer to the latter question even more than they did. So he decided to go along with the program, at least for now.

The guard led him down a long corridor. As they neared the door at its end, a green light flashed in their faces and a voice spoke from a hidden speaker. *"Identification failure. Doors are sealed."*

The guard motioned for Peabo to stop. "Security override: Alpha Charlie X-Ray Baker Baker Three."

"Voice pattern matched. Security override confirmed. Officer Daniels, please state destination."

"The research wing of the RBI headquarters. Direct transport via secure route."

"Confirmed. Private tube transport for Officer Daniels and unknown person to the headquarters of the Regional Bureau of Investigation, Research Wing."

Peabo heard the sound of rushing air behind the door, and then it slid open with a hiss, revealing a tube-shaped compartment with two padded armchairs inside.

"The capsule is now ready for boarding."

Peabo followed the guard into the tube, trying not to look surprised at what he was seeing. The tube was small—about fifteen feet long and eight feet wide—and the walls were transparent, probably some kind of reinforced glass. As soon as both Peabo and the guard were seated, the door closed, and the air pressure changed.

Speakers set within his chair's headrest crackled, and a new voice said, *"We are about to depart."* This voice was a woman's, and she spoke with a cheerful tone, as if he'd won a prize or something.

Safety harnesses built into their chairs activated, and a gauze-like mesh wrapped itself around Peabo's legs and chest. He looked over to the officer and saw the same thing had happened to him. The officer looked unconcerned, even bored, so Peabo tried to stay calm.

The capsule began to move soundlessly forward, and the two chairs swiveled smoothly so that the passengers were facing in the direction of travel. Then they accelerated, and Peabo felt himself being pushed against his chair.

"The capsule is departing Myrkheim Station."

Peabo turned to the guard. "How long does it take to get to the headquarters?"

"It's a quick journey. It's only about five minutes from the switching terminal."

Peabo looked through the clear walls of the capsule as it accelerated through a concrete tube. The entire thing must have been riding on some kind of frictionless support, because there was utterly no sound in the capsule's cabin. At first, a black stripe on the wall raced past every second or so, but in no time at all, the black stripes had become a gray blur.

Then suddenly the tube vanished, and the capsule was flying through empty air. Peabo felt his stomach muscles clench as they veered hard to the right, his chair swiveling with the shift in momentum. Only then did Peabo realize that they weren't actually flying through the air, but were in a clear tube of some kind.

In fact, now he could see, in the distance, a maze of semi-opaque tubes, looking like a snarl of fishing line.

It was becoming very, very obvious that this world was far more advanced than anything he'd ever seen before.

"Passengers, we are arriving at the Brevard switching terminal. Please remain seated. Your car will automatically be routed to the proper queue for high-speed transport."

High-speed transport? Peabo thought. *You mean that wasn't high-speed already?*

The capsule rushed into a concrete structure, and with a flicker, a hologram of a man wearing a lab coat appeared in the capsule directly in front of Peabo and the officer. If it weren't for the occasional flicker, Peabo would have sworn the man was there in flesh and blood.

"Welcome, neighbor!"

The man sounded bright and happy. A white-coated version of Mr. Rogers.

"You're about to embark on a transport that will see you traveling across our sovereign nation at hypersonic speeds. Some passengers may have moments of discomfort upon seeing the land streaking by at these rates, so be aware that all our capsules are equipped with dimming portals if needed.

"Because you are in a priority queue with a classified arrival gate, you will not be given the option to interrupt this travel. The red emergency button on each chair will not be operational during your trip. Thank you for your cooperation."

The hologram vanished and the capsule shifted sideways onto another of a myriad of tracks.

The speakers in his chair came to life once more, and the

cheery woman's voice returned. *"Your car is next in line for departure. We are departing the Brevard switching terminal in three... two... one..."*

The capsule accelerated so quickly that Peabo felt like an invisible hand was pressing him back against his seat. The g forces he'd experienced on the Seeker were like nothing compared to this. He started experiencing the tunnel vision he'd only read about, the kind that occurred when pilots experienced increased intraocular pressure.

The pressure-induced tunnel grew narrower, and Peabo grunted, trying to push some blood up into his head. As the narrowing stopped, it was all Peabo could do to not pass out altogether. Then, suddenly, the pressure eased, and his vision returned to normal.

A wave of exhaustion washed over Peabo as their capsule entered a darkened building. The only lights were the ones in the capsule itself.

The capsule lurched upward and red lights flickered ahead as they slowed and coasted to a stop.

Peabo had no clue how far they might have traveled or where he was at the moment.

"Oh, that's unexpected," said the guard, motioning to the platform, where a wiry man in a lab coat was walking toward them. Behind him were a half dozen burly men who made the average gorilla look scrawny. "That's Director Clearwater. He's the new head of RBI research."

The director pressed a flashing button on a column, and the red flashing lights turned to solid green.

"Secondary authorization received."

The mesh restraints that had held Peabo in place vanished in a puff of odd-smelling smoke, and the capsule's door slid open.

Peabo stood and exited the capsule, feeling a bit unsteady, but happy to have his feet back on unmoving ground.

The director walked right up to Peabo and stared at him for a full two seconds before extending his arm. Peabo clasped the man's forearm uncertainly, and the man grinned.

"I'm Jonathan Clearwater, head of research. I have many questions for you… Mr. Smith, is it?"

"Please, the name is Peabo."

"Peabo then." Clearwater motioned down the platform. "Let's go directly to the lab."

The man's guards formed a semicircle around the two as Peabo followed the director, his senses on high alert.

"Peabo, the physician says you have some form of dissociative amnesia." The director pulled a leather pouch from his coat pocket and opened it. Light poured forth from within. "Do you recognize this item?"

Peabo nodded. "I remember having that pouch on me when I was found. That and a sword."

"Yes, the sword. That's another item we need to talk about. But this one… this charged gem… this is what has brought you to my attention." He cinched the pouch and put it back in his coat pocket. "My team is working on a related project, one that very few people know about, commissioned by our sovereign. But it's only very recently—by which I mean only days ago— that we managed to capture energy within the matrix of a crystal." The director patted his pocket. "And now you show up, carrying something that we at STAG have been working on for nearly a decade. I'd say that's more than a coincidence."

Peabo's eyes widened and his step faltered.

The man stopped midstride and grinned. "What is it? I can tell something that I just said struck a nerve."

"What is it you called your group? I thought this was supposed to be RBI—"

"Yes, yes, Regional Bureau of Investigation. My group falls under their domain, but RBI's research wing is compartmentalized with several different charters." The director's icy blue eyes looked directly at Peabo. "STAG stands for the Special Technologies Analysis Group, and we're chartered to do some very advanced research."

Peabo's mind flashed back to a year ago, to a time before he'd ever even started on this crazy adventure. In a different world, a different universe.

He'd walked into a new job. It was a hush-hush operation, and on the very first day bright lights flashed into his eyes and a disembodied voice said, *"Mr. Smith, welcome to STAG."*

His ears started to buzz with static.

Director Clearwater pointed at a pair of thick metal doors that lowered into the ground. "Mr. Smith," he said, "welcome to STAG."

AUTHOR'S NOTE

Well, that's the end of *The Sage's Tower*, and I sincerely hope you enjoyed it.

If this is the first book of mine you've read, I owe you a bit of an introduction. For the rest of you who have seen this before, skip to the new stuff.

I'm a lifelong science researcher who has been in the high-tech industry longer than I'd like to admit. There's nothing particularly unusual about my beginnings, but I suppose it should be noted I grew up with English as my third language, although nowadays, it is by far my strongest. As an Army brat, I traveled a lot and did what many people do: I went to school, got a job, got married, and had kids.

I grew up reading science magazines, which led me into reading science fiction, mostly the classics by Asimov, Niven,

Pournelle, etc. And then I found epic fantasy, which introduced me to a whole new world, in fact many new worlds, it was Eddings, Tolkien, and the like who set me on the path of appreciating that genre. As I grew older, and stuffier, I grew to appreciate thrillers from Cussler, Crichton, Grisham, and others.

When I had young kids, I began to make up stories for them, which kept them entertained. After all, who wouldn't be entertained when you're hearing about dwarves, elves, dragons, and whatnot? These were the bedtime stories of their youth. And to help me keep things straight, I ended up writing these stories down, so I wouldn't have it all jumbled in my head.

Well, the kids grew up, and after writing all that stuff down to keep them entertained, it turns out I caught the bug—the writing bug. I got an itch to start writing... but not the traditional things I'd written for the kids.

Over the years I'd made friends with some rather well-known authors, and when I talked to them about maybe getting more serious about this writing thing, several of them gave me the same advice: "Write what you know."

Write what I know? I began to think about Michael Crichton. He was a non-practicing MD, who started off with a medical thriller. John Grisham was an attorney for a decade before writing a series of legal thrillers. Maybe there was something to that advice.

I began to ponder, "What do I know?" And then it hit me.

I know science. It's what I do for a living and what I enjoy. In fact, one of my hobbies is reading formal papers spanning many scientific disciplines. My interests range from particle physics, computers, the military sciences (you know, the science behind what makes stuff go boom), and medicine. I'm admittedly a bit of a nerd in that way. I've also traveled extensively during my life, and am an informal student of foreign languages and cultures.

With the advice of some New York Times-bestselling authors, I started my foray into writing novels.

My first book, Primordial Threat, became a USA Today bestseller, and since then I've hit that list a handful of times. With 20-20 hindsight, I'm pleased that I took the plunge and started writing.

That's enough of an intro, and I'm not a fan of talking about myself, so let me get back to where I was before I rudely interrupted myself.

Writing fantasy isn't a natural path for me as a person of science, but I should note that this isn't exactly a traditional fantasy novel. As much as practical, I weave in science realities throughout, and sometimes very advanced topics might even come up in context of the story.

I wrote the first book in this series on a dare of sorts. It was asserted that I couldn't write a single book that catered to fans of thrillers and fans of sci-fi/fantasy. I'm glad to say that the first title, *The Plainswalker*, was a success with fans of both genres, which reaffirmed my instincts on a few things: because trust me, doing what others don't do often is usually a recipe for disaster.

I'm going to assume that those of you who have gotten to

this part of the book have at least finished reading it and I've hopefully kept you entertained. I'd like to give a bit of insight regarding my thought process when creating this book and the overall story arc for the series.

As you may realize, there are gaming elements weaved into the story, which I hope by now are relatively seamless. Those thriller readers are sold on the concept of leveling, and the fantasy readers are tolerating my POV character trying to figure out the science of what he's seeing.

This particular part of the series was intended to be a transition point for our main character. By the end of the book, Peabo has gotten pretty powerful. A bit surer of himself, and slightly more comfortable with his current role.

By the end of the book, all of those things change.

For many authors of a successful series, they are asked to write prequels so that people can get a better feel for the back-story of some characters or the history of the world they're reading about. I'd planned from the beginning to do what book #3 promises to bring.

Many of you might have questions about the First Age. We've certainly seen some ruins. Hints of an advanced society. Some God-like creatures are referenced as having been banished, what gives? Something really bad happened back then. And Peabo isn't the first plainswalker to walk that world.

I'll announce now that the next book is entitled, *The Prismatist*. The story should address many of the questions posed above and hopefully many more.

I still struggle with what genre this series would fall under.

The Plainswalker was clearly a combination of technothriller and fantasy, with some science fiction tossed in. The Sage's Tower probably has more focus on fantasy with some science fiction tossed in. *The Prismatist* may flip that script and have a lot of science fiction with fantasy elements tossed in.

Many of you have written me with thoughts on what genre The Plainswalker fit into, and the responses were all over the map, which was amusing to me. One thing that was a common theme was that it read very much like a "Rothman" novel, which I suppose is a good thing—at least I hope it is.

As always, I'd love to hear comments and feedback.

Please share your thoughts/reviews about the story on Amazon and with your friends. It's only through reviews and word of mouth that this story will find other readers, and I do hope this book (and the rest of my books) find as wide an audience as possible.

Again, thank you for taking the chance on a relatively unknown author. After all, I'm no Stephen King.

It's my intent to release two to four books a year, and I'll be completely honest, I'm heavily influenced by my readership on what gets attention next. An example of that being my first book, Primordial Threat, a book that was not going to have a follow-on title. But when I released it, it became a hit in the US and abroad, so due to demand, I released a second in what is now known as the Exodus Series.

I should note that if you're interested in getting updates about my latest work, join my mailing list at:

AUTHOR'S NOTE

https://mailinglist.michaelarothman.com/new-reader

Mike Rothman
December 1, 2021

ADDENDUM

If you've read my books in the past, you've come to expect this scientist to weave in some science regardless of what genre the book is. I don't like to be predictable, but in this one sense, I feel the need to go into some of the science that is covered within the story.

As I give very brief explanations of what may be very complex concepts, my intent is to only leave you with sufficient information to give a remedial understanding of the subject. However, for those who want to know more, it is also my intent to leave you with enough keywords that would allow you to initiate your own research and gain a more complete background understanding of any of these topics.

This should also give you a peek into some of the things that have influenced my writing of this story, and maybe have you start asking what all authors inevitably ask themselves, "What if?"

Teleportation (Gating):

In this story we introduce the concept of gating, which is very much a term used in gaming systems such as Dungeons and Dragons and many other role-playing games. As always, things in this story aren't always obvious whether they fall into the pure fantasy category or the science-based category. Sometimes it's a little mix of both.

Often, things that look to us like fantasy today are the science-fact of tomorrow.

For instance, the telegraph must have seemed like magic to those in the 1800s. The idea that you could do something in one place, and almost instantly have it translated into words many miles away was the equivalent of magic to most people. As was the first playback of a human's voice, or the phone.

In the use of the term gating, we really are talking about teleportation. It's the concept of moving an object from one place to another, and it too seems like magic to us. Or at least, like science fiction.

Yet the most fundamental aspects of teleportation are science fact.

Granted, the teleportation that has been demonstrated to date has been at the atomic level. Nonetheless, real experiments have demonstrated some measure of success. For instance, particles have actually been teleported up to eighty-nine miles between two of the Canary Islands.

Suffice it to say that this is a topic that is vastly too

complex for true engineering-level discussion as an addendum to this novel, but the topics one could research further if you are interested in learning more would be Quantum Entanglement and Quantum Teleportation.

Another fascinating scientific topic that demonstrates that teleportation is theoretically possible, at least on paper, is the concept of a wormhole. This is, simply put, the ability for two points in space-time to be connected together as a "shortcut" of sorts. Imagine if you were standing in Spain and wanted to travel to New Zealand on the other side of the world. If there were a direct flight, it would be approximately 12,000 miles. But if there were a wormhole between these two locations, it would only be roughly 8,000 miles. Such shortcuts are the exotic areas where science fiction meets the world of the possible. Not only could one potentially be zapped from one place to another, a thing such as a wormhole can even establish a means to travel backward in time.

And speaking of travel backward in time...

Time Travel:

When Einstein first described general relatively in 1915, he described our universe in terms of the three dimensions of space that we're very well aware of and the fourth dimension being time itself. This is where the term space-time comes about, it's the term scientists use to describe all four dimensions of our universe.

General relativity is describing spacetime itself. Spacetime is actually a model in which space and time are woven together to simplify talking about the four dimensions that would normally involve space and time. Here, Einstein determined that large objects cause a distortion in spacetime, and that distortion is known as gravity.

The idea of traveling forward in time isn't at all controversial. In fact, it's been proven to be true.

In science the affect is generally called time dilation, and it has been experimentally verified. I'll refer you to the U.S. Naval Observatory experiments by Hafele and Keating, which documented what happened when four incredibly accurate atomic clocks were synchronized and two of them were flown around the world while the other two remained stationary. When the clocks were brought back together, the time had shifted ever-so-slightly for the clocks which had been traveling at jet-like speeds. For them, they'd traveled forward in time by a fraction of a second. Admittedly nothing too exciting, but it proved a principle of time travel in a forward direction was possible.

However, going back in time poses interesting issues.

In 1974, Frank Tipler took Einstein's equations for relativity and realized that it was at least logical that a time-traveling device could be constructed.

Of course, the equations described on paper don't translate well to practical solutions with the level of science and know-how we have today. But as a thought experiment, Tipler posed what such a thing might look like if we ever had such technology.

Let's start with a huge amount of mass: the equivalent of ten sun's worth of mass. I know, I know, you're already thinking, we've gone off the deep end and are in crazy town. Bear with me.

If we packed that much mass in the equivalent space that a black hole would occupy, we would be talking about something less than twenty miles across.

All things considered, that's not *that* big, at least in size.

Tipler proposed that this amount of mass, instead of a ball, let's create a cylinder. Sort of like the cardboard center of a roll of paper towels—just bigger.

Imagine that the cylinder was rotating very very fast.

When you combine the immense gravitation pull of the mass, coupled with the very fast rotation, you get something called a frame-dragging effect.

What is that?

The cylinder would in fact be dragging space-time along with it, and if you followed the rotation in one direction, you'd find yourself in a CTC (closed timelike curve) that rockets you into the past.

A CTC is essentially where time loops back on itself so that when you believe you're moving forward, ultimately you come back to where you started and realize that along the way you were actually going back in time. Expand that out to eternity and you can imagine yourself going back an arbitrary amount of time.

If you moved in the other direction, you'd be going into the future.

I know, I know – this is very advanced concepts in theoretical physics, but these are all things you can look up if you so desire.

There are of course a variety of huge difficulties in constructing such a thing. Variables such as having exotic matter that contained negative energy, or an infinite-length construction.

But what about paradoxes? Like killing your ancestor and such.

Well, there is something called the Novikov self-consistency principle. Its entire premise is to address the paradoxes associated with time travel, which is a hidden "feature" of general relativity.

The implication is that there is a single timeline for the universe you're in, the time traveler would not be permitted to affect the past so that it perturbs the future.

That does sort of play into the idea of free will and such, but the idea being you'd physically be unable to affect the past.

But if that's the case, why did Peabo seemingly go back in time? What's the point then if he can't change the past?

This is where I as a scientist shake hands with myself as the author and make a gentleman's agreement. We're going to take things that are already advanced, and kick it up a notch with actual scientific concepts that hurt most people's heads.

The rules above apply for the universe that we're in.

Theoretically, everyone was born in the universe they're in, right?

But Peabo isn't from the universe that he's currently in. Remember? He travelled from one brane (universe) to another brane (see "The Plainswalker" for details) and landed in the universe he's currently in.

He wasn't there from the beginning. He's a new variable. And from the beginning, someone in the story who knows a thing or two about how such things work has introduced a wildcard into the equation that makes it possible for things in the past to change, thus a loophole in the self-consistency principle.

That wildcard is Peabo.

Light and prisms:

In this book we see Peabo experience a lot of things having to do with light, so I wanted to at least give a remedial background on what light really is, especially since there are hints of colors and rainbow effects that are referenced throughout the book.

First of all, light is composed of tiny energy packets called photons. They have an interesting characteristic since they can be viewed as both a wave and a particle. For purposes of this description, let's simply focus on light being a wave.

What does that mean?

Well, let's talk a bit more generally first about light: the way you see an object is based on the light that's being projected from it or reflected off of it. In the case of stars, they're projecting light.

But the way we humans perceive light is as a wave with a

certain frequency. For example, let's say that you have a long string that you're waving back and forth. Imagine that the waves in the string is what light really looks like. It's simply a series of energy waves. Those waves all have a certain length to them. If you ran farther away with the end of the string, the waves would get longer. Light does the same thing when you move away from it. The wave still catches up to you, but from your perspective, the length of the wave seems to be just a little bit longer. The longer the wave, the redder it appears. The shorter the wave, the bluer it appears.

We are only able to detect these light waves in a very narrow band of lengths. If they're too long, it would go beyond red, into the infrared spectrum. If they're too short, they go beyond blue and violet and ultimately cross over into the ultra-violet range.

The waves are measured from one peak to the next peak, so it's easy to imagine that the less energetic the light is, the longer the wave length. The more energetic the light is, the shorter the wave length.

The light we normally see is a mixture of many different wavelengths, but when we encounter a rainbow, what you're seeing is the light being refracted, bent in such a way that the wavelengths are sorted into their component wavelengths. Many people don't realize that the light we can see is a very small portion of all the light that is around us.

If you are ever near a radio tower that is broadcasting a signal that your car radio receives, even though you can't see the waves hitting your receiver, that tower is most definitely broadcasting "light" at an energy level we can't actually see with our eyes, but the receiver in your radio can.

The illustration below gives an indication of just how narrow the range is that we can actually see.

VISIBLE SPECTRUM

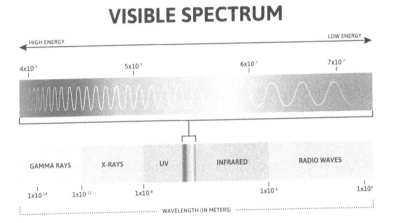

However, Peabo is starting to experience things that he's unused to. Imagine you were looking at your TV's remote control and could see the light being transmitted from it. It wouldn't necessarily show up as one of the colors you recognize. It would be something further out on the red scale than we have a word for, other than infrared.

What is interesting is that as we get older, our range narrows a bit. Some kids and even young adults have been tested and can actually detect some forms of light that most adults wouldn't even see.

This is probably more than you wanted to know about light and some of the science behind it, so I'll leave the rest as an exercise for those of you who are interested in researching the topic further.

Power Crystals:

In this story, I cover a concept that may seem fantastical... the ability to store a vast quantity of energy in what is relatively a small space. Recall the crystal that Grundle had routed lots of energy to, and that Peabo ended up using as a source of power. We all know what batteries are, and often the bigger the battery the more "oomph" it has. Oomph being a technical term, of course. The idea that so much energy could be stored in a thumb-sized crystal seems ludicrous, right?

Let's talk a bit about the relationship between energy and mass. Even though bigger batteries tend to store more energy than smaller ones, our technology is crude compared to what is physically possible. This explanation will at least give you some insight on how far we are from what could be done in the future.

I'll use an example that people might be able to relate to. In the past, I've been asked a question that relates to this topic: "Does a battery lose mass when it discharges?"

Well, there's an imprecise answer and a precise one.

The imprecise answer would be no.

However, let's peel that onion a bit.

The difference boils down to Einstein's $E=mc^2$ that

follows from his special theory of relativity. Energy is equivalent to mass times the squared speed of light.

When a battery discharges, setting aside leaks and the collection of dust or humidity and other environmental factors, the atoms inside the battery are only rearranged into different configurations or different molecules but the identity and the number of the nuclei inside the battery is constant.

Let me just emphasize that the energy can't be calculated from masses of the electrons. Electrons are not lost when a battery is discharged. If a battery is losing electric energy, it doesn't mean that it's losing the electric charge! They're just moved from one electrode closer to the other and it's just the motion through the wire stretched between the electrodes (and the electric field inside the wires) that powers the electric devices. But the whole battery is always electrically neutral; because it contains a fixed number of protons, it must contain a fixed (the same) number of electrons, too.

Instead, the energy difference really boils down to different electrostatic potential energies of the electrons relative to the nuclei. One could say that when a battery is being discharged, its electrons are moving to places that are closer to the nuclei, perhaps other nuclei, on average and the modified interaction energy affects the amount of energy/mass stored in the electromagnetic field.

For example, the top-of-the-line P100 Tesla has a roughly 100 kWh battery capacity. Multiply it by 1,000 and 3,600 to get the value in Joules; divide it by 10^{17} which is (approximately) the squared speed of light and you get the mass difference in kilograms.

It's about $100 \times 1,000 \times 3,600/10^{\wedge}17 = 3.75 \times 10 - 9$

That's almost 4 micrograms—for this huge Tesla battery. So, a poppyseed weighs about 75 times more than the weight difference between a fully charged Tesla P100D and a completely discharged one.

So, technically—yes, there is a weight change, but realistically—not really.

Confused yet?

Well, let's summarize:

If we were storing energy as efficiently as physics would allow, something with the mass of a single poppy seed would be able to power the average US 2,000 square foot home for over half a year.

Compare that to any battery we have nowadays and that gives you an idea of how far we have to go, just using known physics.

ABOUT THE AUTHOR

I am an Army brat, a polyglot, and the first person in my family born in the United States. This heavily influenced my youth by instilling in me a love of reading and a burning curiosity about the world and all of the things within it. As an adult, my love of travel and adventure has driven me to explore many exotic locations, and these places sometimes creep into the stories I write.

I hope you've found this story entertaining.

- Mike Rothman

For occasional news on my latest work, join my mailing list at: https://mailinglist.michaelarothman.com/new-reader

You can find my blog at: www.michaelarothman.com
Facebook at: www.facebook.com/MichaelARothman
And on Twitter: @MichaelARothman

CPSIA information can be obtained
at www.ICGtesting.com
Printed in the USA
LVHW010903181122
733278LV00011B/284